PUSHING

THE GILROY CLAN VOL. 1

MEGYN WARD

Also by Megyn Ward

The Gilroy Clan
Pushing Patrick
Claiming Cari
Having Henley
Conquering Conner
Destroying Declan
(Coming October, 2018!)
Taming Tesla
(Coming December, 2018!)

The Kings of Brighton
Tobias
(Coming August, 2018!)

City Nights
Drive
Grind

With Shanen Black

Paradise Lost
Diving Deep
Hard Dive
Tidal Wave
(Coming September, 2018)

Patrick & Cari's Playlist

1) Jet Pack Blues – Fall Out Boy
2) Desire – Meg Myers
3) Do I Wanna Know – Arctic Monkeys
4) Complicated – Fitz and the Tantrums
5) Nicotine – Panic! at the Disco
6) Magnets – Caracal (feat. Lourdes)
7) R U Mine – Arctic Monkeys
8) The Kids Aren't Alright – Fall Out Boy
9) Issues – Julia Michaels
10) Graveyard Whistling – Nothing but Thieves

ONE

Patrick

2014

Fuck me, I'm tired.

Like, *forget-food-fuck-showering-on-the-verge-of-passing-out* tired.

Unfortunately, sleeping isn't on the short list of my fraternity brothers' priorities. Ever seen *Animal House*?

That's where I live.

How I—straight-laced, study-groups, bed-by-ten-on-a-school-night *me*—managed to pledge the fraternity that thinks the fact that it's Wednesday is cause enough to tap a half-dozen kegs and invite the known universe over to party, I'll never know.

Wait. Yes, I do. Conner.

I pledged Kapa Sigma Pi because my cousin convinced me that if I wanted the full college experience, I needed to join a fraternity.

Two years in and I want to kill Conner. Sometimes more

than I want to sleep.

You need to loosen up on the reins a bit, Cap'n. Live a little. You've got your whole life to grow old.

Cap'n. Short for Captain America. He's been calling me that since we were kids, reading comics in the storeroom of his father's bar. Because, according to him, I'm a *paragon of virtue and defender of justice.* I used to like it—when I was nine.

So, yeah. It's Wednesday night, and the front lawn of our fraternity is littered with plastic cups and clothes. Yup— clothes. Because Sigma Pi parties aren't clothing optional, they're nudity required.

Not all the way naked. You can keep your underwear on. If you want to.

That part is optional, at least.

I'm sitting in my car. Considering sleeping in it. Maybe heading back to the library and bedding down in the stacks. Just as I decide that it might actually be preferable to listening to sorority girls vomit all night long, my phone rings. It's Rob, my roommate. I pretty much hate everything about him, but I tolerate him because he's my fraternity brother and I take his shit because that's what I do. I take shit. Keep the peace.

"You try sleepin' in your car again," he shouts into the phone, loud enough to have me pulling my cell away from my ear. "The brothers and I are gonna gift wrap it."

Shit. That means they're going to plastic wrap my car. With me inside. "Actually, Conner just called. I think I'm going to head—"

"Nice try, pussy," Rob says over the loud music and

shouts coming from inside the house. "Your cousin's in the kitchen."

Of course, he is. Because the real reason Con pushed me to join Sigma Pi was so, he'd have open access to all their parties. And all the girls who attend them. "Okay," I say, giving in. "One beer and I'm out—got it."

"Yeah, whatever, bitch," Rob says, laughing. "Just get your ass in here."

I hang up and get out of my car, slamming the door a little too hard, before walking around the side of the house toward the back door. If I go through the front, someone will be there to confiscate my clothes for sure. At least this way, I have a chance of keeping my pants on.

No such luck. Rob greets me at the back door, paintball gun slung over his shoulder. He's completely naked. "Strip, motherfucker," he says, giving me that douchey grin of his that makes me want to break his nose.

We're standing in the kitchen, and we're not alone. There're a few dozen partiers standing around, talking and drinking. Con's one of them. He's leaned against the counter, wearing nothing but boxer briefs and a pair of half-naked Deltas hanging around his neck, laughing his ass off. I flip him the bird. Finally, he recovers enough to attempt a rescue.

"Come on, man," he says, throwing his empty beer cup in Rob's direction. "Give him a break."

"House rules." Rob slings the paintball gun off his shoulder and points it at me. "Strip or suffer the consequences."

Pro tip: Getting shot with paintballs hurts like a

motherfucker.

Smelling a confrontation, people are gathering and staring, waiting for me to either drop my cargos or get splattered with a couple dozen paintballs. "You're a dick," I mutter, dragging my T-shirt over my head before tossing it up the stairs. "And awfully invested in seeing me naked." I unbutton and unzip my cargos, letting them drop around my ankles.

Rob narrows his eyes at me for a second before giving me a smirk. "You said the magic word, bro," he says, motioning at me with the business end of his paintball gun. "Boxers too."

He thinks I'm going to refuse. That I'll be too embarrassed to follow through and he'll finally get a legit chance to humiliate me. Two years in this fucking fraternity and somehow I've managed to avoid getting naked, and now here I am, dick swingin' in the wind because my roommate is an asshole who thought he was going to cock shame me.

"Let's go, Gilroy," Rob snipes at me, motioning with the barrel of his paintball gun. "Drop 'em or I drop you."

"Remember you said that," I tell him, hooking my thumbs into the waistband of my boxers and jerking them down before I have a chance to think too hard about what I'm doing. According to Conner, that's my problem. I think too much.

Sometimes I think he might be right.

"Holy. Shit."

I look over Rob's shoulder at the pair of girls hanging around my cousin's neck, fighting the flush that's forcing its way up the back of my neck. I'm not sure which one of them said it, but they're both staring at me. Everyone is.

"Jesus Christ, what do you feed that thing?" someone shouts from the doorway and everyone erupts into a flurry of shouts and laughter. I'm pretty sure people are taking pictures.

Rob's dick just died of shame!

Is this real life?

They're shooting porn in the kitchen!

Boogey Nights!

It's high school all over again.

I look back at Rob and give him a one-thousand-yard stare. "Happy?"

He doesn't look happy. He looks like he wants to tell me to put my pants back on. I smile at his obvious discomfort and give him a rough shoulder check, pushing past him toward the keg. No matter how much I want to, I'm not running now. Pulling a cup from the stack, I give the tap a couple of pumps before angling my cup under the nozzle, trying to pretend the way people are staring and talking doesn't bother me.

"Hey."

I look up to find Conner standing on the other side of the keg, sorority girls still hanging around his neck. Still staring at me. *I am not naked. I am not naked. I am not naked…*

"What?" I say, righting my cup before tossing the nozzle. I'm not exactly in the mood for my cousin's shit.

"Fuck that prick," he says, tapping the rim of his cup against mine. The girls hanging on him let out a high-pitched titter like he just said the funniest thing ever.

"Want me to throw him out a window?"

"No," I say, my shoulders relaxing a bit. Con is an unbearable jerk half the time, but he's loyal. All I'd have to do is say the word, and Rob'd be in the hospital within the hour. "I think meeting my sidekick is humiliation enough, don't you?"

Con throws back his head and laughs. "Holy shit, Cap'n—did you just make a joke about your dick?"

Because I did and I'm suddenly feeling awkward about it, I ignore the question. I set my beer down without taking a drink. "I'm going to bed," I say. "Some of us have class in the morning."

"You're such a grandma," Con says, giving me a disapproving look.

"This grandma has a test tomorrow," I tell him.

"So?"

"So, not all of us graduated college at sixteen," I remind him. "Some of us have to put real, actual effort into our educations."

Con gives me one of his conspiratorial grins that almost always means he's about to suggest something I won't like. "You know, I'd be happy to—"

"No." I shake my head. "You're not taking my tests for me."

"Whatever, Granny," he says. "You're gonna be sorry."

"Yeah… I don't think I am," I say with a laugh. "I'd rather—"

"Hey," Half-naked Delta #1, unhooks an arm from Con's neck and drags a glitter-polished nail from my pecs to my package. "Are you guys twins, or something?"

I grab her by her wrist before her fingers make contact with my groin, giving Con a *make it stop* look because I can't. I cannot stand here naked and have this conversation.

"We're actually the same person," Con tells her, drawing her hand from my grasp so he can lift it to his mouth. "It's all very complicated and science-y—alternate dimensions. String theory."

Delta #1 scrunched up her nose. "What's that?"

Good Christ. Someone shoot me.

Con kisses the tip of her glittery fingers and smiles. "Why don't we all go back to your place so I can explain it to you? I put on a hell of an interactive puppet show."

That's my cue.

"You should totally do that," I say, heading for my pile of clothes. Con laughs while I snatch my cargos and boxers off the ground.

"Please tell me you're packing one of those," Half-naked Delta #2 stage-whispers behind my back.

"Who do you think stars in my puppet show?" Con says, evoking another volley of giggling. "You sure you don't want in on this?" he shouts at me as I mount the stairs.

So. Fucking. Sure.

"Yup—have fun," I call over my shoulder, halfway up the stairs. I just want to get to my room and put some fucking pants on.

"Boogey Nights!" he shouts because being loyal doesn't make him any less of a dick.

The answering shout that erupts throughout the house seals my fate. "Boogey Nights!"

Shit. That one's gonna stick.

Someone's knocking. And crying.

I lift my head from the pillow and listen. The music is no longer at an ear-splitting volume. My asshole fraternity brothers have finally stopped shouting my newest nickname, and I can hear someone puking in the bathroom across the hall. The party is finally trying to die.

Thank Christ.

"Hello?" The muffled word is followed by a flurry of soft knocking, like whoever it is doesn't want to wake me up but needs to for some reason.

I pick up my cell and peer at the display. It's 3AM. I've been asleep for approximately two hours. I have class in four. Kill me now.

I peel myself off my bed and stumble over Rob's mess, toward the door. Yanking the door open, I'm too goddamned tired to remember that I barely got my boxers back on before I fell, face-first, into bed. Bleary-eyed, all I make out is a tousled fall of caramel-colored hair, and the skimpiest bra and panty set I've ever seen, all of it wrapped around a body that suddenly makes it hard to breathe.

"Bathroom's over there," I say, nodding my chin across the hall. "Sounds like someone else is making a deposit, but I'm sure—"

"I don't need to throw-up," the girl sniffles, pushing her hair out of her face before brushing shaky fingers across tear-stained cheeks. She's obviously drunk. Tequila, if my nose is any judge. "I need my clothes."

Her clothes? I look over my shoulder like I expect them to be carried out of the rubble by woodland creatures or some shit. "Yeah, I don't think—"

"I thought you had tattoos," she says, raking her gaze over my bare chest and arms like I'm trying to pull a fast one.

"Nope." I sigh, grappling with my patience. She's not the first person to mistake me for Conner. She won't be the last. "What I have is class in a few hours, so…"

"Cari, you're being stupid." It's Rob, I'd know his douchey voice anywhere. Craning my neck past the door frame, I can see him barreling down the hall. Yup. Still naked. "Just let me explain."

"Explain?" The girl rolls her eyes and pushes past me. "Seriously? I turn my back for ten seconds, and you're in the laundry room getting your dick sucked by some *rando*." She starts digging through Rob's side of the room, tossing his shit everywhere. "Pretty sure I can figure it out on my own." She comes up with a pair of jeans. "Hold these," she says, tossing them to me. I catch them just as Rob appears in the doorway.

"Where do you think you're going?" Rob says, standing in the doorway like he's going to try to stop her from leaving. I stand up a bit straighter. The palms of my hands start to itch.

"*Uhh*—home," the girl says, pulling a shirt from the debris. She lifts it to her nose and gives it a sniff before focusing on me. "Can I wear this?"

Somehow, she knows the shirt is mine. "Yeah," I say, but I'm not really looking. I'm too busy watching Rob. If he touches her, he's gonna get a trip to the hospital after all.

"Thanks," she says, pulling it on before holding out a

hand. "Can I have my pants, now?"

I hand them to her, and she bends over to tug them on over her legs. I look away, but not before I get a flash of what might be the most perfect ass I've ever seen.

"Home?" Rob laughs, folding his arms across his chest so he can look down his nose at her. "You live forty-five minutes away, Cari."

"So?" she says defiantly.

"*So*, I'm not driving you," he says like she's being petty and childish for even suggesting it. "*So*, have fun walking."

Dressed, she turns to look at me. "Do you have a car?"

I stifle a sigh. "Yes."

She gathers her mass of thick, wavy hair and pulls it back into a ponytail. "Will you drive me home?"

I have class in less than four hours. This girl lives forty-five minutes away. Ninety-minutes round trip, minimum. I should be sleeping. I have a test I can't afford to miss. The last thing I should be doing is getting in the middle of this shit, but then I make a mistake. I look at her. Really look at her. She's beautiful, yeah—but she's also desperate and drunk. If I say no, she'll ask every guy in this house to take her home. As much as I'd like to believe that she'd get home safely, I wouldn't bet on it.

"Please," she says, "I can't stay here."

Fuck.

"Cari, if you leave with him, it's over," Rob fumes from the doorway, arms crossed over his chest. "I won't take you back."

She doesn't answer him. She just stands there, her wide, blue gaze fixed on my face, waiting for my answer.

If I do this, it won't just be back-handed insults and passive-aggressive shit-talk anymore. It'll be all-out war between us. Not because Rob's an asshole and we don't like each other. Because, after what he saw in the kitchen, he's intimidated by me. Doesn't want his girl anywhere near me or my sidekick, no matter how much of a pussy he thinks I am.

I'd be lying if I say I didn't like the way that feels.

I pass a rough hand over my face while ignoring the daggers Rob is staring at me. "Alright—let me get dressed."

Two

Cari

"I'm Patrick, by the way."

I look across the center console at the guy who agreed to drive me home. A stranger. I asked a total stranger to take me home. A ridiculously hot stranger who nearly made me swallow my tongue when he opened his bedroom door. But a stranger, nonetheless.

I caught my boyfriend with his dick in some girl's mouth, and that's all it took for my drunk ass to lose every ounce of self-preservation I possess. For all I know, this guy is driving me to his kill shack in the woods. And I asked for it. Sure, he's gorgeous, but you know who else was good-looking?

Ted Bundy.

Tears start to well up again, and I let out a long, slow breath, trying to keep them at bay. It didn't work. "I'm Cari," I say, knuckling tears off my cheekbone.

"Are you hungry?" he says, shooting me a quick look, like, *See, I'm normal. I eat food and everything. Totally not a psychopath.* "I'm starving."

We're stopped at a stoplight, not far off campus, and I'm considering jumping out of the car. It's pretty obvious he's trying to put me at ease, but it's not working. But then I look at him. It's still dark outside, and the red glow of the stoplight washes over the features of his face, and that's when I see it. He's not just hot. He's perfect.

"I could go for some pancakes," I say, tilting my head to give him a smile. "Might help soak up some of this tequila."

"Excellent." He thumps the heel of his hand on the steering wheel. "I know a place that has the best pancakes in Boston."

Fifteen minutes later, we're parking in the lot across the street from a little hole-in-the-wall diner that has a line out the door that's comprised of mostly still-drunk college kids with a liberal sprinkling of white-collar business types. By the looks of it, it'll be hours before we get a table.

"On second thought, maybe you should take me home," I say, slowing my stride. "They look crowded, and you probably have stuff to do—like get to class."

Patrick stops walking and turns to look at me. Smiles at me and it's like staring into the sun. He shines, so perfect and bright, it almost hurts to look at him. "I do need to get to class... but I *want* pancakes," he says, his dark green eyes glittering with humor. "And bacon. Do you like bacon?"

"What kind of girl do you take me for?" I say, fighting the smile threatening to break over my face. "Of course, I like bacon."

He splays a hand across his chest and lets out what

sounds like a relieved breath. "Thank god—I thought I was going to have to leave you here." He holds his hand out to me, and I take it so he can pull me onto the sidewalk. As soon as I'm standing beside him, he leans in to press his mouth to my ear. "Stick with me, and don't talk to Nora unless she talks to you first, okay?" he says, straightening to look down at me. That's when I realize how tall he is. I'm five foot nine, and I feel tiny standing next to him. The second thing I notice is how amazing he smells. Like sunshine and sawdust. I recognized it as his scent the second I picked his shirt up off the floor. Rob's douchey cologne doesn't smell half as good.

He's still looking down at me, waiting for me to answer him, so I nod like an idiot. "Okay." For all, I know he *is* Ted Bundy, and he *is* going to take me to his kill shack in the woods. But I don't care. Not as long as he keeps looking at me like that.

He smiles again. "Here we go," he says, swinging the door open, stepping aside so I can pass through it first. As soon as we're in, Patrick takes the lead, grabbing my hand so he can pull me in his wake, past a massive swarm of people crowding the hostess station. Behind the podium is the frailest, scrawniest old woman I've ever seen. She can barely see over the hostess station, but the gaze that focuses on me is laser sharp. "Hey—hey, Veronica," she barks at me, and I'm instantly confused. Veronica? She must see the confusion on my face because she points at me, her bony finger hovering in the air between us. "Yeah, you—you ain't special. You see that line?"

"Nora," Patrick reaches for the hand that's pointing its

finger at me and lifts it to his lips. "As beautiful as ever."

As soon as she sees Patrick, Nora seems to grow six inches, and a slow smile spreads across her face. "I was wondering when you were gonna show up," she says. Hand still held aloft, she skirts the podium, neck craned to look up at him with total adoration. Her forehead barely clears his belly button, but she gives him a disapproving *tsk*. "It's been weeks."

Patrick nods his head while people behind him start to grumble. Without looking away from the old woman in front of him, Patrick reaches a hand between us to catch me by the wrist. "I've been busy with classes," he tells her, pulling me closer.

"No excuse. Con makes it in to see me." She gives him another disapproving glare, but it's thin enough to show the affection underneath.

"Con isn't in college anymore." Patrick's mouth quirks as he fights to suppress a smile. "I'm sorry, Nora—I didn't mean to stay away so long. Got room for me and my friend?" The request ups the volume on the grumbling crowd to near-riot levels.

"Hey," Nora shouts, her voice loud, tone drill-instructor sharp. "You're gonna shut your damn cake-holes, or you're gonna leave my damn restaurant. Ain't gonna be both ways."

It's like someone hit the mute button. That's how quiet it is. I can feel a grin coming on, but then she shoots me a look so sharp I can feel it withering on my face. "Somethin' funny, Veronica?"

I shake my head, fast and sure.

"Got Con and Audrey in the back," Nora says, tilting her head toward the dining room.

Patrick seems to hesitate for a second before he nods. "That'd be great, Nora." He leans down to press a kiss to her soft, wrinkled cheek.

She beams at him, pulling her hand free. "Next time, don't stay away so long," she tells him, giving him a pat on his cheek that sounds more like a smack. I'm chewing on the inside of my cheek to keep from laughing.

"Promise," Patrick says, rubbing the feeling back into his cheek.

Satisfied, Nora moves back behind the hostess station. "I'll send Tina over with coffee."

Patrick leads me through the diner, to a booth near the kitchen. Sitting across from each other is a couple in their early twenties. They're arguing.

"I will not admit it," the girl says, small hands flat on the table. She had short, dark hair with long layers falling across her brow that accentuates sharp features and a full mouth, currently set in a hard line that borders on hostile. "Matter of fact, the only thing I'm going to admit is that you're a moron."

"There's no shame in being wrong, you know—" The guy is leaned back in the booth, sleeved-out arm draped across the back of it, laughing loudly. "and there's no need for name-calling," he tells the girl, a smirk playing at the corners of his mouth. Getting a good look at him, I stop in my tracks. I'd seen this guy at the party tonight. I thought he was Patrick when he opened his door an hour ago. It was the lack of tattoos that threw me.

"Is he your—"

Patrick's hand tightens on my wrist for a moment. "No," he says, letting go of me completely. "He's my cousin."

"I'm not wrong," the girl hisses, lifting herself out of her seat just a smidge. "Superman *is* better than Batman. He has quantifiable super-powers. Batman is nothing but a trust-fund baby with a cool car and mommy-issues." She returns the guy's smirk. "Sound familiar?"

"You're mean." The guys sounds genuinely wounded. I would've bought it, if not for the grin plastered all over his face. "Hey, Boogey Nights," he says, turning to look at us, still grinning. "Thought you had class."

Boogey Nights? Patrick visibly flinches at the nickname, the look on his face unmistakable—*don't.*

"Yeah?" he says, casually, sliding into the booth next to the girl. "Thought you had a threesome."

"I did—and it would've been a foursome if you weren't such a prude," the guy says, shooting Patrick a shit-eating smirk before looking at me. "Have a seat, Legs, tell me your safe word," he says, giving me a grin that I'm sure has melted plenty of panties. "Mine's peppermint."

Threesome? Safeword? I look at the girl next to Patrick, waiting to see how she's going to take having her boyfriend's cheating rubbed in her face. I know from recent, personal experience that it's not fun. Suddenly, I'm angry. Really angry. "What the fuck is wrong with you," I seethe. "Talking about fucking other girls in front of your girlfriend doesn't make you a man. It makes you an asshole."

All three of them look at me like I sprouted a second

head. Then the girl starts to laugh. "Oh…" she keeps laughing. "You think… no," she says, shaking her head while wiping tears from her eyes. "We're not together," she finally manages, hand pressed to her middle like her stomach hurt.

"Oh." A warm flush creeps across my chest. "I thought…"

"She's laughing to cover up the fact that she secretly—*not so secretly*—wants to fuck me," the guy who looks like Patrick says, giving the girl a sweet smile. "Isn't that right, Tessie?"

The girl lets out another hoot. "I wouldn't let you fuck me with Cap'n's dick."

Tessie? "I thought your name was Audrey."

"That's just what Nora calls me," the girl says, waving her hand. "As in Audrey Hepburn—it's her thing. What she'd call you?"

"Veronica."

"Veronica…" The girl gives me an appraising look. "Veronica Lake, I bet." She nods. "I can see it." She lifts her hand and aims it in my direction. "I'm Tess. This is Conner—and you're right. He's a total dick."

The guy sitting next to me—Conner—laughs as I take her hand and shake it, returning her smile. "I'm Cari," I tell her, feeling instantly accepted, which is weird because I've never gotten that from another woman before. Instant acceptance.

"Hi, Cari," she says sitting back in her seat, to study her menu. "You have no idea how glad I am to finally have another girl around to help me keep these two fucksticks in line."

THREE

Patrick

Class started twenty-five minutes ago and missing that test is going to cost me. I could've made it if we hadn't stopped for breakfast. Probably still could've made it if Tess and Con hadn't been there—but we did, and they were. But if I'm honest, right now, I don't really care. I can't remember the last time I had this much fun.

"So, what's their deal?" Cari says from the seat next to me. Breakfast is over, and we're finally back on the road, battling rush-hour traffic that's turning a forty-five-minute drive into a two-hour trek across the universe.

I don't really care about that either.

"Tess and Con?" I say, shooting her a quick look. "You mean, why aren't they together?" She's not the first girl to ask, trying to get the all-clear before making a move on Conner. But giving it has never bothered me this much before.

She laughs. "Yeah—they seem perfect for each other."

"They are," I agree with a shrug. "That's the problem."

I watch her brow furrow from the corner of my eye. "I don't get it."

"It's hard to explain," I tell her, trying to find a way to clarify a relationship that defies clarification. "Tess is the one girl Conner would never make a move on."

"Why?" Cari says, a puzzled look on her face. "She's smart, funny and freakin' adorable."

Tess? Adorable? I suppress a laugh. "He loves and respects her too much," I say because there's no other way to explain it. "Like a sister."

"Really?" Cari arched an eyebrow at me. "Because talking about getting in her pants made up about 75% of their conversation."

"That's Con and Tess." I'm the one who's laughing now. "He runs his filthy mouth, and she insults him. Like you said—they're perfect for each other."

We spent the next hour crawling across Boston at fifteen miles an hour, talking about everything from music and movies to where we see ourselves in five years. We're both small-town college transplants—I grew up in upstate New York. She was raised in Ohio—and we both like thin crust pizza, prefer Abbott & Costello to the Three Stooges and hate Tom Brady. The conversation peters out, and we sit for a while, neither of us talking. She's looking at her hands and chewing on her lip like she has something to say.

"Can I ask you a question," she says in a rush. "You don't have to answer, but..." I can tell by the flush creeping up her neck beneath the collar of her shirt what she's about to ask. She's going to ask me if Con has a girlfriend or is seeing anyone or thinks she's hot. I'm nothing if not my cousin's perpetual wingman.

"Shoot."

"Why did your cousin keep calling you Boogey Nights?"

Jesus. I nearly swallow my tongue—have to literally force it out of my throat, so I don't choke and pass out in the middle of cross-town traffic. Seriously? Why can't she just ask me about Con's relationship status like every other girl on the planet?

"Because Conner's an asshole who experiences joy at the discomfort and embarrassment of others," I tell her.

Because this girl doesn't seem to know when to quit, she double-downs. "People kept shouting it all night and then—*ohhh*," I can feel her gaze zeros in on my lap. Because it's also an asshole that experiences joy at the discomfort and embarrassment of others, my cock twitches under her heavy stare. "You're the guy Rob made strip in the kitchen." Realization dawns and a flush creeps up her neck from under the collar of her shirt. "The guy with the…"

Enormous dick. "Roller skates? Raging coke problem? Best friend who wants to be a famous magician? Yeah, that's me." I deflect and thankfully, she lets me. Clearing my throat, I change the subject. "Can I ask *you* a question?"

The question is intrusive enough to draw her attention away from the front of my shorts. "Why am I dating Rob?"

"More like *how*," I say. "Rob and I have been roommates for almost two years, and I've never seen you before tonight. I didn't even know he has a girlfriend." As soon as I say it, I want to kick myself. "That didn't come out right. What I mean is—"

"It's okay," she says, offering me a smile that looks too

practiced to be genuine. "Rob and I met over the summer—his friend is dating my roommate—and we just started hanging out." She shrugs. "It's not that serious." She rolls her eyes. "I don't even know why I got so upset over catching him with that girl." She sounds like she's trying to convince herself that what she's saying is the truth. For some reason, the fact that she's making excuses for that asshole pisses me off.

"He's not a good guy, you know," I blurt out because, apparently, putting my foot in my mouth is my signature move when it comes to this girl.

"I know." She sighs, gaze aimed out the passenger side window. "Unfortunately, good guys are hard to come by."

I'm a good guy. I want to say it, but somehow I manage to stop myself from making a total ass of myself. Instead, we spend the rest of the car ride in silence. When I finally pull into her driveway, next to a beat-up, powder blue Karmann Ghia. It's nearly nine in the morning, and the house seems quiet, making me wonder who she lives with.

I put the car into park and look at her, intent on apologizing. Her relationship with Rob is none of my business. No matter how much I like her.

"Hey, look..." I say, turning in my seat. I watch her take off her seatbelt. "I shouldn't have said anything about you and Rob. It's none of my—"

And then she's kissing me.

She leans across the gear shift, laying her hand on my thigh, fingers brushing, almost carelessly, against the shaft of my cock and it hardens instantly. Her lips are soft, slightly parted. Her tongue slips into my mouth, rubbing and sucking against mine. Her teeth, nipping and grazing until I'm fucking drowning in her.

My hands lock around her upper arms, and I keep them there because I want to drag her into the backseat of my car and get her naked. I wanted her to straddle me, impale herself on my cock and fuck me stupid in her driveway. In broad daylight. But guys like me rarely get what we want. We're usually too worried about doing the right thing, and while she's not fall down drunk, she's not sober either. Dragging her anywhere is definitely off limits. Before I can push her away, she beats me to it, pulling back to look at me, waiting for me to say something. Do something.

I let her go. That's what I do. "It was nice to meet you, Cari." That's what I say. The most amazing girl I've ever met just had her tongue in my mouth, and her hand on my cock and I say, *nice to meet you.*

I should've gone with my first instinct and thrown myself into traffic when she asked me about my dick.

She sighs, the breath of it skates across my mouth, just before she gives me a soft smile. "Thanks for the ride, Patrick," she says, trailing her fingers across my obvious erection as she goes. She slips out of my car and leaves me sucking wind while she walks up the drive without a backward glance.

FOUR

Patrick

Three years later....

"Hey, boss," the voice below me calls out, bouncing off me like I'm made of rubber, the word *boss* making it easy to ignore. That's my cousin, Declan. He's the boss. It's his initials on the work trucks parked outside— DG Contracting—not mine.

I'm on the second floor of the six-thousand square foot custom home we're building, standing in approximately the same place there's supposed to be an upstairs laundry shoot. It isn't there. Moving down the hall, I head toward the master suite where there's space to spread out my blueprints and check before I find Jeff, the crew foreman.

I find my table—just a sheet of plywood balanced on the backs of a couple of paint splattered saw horses—and spread out my blueprints. The embossed seal pressed into the lower left-hand corner bears my name. *My blueprints* because I drew them up. I designed this house. And now, we're building it. I'm an architect, but I also act as the go-between between Declan and his crew because he's not exactly what would be considered a *people person*. Left to deal with it on his own, he'd fire everyone and just build the house himself.

"*Boss!*" The bellow is directly below me now, and I look down, weaving my gaze between the cracks in the yet to be finished sub-floor to find Jeff looking directly at me.

He's talking to me.

"Something wrong?" I say, instantly concerned. Declan isn't here—something about him and his fiancé going to register for wedding gifts at some pricey department store. When he left, Dec looked like he wanted to hang himself.

"Nah, nothin' wrong, boss," Jeff said, breaking out into a wide grin. "Your girlfriend's here again."

I don't have a girlfriend. What I have is Cari. She's not my girlfriend but trying to convince the crew of giant adolescents, masquerading as grown men that I work with is nearly impossible.

Letting the plans roll closed, I snatch them off the table on my way down the hall and to the stairs. Jeff is waiting for me at the foot of them, hardhat pushed back on his forehead, tool belt dragging at his worn jeans. He's a good guy, just a few years older than me. He dropped out of high school in the tenth grade and worked construction with his dad until he died a few years back. He's a hard worker. Doesn't have to be told more than once to get shit done and the rest of the guys respect him, which is why he's foreman, as opposed to someone who is older or has more experience.

"She's not my girlfriend," I say, casting what I hope looks

like a casual glance past him at what will, at some point, be a limestone portico. She's standing in the sun, leaning against my dusty work truck. Seeing her makes me want to say it again—*she's not my girlfriend*—just so I can remind myself.

I had my chance a long time ago, and I blew it.

A few days after I took her home all those years ago, Cari showed up at the fraternity. She wasn't there for me. She was there for Rob, deciding to give him *one more chance*. One more chance turned into eight but over the course of the six months that it took him to really fuck everything up, Cari and I became friends. And that mind-blowing kiss she laid on me three years and a seemingly endless parade of douchebags later—it was like it never happened.

"Why the fuck not, bro?" Jeff says, jerking my attention away from shit that happened a long time ago. While more responsible and intelligent than most of his counterparts, he's just as nosy and irritating.

Thanks, Patrick. You're the best friend a girl could ask for.

That's the text I got back after wishing her luck on her interview today.

Friend. That's what I am to her, and that's all I'm ever going to be. Not that it's any of Jeff's business.

"Your boys forgot to install the hallway laundry shoot." I slap my blueprints into his hand. "That's gonna set the drywall crew back a day, easy," I say, breezing past him, smiling when he hisses out a curse before stomping away, to round up his crew for a tongue lashing.

Tossing my hard hat on a work table by the front door, I run a hand through my hair and fix a friendly smile on my face before emerging from the dark mammoth of glass and wood and into the sun. "Hey," I call out to her as I stride forward. She's dressed in what she's dubbed her *interview costume*—a tight, knee-length black shirt and a silky white top that dips just low enough in front to offer a hint of cleavage. The only difference is the low-heeled pumps she'd bought specifically for interviews were replaced with a pair of cherry red stilettos I've never seen her wear. They had to be at least five inches, lifting her from her usual 5'9 to something closer to my own 6'4. There was something strangely erotic about having her nearly tall enough to look me in the eye.

Tucking away my decisively *unfriendly* thoughts, I forced an easy-going smile onto my face. "How'd it go?"

"I got the job," she squeals, throwing herself at me, and I steel myself against the feelings I'm about to be assaulted with. She wraps her arms around my neck, giving me no choice but to catch her, letting my hands land lightly on her waist. She smells like Cari—flowers that bloom in the dark and night falling rain. The scent of her, combined with the shoes that bring us hip to hip, goes straight to my cock and I have to set her away before she feels it stiffen against her belly. If I'm too abrupt, she doesn't seem to notice.

"Told ya so," I say, giving a lock of her long, caramel-colored hair a playful tug.

"I start Monday," she crows, so proud and excited, the smile on her face threatens to split it wide open. "Want to know what sold her on hiring me?"

"The fact that you're talented, brilliant and excited at the prospect of making her coffee every morning for the unforeseeable future?" I'm teasing her, and she rewards me with a playful punch on my shoulder.

"No, jerk," she shoots back, clear blue eyes narrowed down to slits. Despite the fierce look she's giving me, I know she's not really mad. She's got a strawberry birthmark that goes from pale pink to fire engine red in about 2 seconds when she's pissed or excited. It's peeking out beneath the neckline of her blouse, the color of cotton candy. "This." She shifts to the side to show off the ratty, paint-splattered canvas bag she carries everywhere. Before I can ask, she explains. "She said it was a painter's bag. She could tell I was serious about art, not just some fresh out of college bimbo applying because I want to use the position to meet a rich man."

"Speaking of rich men, is James taking you out to celebrate?" The second I say it, I want to punch myself in the face. She's grown out of college bros, but she still dates assholes and James is her latest. He's in his mid-thirties and just made junior partner at a law firm downtown. He's financially solvent, good-looking and treats her like shit. Which means he's the perfect guy as far as Cari's concerned.

The smile on her face starts to crumble, but she gives it a boost, smoothing her hands down the front of her skirt. "It's just a stupid receptionist job at an art gallery," she says, immediately discounting herself. I can imagine it's something she's heard James say to her a hundred times. "It's not a big deal... it's just that you texted me this morning and I thought you'd want to know how it turned out." She offers me a weakened version of her earlier smile.

I briefly entertain thoughts of kicking the shit out of James for making her feel like her accomplishments don't mean anything.

"Look," I say, noticing the whining screech of power saws and the *thunk* of nail guns have gone silent behind me. "First of all," I start over, lowering my voice so the gaggle of hard hat-wearing gossips I know is watching us from the house can't hear me. "You're not a receptionist. You're the personal assistant to Miranda McIntyre—*the hottest, up and coming, art broker in Boston*." The last is a direct quote from our text conversation last night, and it pulls another smile out of her. "Second of all, it's dollar shots at Gilroy's tonight. I'll round up the crew, and we'll celebrate. Drinks are on me," I say, just to make her smile again.

It works. She doesn't just smile, she laughs. "Can I bring James," she says, moving toward the ancient Karmann Ghia she brought with her when she moved here for college.

The thought of spending all night watching her make eyes at James while he paws at her and scopes the bar for his next victim makes me want to vomit. I want to tell her no. That he's an asshole and I want to kill him every time I have to watch him put his hands on her. But I don't. I can't. Instead, I just smile and say, "Of course."

FIVE

Cari

I woke up late. My interview at Gallery Blu was at 10 o'clock, so I set my alarm for 7, giving myself plenty of time to get ready. I woke with a jolt at 8:30 and scrambled out of bed and dove into the shower, only to find that my roommate, Nia, used all the hot water.

Typical.

Teeth chattering from the cold, I quickly dried and dressed, progress stalled when I couldn't find the subdued black pumps that I've been wearing on job interviews. So, I was stuck with wearing the only other pair of heels I own, a pair of bright red stilettos I'd bought on a whim and never wore because they make me look like an Amazon warrior who moonlights as a hooker. Irritated, but in a rush, I stepped into them and hurried into the kitchen to grab something for breakfast that I can eat in my car. Rummaging through the fridge, I found the carton of blueberry yogurts I bought yesterday at the store. Where there should have been four, I found only one. Again, typical. My roommate's motto is: *what's mine is mine and what's yours is mine too.*

I yanked the last yogurt free from the carton and straightened, slamming the refrigerator closed. The rush of air fluttered a piece of paper trapped under magnetic Tiki bottle opener a girlfriend brought me back from a trip to Hawaii.

C ~

Justin proposed!!! We're getting married in a few weeks, so I need you out by the first of the month.

Thx,

N.

p.s. I borrowed your black heels. ♥

I let out a strangled scream, crumpling the note in my fist before tossing it in the sink. Bitch ate all my yogurt, stole my shoes *and* kicked me out, all in one morning. The worst part is that the first of the month was less than a week away. Left with nothing else to do, I pulled my Tiki bottle opener off the freezer door with an angry jerk and jammed it into my bag along with the last of my yogurt and a spoon before storming out the door.

God must've felt sorry for me because, despite my perpetual tardiness, I arrived at the art gallery with ten minutes to spare. Deciding to use my time wisely, I dug into the nuclear wasteland I call a purse and pulled out my yogurt. Between bites, my phone let out a chirp. I had a text. It's either my roommate telling me she'd packed my room up and left the boxes on our front porch or it was James, bored at work, asking me to send him nudes. Not that I ever did. When he asks, I just send him a stock photo off Google of a pair of tits. He's never noticed the difference.

Looking at the screen, I see that the text is from neither of them. It's from Patrick.

Patrick: Good luck today!

Just seeing his name on my cell screen makes me feel better. Smiling, I tap out my answer and hit send, strangely anxious while waiting for his reply.

Me: Thanks… I'm nervous.

He replies almost immediately. Patrick's never been one of those guys who takes forever to text back.

Patrick: Why? The luck was just a formality. You're gonna get this job. I know it. Now get out of your car and get in there before you're late.

He's on a construction site, 30-miles away and he knows exactly what I'm doing. Sitting in my car in front of Gallery Blu, trying to calm my nerves before I go in and try to land my dream job. Well, not my dream job *exactly*. I want to own my own gallery someday. But that takes time and someone willing to show you the ins and outs of the art game. I'm hoping Miranda McIntyre with be that someone for me.

Me: You're the best friend a girl could ask for. ♥

I don't wait for a reply this time. He's right, if I don't hurry, I'm going to be late. Sliding out of the driver's seat, I sling my paint-splattered canvas bag over my shoulder and hurry across the street.

The interview takes less than twenty minutes. Miranda, while intimidating at first, with her jet-black hair and flawless porcelain complexion, set me at ease almost immediately. "Nice shoes," she said while I settle into the seat across from her, gaze roving over my clothes, probably trying to reconcile my professional outfit with the canvas satchel that James makes me leave in the car whenever he takes me to dinner. "You're an artist."

I look down at the bright red stilettos and feel the blood rush upward to collect in my chest. I don't blush like normal people, but anyone who knows me and cares to pay attention can tell how I'm feeling by gauging the strawberry birthmark, just below my collarbone. Right now, it feels like a red-hot brand against my skin. "Oh…" I look down at my ridiculous red shoes for a second. "I'm not—not really. It's more of a hobby." It feels like more than that to me. Painting is something I have to do. Compared to it, even breathing feels optional. "Or maybe therapy."

When I look up, I find her studying me, eyes narrowed, trying to figure out if I'm for real or not. "You feel like you need therapy?"

I fight the urge to look away again. "Don't we all?"

She doesn't answer me, she just smiles. "Let's take a walk."

She gives me a tour of the gallery, and it's beautiful. A second-floor loft space with floor-to-ceiling windows that let in gorgeous light that sparkles against the black granite floors. She asks me about my tastes in art, half testing me but also half interested, and seems surprised when I'm not afraid to disagree with her about preferences in style and medium. "Usually, the people who come in here for interviews wouldn't know a Pollack from a Warhol. They think selling a painting is like selling a car," she tells me, her tone thoughtful. She stops in front of the bank of windows looking over the street, directly above where I parked my car. "Yours?" She says it without looking at me, pressing a perfectly manicured nail against the glass.

Despite the fact that she complimented me on my worn bag and ridiculous shoes, I'm embarrassed. James calls my beloved Kharmann Ghia a death trap and refuses to be seen in it. "Yes," I say, feeling warm blood creep across my chest. "I worked summers all through high school to buy it. When I came here from Ohio for college, I couldn't bear to leave it behind."

"Ohio?" Miranda says, shooting me a sidelong glance. "I had you pegged for California. One of those ritzy little beach towns… Santa Barbara or maybe Malibu."

The only thing ritzy about the tiny town I grew up in were the crackers in our kitchen cabinet. I don't know why, but for some reason, the fact that she took me for a rich California girl makes me feel good. "I've never been to California," I tell her. "Before I moved here, I never even saw the ocean."

She makes a small sound in the back of her throat that might have been approval before she looks back at my car. "It's long hours. Hard work. You'll be dealing with temperamental artists and jackhole customers who'll treat you like hired help. I'm a raging bitch most of the time, and I'm not likely to apologize for it—to you or anyone else," she tells me plainly, shifting her gaze, so she's looking directly at me. "But I can pay you enough to keep you just about the poverty line and offer you 2% commission on any paintings we sell. If you're interested, you can start on Monday."

Driving back into the city, I'm feeling pretty good. It's been nearly a year since graduation, and it's been rough watching all my friends move on from college life to stable adult living. Before Miranda McIntyre offered me the position as her personal assistant, my life felt about as stable as a skyscraper built on the San Andreas fault line.

When we graduated, he immediately started looking for a position in an architecture firm, and the job offers started rolling in almost as fast. The problem was they were all thousands of miles away from Boston. Thinking about Patrick moving away was unbearable. Besides Tess, he was my best friend. Living here wouldn't be the same without him.

He'd been about to take an offer in Seattle and been miserable about it when his cousin, Conner offered him the solution to everything. "Why don't you and Dec go into business together? He's already got the construction thing locked down—you design them, he builds them. Should be a piece of cake," he said, gesturing with a beer between his cousin and his older brother before he set it down in front of the guy who ordered it. It was Thursday—Ladies Night at Gilroy's, the family bar—and Conner never missed a Ladies Night.

It had been the perfect solution, the fact that it'd come from Conner, notwithstanding. Three years in and Patrick and Declan are flying high, designing and building custom homes for Boston's mega-rich.

Pulling up the drive, seeing the house Patrick designed, knowing his dreams were coming true was almost enough to take my mind off the fact that while I'd landed my own dream job, it didn't fix the fact that I was on the verge of homelessness. Not wanting to worry him, I kept it to myself. There would be plenty of time to figure it out tomorrow.

Now, chugging down the freeway, I think about the glass and metal buildings clustered together, skyscrapers wedged between Old City Hall and the Old State House. That's where James is.

On impulse, I dive off the freeway and pilot my death trap to the parking garage attached to the building that houses James's law firm. I flash my parking pass and smile at the attendant, and he lifts the gate with a tip of his hat. James gave me the pass a few months ago, so I can bring him lunch. Lunch inevitably leads to a quickie in his office. The prospect usually excites me. Today, I wished I had a sandwich to throw at him instead.

Parking as close to the elevator as I can manage, I grab

my bag and hustle toward it, catching the car just before it started its way up. Leaning over, I tap the button for the 22nd floor, smiling at the young mother and her daughter who were getting off on the 7th.

I know what he'll say when I tell him I got the job. He'll give me a bland, vaguely annoyed smile that I bothered him at work and say, *Congratulations, babe. How 'bout you lift your skirt so we can celebrate.*

When the doors slide open on seven, I almost get off with the mother and her daughter. Telling James can wait. I want to go home and change. Go get Tess and head to Gilroy's so we can plot how to get my roommate back and toss back too many dollar shots while we wait for Patrick and Conner to get off work.

Instead, I stay put, offering the little girl a small smile when she waves at me while her mom drags her off the elevator. I'll tell James. Maybe he won't be a complete dickface about it. Maybe he'll tell me I look nice and take me out to lunch to celebrate.

I step off the elevator and into the small reception area at the center of the pod of offices where James's is located. As a junior partner, he shares an assistant with four other lawyers, but it's still a big deal. He's an attorney at one of Boston's biggest firms and set to make full partner before he turns 40. He's successful, and soon, I will be too.

"Hi, Janine," I say, breezing past his assistant and she looks up from a stack of files, a ready greeting on her lips that falters when she sees me.

"Hi—oh, Ms. Faraday," she says loudly, scrambling from behind her desk to wedge herself between me and the door to James's office. "Mr. Templeton isn't here. He's at—in with one of the partners, discussing a case."

I know she's lying. When James is in a meeting, she lets me wait in his office, no problem. I reach past her and turn the knob, pushing the door open. Janine makes a small sound and turns her face away. "I'm sorry, Mr. Templeton—I tried to…"

Her voice, directly in my ear, fades away. James isn't in a meeting with a senior partner. He's in his office with someone who looks barely old enough to wear make-up. He's got her bent over his desk, her skirt jacked up around her waist. His pants around his hips. The girl—and she *is* a girl. If she's older than eighteen, I'm the Queen of England—has James's tie stuffed in her mouth to muffle her moans while he pounds into her. Despite the tie in her mouth, she doesn't look like she's under duress. She looks like she's loving every minute of it.

James looks up from the girl sprawled across his desk and glares directly at me. The worst part of it is that when he sees me, he doesn't even stop fucking her. Doesn't try to explain or make excuses. He just looks at me like I don't matter. Like I'm nothing.

I leave quietly. Calmly, with Janine following me to the elevator, her short, stocky legs working double time to keep up with me. "I'm so sorry, Ms. Faraday," she huffs softly behind me. "You're such a sweet girl, and I wanted to tell you, but..." she trails off when the doors slide open, and I step inside and turn to look at her. I think she's expecting to see tears. That I'm going to lose my mind, ride the elevator all the way to the roof and fling myself off it.

Nothing could be further from the truth.

"I really *am* sorry, Ms. Faraday," she says softly, her hands chest-high, churning themselves into knots. I've been dating James for almost a year, and she's the only person in this entire building who ever called me Ms. *Anything*. To everyone else, I'm nothing more than James' hot young girlfriend. The girl who'll get out of bed to bring him coffee at 3AM when he's working on a big case or pick up lunch for the team while they're prepping for court, even though he has an intern for that. But why ask your intern to fetch you lunch when you can just as easily ask her to lift her skirt and bend over your desk?

Laughter bubbles on my lips and I fight hard to suppress it. "It's alright," I say, pressing my thumb against the button marked G for garage. The day I hurdle myself off a building over a guy like James Templeton is the day I sprout wings and fly. I offer her a smile to show her that I *really* am alright. "I understand, Janine, and it's okay," I tell her as the doors slide closed.

It doesn't really hit me until I pull into my driveway. I just walked in on my boyfriend fucking someone else, and I'm four days away from sleeping in my car. Nia's here. I can hear the TV blaring the divorce court show that comes on after her soap. Over the din, I can hear her on the phone, babbling away about how Justin popped the question and about how she wants to get married in Belize. Her parents are loaded, so she'll get her way.

Because I don't want to go in and deal with her and because I'm a total glutton for punishment, I sit in my car and use my phone to Google James' law firm and search their employee directory. I clicked the tab marked SUMMER INTERNS, and there she is in a group photo. Elisabeth Lindstrom, looking fresh and wholesome and not at all like the kind of girl who would let someone who is practically old enough be her father, stuff a tie in her mouth and pound her into the side of his desk.

Looking at her, I realize I don't care. Which is sad, really. I've been cheated on so many times by so many guys that I can't even work up a decent rage over the fact that I caught my boyfriend cheating on me. Again.

I close my browser but don't put my phone away. Fingers poised above my cell's screen, I contemplate calling Patrick. Even though he tries to hide it, I know he doesn't like James. Telling him what James did would confirm everything he thinks about him. And about me. Instead of calling Patrick, I call Tess, but it goes straight to voicemail. I leave her a message, telling her that I got the job and that we're all meeting at Gilroy's to celebrate before hanging up.

Even though he literally got caught with his pants down, I have no doubt James will show up at Gilroy's tonight and somehow manage to turn this whole thing around on me. Somehow make me responsible for the fact that he can't keep his dick in his pants.

The real sad part is that yesterday, I would have gone for it. I would've bought his half-assed apologies and promises that he'd never do it again. I'd probably even apologize to him for showing up at his office unannounced and promise to be a better girlfriend. More attentive. More giving. An even bigger doormat.

Because not only am I a glutton for punishment, I'm also a dumbass.

"*Was,*" I say out loud. As in not anymore. James can apologize and gaslight me until he's blue in the face. This time, I'm not buying it. I'm over it. I'm over him.

I get out of my car, slamming its door behind me. Despite My yogurt-stealing bitch of a soon-to-be ex-roommate and my intern-fucking ex-boyfriend, today is a day for celebrating. I'm going to put on my favorite dress, even though it's a little too extra for Gilroy's. I'm going to drink a little too much. I'm going to flirt, and dance, and have a good time.

And when James shows up, expecting me to forgive him and act like nothing happened, I'm going to tell him to go fuck himself.

SIX

Patrick

I didn't hear him knock. Probably because he didn't. Conner isn't really the knocking type, he just lets himself in. Wherever he pleases, whenever he feels like it. One of the several hundred things I envy about him. I look over to find him leaning against the door jamb, trying not to look impressed with the work I've managed to put in on the room, despite the fact I'm working sixty-hours a week with his brother.

"Come on," he says, giving me an impatient clap of his hands. "It's quittin' time Cap'n."

"I wish you'd stop calling me that."

"You'd rather I call you Boogey Nights?"

I bend over to load paint onto my roller, barely sparing him a glance. "I fucking hate you sometimes, you know that?"

"Cap'n it is." Conner grins at me, pleased with himself for getting a rise out of me. "You gonna come downstairs at some point or are you too busy to drink beer with your favorite cousin?"

I look over my shoulder, pushing the paint roller upward, as close to the ceiling as I can get.

"Declan's working?" I say, laying the roller in its paint tray to step back so I can admire my work. I've been renovating the apartment over Gilroy's for the past few years, and this bedroom is the last piece of the puzzle.

"Fuck you," Conner says, laughing despite his harsh words, casting his gaze around the room. "Looks pretty good in here, man," he concedes with an approving nod. "When you moving in?"

I've been living here while I work on the place, but I've been camped out in the room down the hall, which is cramped and dim—nothing like the room we're in now.

"As soon as the paint dries," I say with a grin, taking a long, appraising look of my own. I'd expanded the space, knocking down the wall between this room and what used to be our grandmother's sewing room, adding another hundred square feet of space. Now there's plenty of light and space for my drafting table and the king-sized bed I'd bought at a flea market a few weeks ago.

"Well, come on then," he says, giving his hands an impatient clap. "Tess is whipping my ass at pool. I need back-up, and it's hot as balls up here."

"Alright," I say, lifting the hem of my shirt to wipe sweat off my face. I'd been putting off opening the vents that lead up from the bar. My uncle Paddy—Con and Declan's dad—rents the place to me, utilities included, but I don't like the idea of jacking up Gilroy's electric bill just so I don't have to sweat. I pick up the roller and disposable paint tray off the drop-cloth covered floor and tossed it in the trash. "Cari show up?" I say as casually as I can, but Conner isn't buying it.

"Legs?" he says, using the nickname he gave Cari the night he met her. The smile on his face says he used it just to piss me off. "No—although, I've been up here with you for about fifty-seven years, so who knows? She might've shown, met the love of her life, gotten married, had kids and died by now."

"Okay, okay..." I push past him on my way down the hall, "Get out of here so I can shower," I tell him as I strip off my shirt, heading down the hall to the bathroom.

"You don't want me to wash your back, Cap'n?" Conner calls after me, grinning so wide I can hear it in his voice.

"Fuck off," I say, just before I slam the door.

"Are you guys twins?"

I'm about three pints in, building a good buzz, when she finally asks. I knew it was coming—they always ask—but even though genetically, my cousins and I are siblings, the idea of Conner and me sharing a womb still makes me laugh.

"No." If she'd asked Conner, he would've given her some bullshit answer like he made me with one of those 3D printers or that I'm a sentient robot he built his freshman year at MIT. "We're cousins," I say, draining my pint. "Our identical twin fathers married identical twin sisters. Stir that together, and you get us." I look at Conner, standing on the other side of the pool table, head ducked so he can talk to Tess. Looking at Conner is like looking in a mirror.

Or it would be if I stopped shaving, cutting my hair and giving a shit about my general appearance. Same dark hair. Same green eyes. Same everything... right down to our dimples. Well, almost everything. His jawline is a little leaner. I'm an inch and a half taller. His left arm is completely sleeved out with tattoos, with more splashed across his chest and back. We're not truly identical, but we look enough alike to give people pause.

The girl bounces a look between Con and me before landing on me with a smile. "You're way hotter."

I don't know what to say to that. Despite his worn jeans, three-day beard, and IDGAF attitude, Conner is the heavy hitter between the two of us. In fact, I'd be hard-pressed to look around Gilroy's and find a girl he hasn't had under him. Me? Well, let's just say it's been a while.

I clear my throat. "You want to break?" We're playing pool—Con, Tess and some girl he sweet-talked into being my partner. I think her name is Sara. I'm not 100% sure, but I don't want to hurt her feelings by asking.

"You do it," she says, laying a hand on my bicep, fingers digging in just enough to let me know she's interested in more than playing pool. "I'm good at a lot of things, but pool isn't one of them."

I give her a noncommittal smile, leaning over the table, positioning my cue in front of the balls Con just racked, giving them a serious crack that scatters balls across the felt. She's cute, but I'm not really feeling it.

That's when I see Cari through the window, standing on the sidewalk outside the bar on her cell. She's still wearing those red heels, only this time she's wearing a dress that makes me glad I'm hunched over a pool table. Tight black lace, barely this side of decent with whisper thin straps that leave her shoulders and back bare. As usual, the sight of her makes me hard.

It takes me a second to realize she's arguing with someone, mouth moving rapidly, voice raised so I can hear the hum of it through the glass. Ending the call in what looked like mid-sentence, she jams the cell into her bag and disappears around the corner, heading toward the front door of the pub.

"There's Cari," Tess says, fitting her fingers into her mouth to give a short whistle to get her attention. As soon as she sees us, Cari smiles and points, signaling she's making a trip to the bar before she heads our way.

"Another drink?" I drain my pint before nodding at my pool partner's empty glass. She shoots a quick glance at the table where a bunch of her girlfriends are watching us. Letting some random guy at a bar bring you drink isn't smart, but I can tell she's about to say yes, against her better judgment. "Why don't you come with me?" I say on impulse. I don't want to be responsible for this girl trusting the next guy who makes the same offer.

I take Tess and Con's order before leading Sara through the crowded bar. At some point, she threads her fingers through mine. "I almost lost you," she says with a laugh, giving herself an excuse to grab my hand. I give her another smile and don't pull away because I don't want to be rude.

Declan is behind the bar tonight and seeing me push my way to the front, he ignores the crowd of frat boys and college bros, flipping a pint glass off the rack to build me a Guinness. Cari is standing a few feet away. With James. He must've been hiding out at the bar, waiting for her to show up. They're being quiet about it, but I can tell that they're arguing. He must've been who she was on the phone with.

With one eye on Cari, I watch Declan set my pint down before he holds up the mixer gun. "Cran or sour?" he says loudly, smiling at the girl next to me. Gilroy's college girls drink one of two things—whiskey sours or cranberry and Malibu.

She flushes. She's been drinking whiskey sours all night. "I'll take a Guinness," she says, tightening her grip on my hand.

Declan gives her a dubious glance but builds her a pint anyway. "Con too?" he says, already moving for another glass.

"Yeah," I say, distracted by the drama unfolding a few feet away. James keeps reaching for Cari's arm, and she keeps pulling away, shaking her head. "Tess wants a—"

"I know what Tess drinks," Declan says, his tone tight enough to pull my attention away from Cari. I watch as he places a single ice cube in a rocks glass before adding two fingers of Jameson.

"*I said no!*" Cari says loudly, and I look back just in time to see her throw her drink in James' face. She turns to make her getaway, but he's too fast for her.

"Bitch," he shouts, reaching for her arm, his fingers so tight around her bicep the tips of them disappear into her flesh as he starts to haul her close. People are paying attention now, the immediate crowd surrounding them gone quiet, but no one tries to intervene.

Drinks and the girl standing next to me forgotten, I take two strides and push into the middle of it, bringing myself nose to nose with Cari's boyfriend. "Hey, James," I say, keeping my tone conversational. "You're gonna want to let go of her arm. Now."

"Yeah," he sneers at me. From the corner of my eye, I can see his fingers dig deeper. "What are you gonna do about it, boy scout?" We've spent enough time together over the past nine months to decide that we don't like each other, but we've always been nice for Cari's sake. That's over now.

"What am I gonna do?" Without looking, I reach a hand across the bar, smiling a few seconds later when I grip my fingers around the smooth handle of the baseball bat that Declan passes me from behind the bar. "I'm gonna invite you out back, and when we get there, I'm going to take this bat to your fucking head," I tell him, my tone still pleasant. "How's that sound?"

James is drunk, but he's not stupid. His gaze shifting between the four of us, he lets go of Cari. "Keep her," he says, mopping the vodka soda Cari threw at him off his face, before giving her an ugly look. "She's a slut anyway."

The slur has me jerking at the bat, but Declan still has ahold of the other end, and he won't let it go. "Easy," he says under his breath. At least that's what I think he says. My blood is rushing so loud in my ears that he could be reciting the Gettysburg Address for all I know.

We all watch him weave his way toward the door, the crowd parting, making a jagged path for him until he's gone. As soon as the door swings shut behind him, the crowd lets out a cheer.

"That was a new one," Declan says, stashing the bat back behind the bar. James is gone, and Sara is back at the table her friends are crowded around, all of them shooting me looks that range from wary to lustful. I don't really care about any of it though. Tell the truth, I just want them to leave and take Sara with them.

Tess has Cari cornered in Conner's booth, trying to calm her down. Not that she's hysterical. In fact, she looks so angry that I expect her to demand the bat from Dec so she can go after James and finish what I started.

"Why?" I say, cutting Declan a look. I know what he's talking about. "Because I'm a pussy?"

"Bitch, please." Now he laughs at me. "I've seen you go to work—I *know* you're not a pussy. But you usually look for a more diplomatic solution before you ask for the bat."

"So, what?" I'm getting irritated which is a new one for me where Declan is concerned. Out of the three of us, Dec and I are the most alike. It's Conner who usually manages to piss me off. "I'm a nice guy, and nice guys can't stick up for his friends?"

"Is that what that was?" Declan says, calling me on my obvious bullshit. It's last call, and the crowd has moved on to various frat houses and off-campus housing to continue the party. It's quiet, but I pretend not to hear him, even though I can hear him just fine.

No. That's not what that was, and we both know it. That wasn't about me defending a friend, and we both know it.

It was about Cari and the way I feel about her.

Declan shoots a quick glance over my shoulder before looking me in the eye. "Look, cousin, take it from—"

Before he can say what's on his mind, Sara breaks into our conversation.

"That was nice, what you did for that girl," she says, her hand back on my arm. "Not a lot of guys would've done that."

"She's a friend," I say, the automatic answer that explains everything I've done or will ever do for Cari.

I must've said something right because Sara smiles. "Some of us are headed back to my place," she says, looking over her shoulder at the table where her friends are waiting. "Wanna come?"

I might be a nice guy, but I'm not so nice that I don't catch the double meaning in her words. If I go with her, we're going to end up fucking.

I almost tell her she's got the wrong Gilroy. That the one she wants looks just like me and is currently chatting up one of her friends. Instead, I smile and let her down gently. "I've got work in the morning," I tell her, shooting Declan a quick glance. He knows I don't have work tomorrow, but he keeps his mouth shut.

"Okay…" She leans into me, pressing her mouth against mine, her tongue licking at its corner before she straightens. When she does, she has my cell in her hand. "Text me when you've got some free time," she says, putting her contact information into my phone before handing it back.

"Absolutely," I say even though I know I don't mean it.

SEVEN

Cari

My favorite thing about Tess is that she won't ask me what happened with James. She'll let me come to it on my own, in my own time. But I'm not ready. I'm too angry. Too keyed up to answer without losing my shit. When I saw Declan hand that bat to Patrick, I wanted to grab it and use it to cave James' face in. I'm still thinking about it. Which isn't like me at all.

I'm usually the one who goes looking for a reconciliation. Apologizing for things that aren't my fault. Begging for another chance even though I'm not the one who should be on my knees. The shift isn't entirely pleasant, but it's something that makes me feel strong. Ready for whatever life has in store for me. I don't need James. I don't need anyone.

"Are you sure you're okay," Tess says, glaring at my arm. Bruises are already starting to form. "I can get Con to go grab you some ice."

"No," I say. Even though my arm is sore, I don't want

any ice. I like the feeling. It feels like I finally stood up for myself. "But I wouldn't turn down another vodka soda."

Even though Declan's called last call, Tess leans out of our booth to signal Con, and he nods, putting his blonde on ice so he can get us another round. I want to ask Tess why she won't just go up there and get it from Declan herself but I don't. Because that's not what Tess and I do. We don't ask. No matter how much we want to.

My gaze follows him, but it lands on Patrick. He's sitting at the bar, talking to Declan and the girl he's been with all night. She's got her hand on his arm, and she's smiling, gesturing toward the door like she wants him to leave with her. Then she kisses him, and I feel something clench inside my gut. Something that feels a lot like jealousy. When she walks off alone, I let out a breath I didn't know I was holding.

"Well, that's interesting."

I turn my head to see Tess looking at me, a slim dark brown arched over warm hazel eyes. Heat collects below my collarbone, and I know my birthmark is practically glowing, it's so red. Between what happened with James and the embarrassment of getting caught spying on Patrick, it's a wonder the stupid thing hasn't burned a hole in my chest. "How's work going?" I ask, making Tess laugh.

"*Blah, blah,* rebuilt carburetors. *Blah, blah,* clutch replacement. *Blah, blah,* dropped a fuel tank," she says because she knows I don't understand much about her job as a mechanic. She knows I don't really care either. I just want to change the subject. "What about you?" she says, having mercy on me. "When do you start your fancy art job?"

"Monday." The mention of my new job brings on an excited flush. "I'm even more nervous now that I've got the job. I want this so bad, and I'm afraid that I'm going to mess it up somehow."

"Impossible." I look up to see Patrick stand outside the booth, a friendly smile on his face. Not at all like the guy who threatened to put my ex-boyfriend in a coma less than an hour ago. Guinness in one hand and my vodka soda in the other, he hands me my drink, and I smile back, sliding across the seat to make room for him. He hasn't asked me about James yet either. To be honest, I'm not sure what I would say to him, even if he did.

"Is your new boss a guy?" Conner says, sitting down next to Tess, forcing her to scoot across the booth. "Because if he is, all you have to do is wear that dress to work, every day." He gives me the lopsided grin he uses to charm college girls out of their panties. "Because, seriously—employee of the month. Every month."

"Oh, my god," Tess says, jerking her drink out of Conner's grasp. "You are the biggest asshole I've ever met in my life."

Conner leans into her. "You better be glad about it too," he says, flicking the tip of her nose with his tongue, making her squeal. "If I wasn't such an asshole, you'd be panting after me, morning, noon and night."

She pushes him back, and he lets her with a laugh. "You want to know why I'm not *panting* after you like the rest of your groupies?"

Conner gives her a bland smile. "Because you don't know

a good thing when you see it?"

Tess returns his smile with a sweet look that all but guarantees a verbal slaughter. "Because I've seen you naked."

"We were seven, sweetheart." Conner leans back in his seat, full of swagger. "Things change."

Despite the exchange, Conner and Tess sound more like brother and sister, giving each other a hard time. Three years ago, I mistook them for a couple. Now, the thought of them together makes me laugh.

"I'm taking off," Declan appears at the edge of the booth, hands dug into the pocket of his jeans, gaze nailed to his brother's face. "Jessica wants to go look at wedding venues tomorrow." He pulls a key from his pocket and tosses it at Conner. "Lock up."

Something his brother says turns Conner's easy smile black around its edges. "Sure thing, Dec," he says, his tone hard. He snatches the key from the air before cocking his head. "Hey, before you go, can you help me convince Tess to come home with me and sit on my face? So I can show her how a Gilroy's *supposed* to do it."

It wasn't any lewder or more disgusting than anything else he's ever said, but something about his tone sounds off. Angry. Defiant. My gaze instantly flies to Tess' face, but her eyes are glued to the drink in her hand, knuckles white from the force of her grip. Usually, she'd punch him in the arm or smack him upside the head. Right now, she looks like she's having a hard time just breathing.

Something clicks and I take another look at Declan. He's got that same punched-in-the-gut look Tess has.

"Jesus, Con," Patrick says, wiping his hand across his mouth, smothering his words. I feel his knee press into mine, ready to launch himself between the two brothers if it comes to that.

Color drains from Declan's face a second before his jaw flexes, his gaze pulled for a split second toward Tess before landing it on his little brother. "What did you say?"

"You heard me, fuckstick," Conner says, his smile flattening out into something dangerous. "At least I'm loyal."

Declan let out a strangled sound that might have been a laugh. "Loyal? You're fucking kidding me, right?" His hands were working, clenching into fists and then relaxing like he can't decide if he wants to choke his brother or not. "You'll stick your dick into any—"

"*Enough.*" Patrick drops his hand away from his mouth, slamming it against the table in front of him, hard enough to make me jump in my seat. "Leave it alone," he says, splitting a look between them, his tone reverberating with more authority than I thought he was capable of. He and Conner measure in at well over six-feet but eyeballing him, Declan is even taller, his frame packed with an additional twenty pounds of muscle. Despite the size advantage, Patrick's warning seemed to give him pause.

For his part, Conner seemed content to heed his cousin. He just takes a long drink from his pint and holds his brother's glare.

"Fuck you, Conner," Declan says before aiming his gaze at Patrick. "See you Sunday." He turned away and headed for the door.

"Give *Jess* a big, sloppy wet one for me," Conner called after him, refusing to let his brother get the last word. "Oh and fuck you back."

Declan flips him off as he walked out the door.

As soon as he's gone, Conner slouches in his seat and sighs. "Fuck," he mutters, rubbing a hand over the top of his head. He turns toward Tess. "I'm sorry," he says, uncharacteristically contrite. "It's just—I got mad. Mentioning her..." He shakes his head, jaw clenched. "He's such an arrogant prick sometimes."

Tess looked at him, more shaken than angry. "As opposed to you, who's an arrogant prick *all* the time?" she says, pushing her unfinished drink away like looking at it made her sick.

"I deserve that," Conner says, seemingly at a loss for how to fix things before bumping his shoulder against hers, hoping for a smile. "Want me to take you to the bathroom and make you feel better?"

"Thanks, but getting *Gilroyed* isn't going to make me feel better." Tess cracks a smile because where Conner is concerned, it's impossible for her to stay angry for long. "It'll make me vomit."

Crisis averted, Conner grinned for real. "One of these days, you're going to damage my self-esteem."

"Here's hoping," Tess says, picking up her glass and hoisting it high and we all laugh, clinking glasses.

"I'd like to propose another toast," Conner says, lifting his pint again. "To my devastatingly handsome and more than slightly uptight cousin, who *almost*, actually got some tonight. Kudos, Cap'n."

Patrick's shoulder stiffened against mine, but he laughs and clinks his glass against Conner's. "Sara was nice. Just not my type."

"So, you don't go for hot women who are inexplicably into you? Interesting..." Tess says, shooting Conner a perplexed look before aiming it across the table. "If she's not your type, then who is?"

Patrick opens his mouth then clamps it shut, his jaw flexing hard enough to cause a vein to pop in his temple before he opens it again. "I—"

"I have a toast too," I blurt out, picking up my glass. "My roommate gave me four days to move out, and I caught James fucking his intern in his office this afternoon." I force a smile and tip my drink in salute. "So, here's to me."

EIGHT

Patrick

We all sit here for a few seconds, trying to digest what Cari just said. For my part, I'm glad she walked in on James and his intern. Maybe her resolve to break it off with him will stick this time.

"If you take him back, I'm going to kill you," Tess says, reaching across the table to dig an ice cube out of Cari's glass. "Seriously. I'll kill you."

Cari laughs and the sound is easy, like taking James back isn't even under consideration. "If I even *think* of taking him back, I might kill myself."

"Well..." Tess rolls her stolen ice cube across her tongue, eyes narrowed. "Then I'll kill your roommate."

The mention of her roommate deflates Cari's good mood. "I'd *pay* you to kill that yogurt-stealing whore if I wasn't almost homeless and destitute," she says, sitting back to press her shoulders into the back of the booth. "I have less than $200 dollars to my name, and I'm not going to ask my parents. They've done enough for me. Too much, actually."

"What about the new boss?" Conner says, spinning his empty pint in a slow circle on the table in front of him. "You could ask for an advance."

"No way." Cari shakes her head like her hair is on fire. "I'm not starting out what I hope is a long and profitable professional relationship with Miranda McIntyre by begging her for money."

"Wait—your new boss is a woman? Why didn't you say so?" Conner says, giving Cari what I've coined the Gilroy grin. "I'll just fuck it out of her for you. By the time I'm done, she'll be begging *you* to take her money."

"First of all—gross," Tess says, shooting the kind of look martyred saints always wear in religious painting in Conner's direction. "And second—she's right. She can't ask her new boss for money before she's even started her job." She shrugs her shoulders, and I know what she's going to say next. She's going to offer Cari a place to stay.

"Why don't you just move in with me?" I blurt it out, drawing looks from around the table. "I mean, it's not like I don't have the room. In fact, I just finished putting up a fresh coat of paint in the spare room. It's yours if you want it."

Conner, tilts his head, mouth open, ready to ruin everything. I kick him under the table, and he shuts his trap. I smile, hoping like hell I look relaxed and calm. Like it's the perfect solution to Cari's problem instead of the answer to my prayers.

Cari shakes her head. "Thanks for the offer but—"

"I have to go to the bathroom," Tess announces, shoving at Conner's shoulder to let her out of the booth. "Come with me, Cari. You know my bladder doesn't work right unless you're in the same room while I pee."

"You're disgusting," Conner says, helping her out of the booth.

"Guess that means we *are* perfect for each other," Tess says, shifting from one foot to the other, waiting for me to let Cari out.

Cari starts to laugh, but as soon as she's free, Tess grabs her hand and hauls her across the deserted bar, toward the ladies' room.

"What are you doing?"

I look across the table to find Conner watching me— uneasy like he thinks I might have rabies. I can pretend I don't know what he's talking about but that would mean I have hope that he'll just let it go. Which I don't. Instead, I just shrug. "She's broke and almost homeless, what am I supposed to do, Con? She's my friend."

"The two of you aren't friends," Conner says, his tone hard and final. "You might pretend to be, but you're not." He shakes his head at me like I've disappointed him somehow. "You want to fuck her. I don't know about you, but I don't usually fuck my friends."

"You don't have any friends," I say, trying to deny the fact that he's right.

"I have Tess," Conner shoots back, leaning back in his seat.

"She doesn't count," I say shaking my head. Tess and Conner have been best friends since we were kids.

"You know why she doesn't count?" He smiles at me. "Because I don't want to fuck her."

"Stop saying that," I growl at him, throwing a look over my shoulder to make sure we're still alone. "Cari needs my help, and I'm going to give it to her."

"Okay," Conner says, conceding with a toss of his hands. "But at least admit that you didn't offer her a place to live because you're a nice guy. You offered her a place to live because you want to—"

Behind me, I can hear Tess and Cari on their way back to the table. "I will punch you in the face." I said it quietly and Conner laughs just as they made it back to the table.

"Okay," Cari says, the birthmark on her chest a deep, rosy pink. She's excited and I can't help but want to believe it's because she's moving in with *me*, not just because she's successfully avoided homelessness. "If you're serious, I'll do it. I'll move in."

NINE

Cari

As soon as we're in the bathroom, Tess flings me inside and shuts the door, spinning around, to press her back against it. "Say yes."

"Say yes?" I shake my head, instantly dismissing her advice. "I can't *say yes*, Tess."

"Why can't you?" She says it like I forgot to take my medication.

"Because he didn't mean it—it's just Patrick... being Patrick." I cross my arms over my chest. "He was only offering to be nice."

"*Who cares*," she hisses at me, throwing her hands up in the air again. "He's such a sweetheart, he won't back out. Once you say yes, he'll be stuck."

"That's horrible," I hiss back at her, crossing my arms over my chest. "I can't do that to him."

"Bullshit you can't. You've been lusting after Gilroy for *years*."

"What? No." I shake my head, my chest so hot, I can feel

the heat of it in my back. "Patrick and I are friends."

"Really? Friends?" Tess laughs at me. "I *saw* you. You were about three seconds from dragging that little college skank out of Gilroy's by her hair."

I've been caught. There's no use denying it. "So? Moving in with Patrick isn't going to change anything."

"It will if you tell him how you feel." Tess is looking at me but I have a strange feeling she's talking to herself.

"What happened with Declan?" I say, breaking our unspoken vow to not ask. The exasperated look on her face gives way and for a second she looks like I sucker-punched her. "Shit." I suddenly know what it was like to be Conner Gilroy. "I'm sorry. I shouldn't have—"

"We dated the summer before I turned eighteen. He was nineteen. Things were great. Better than great. It felt like forever." She rakes a hand through her long dark hair and lets out a shaky sigh. "And then it didn't."

I don't have to ask what happened. I can see it on her face. Declan broke her heart. "I'm sorry, Tess," I say quietly.

"It was a long time ago. I've moved on." She gives me the kind of smile that almost convinces me she's telling the truth. "Conner hasn't, but I have," she says with a laugh that succeeds in breaking the tension in the air. "I don't understand what the big deal is. You're not exactly shy when it comes to getting what you want."

She's right. As far as partners go, I'm no Conner Gilroy— but I'm no shy virgin either. But just because she's right doesn't mean it doesn't sting to hear her say it out loud. "What's that supposed to mean?"

She must hear the hurt in my tone because she sighs. "You're not a slut. You're not. There's nothing wrong with a woman enjoying sex and fuck James Templeton. He's a dickbag and I've always hated him and his smarmy, smug, dickbag face."

I laugh, even though I know she's serious. She's a solid six inches shorter than I am and tiny. I mean *tiny*—but if Tess ever got her hands on James, I know he'd limp away, missing more than a few vital parts. "You're so adorable when you get angry—you're like a homicidal Tinkerbell."

"Fuck you, Faraday," she says but she's smiling at me, so I know she doesn't mean it. "But seriously, maybe a couple bouts of respectable, puritan sex with Predictable Patrick is just what you need to cleanse the palate."

Predictable Patrick. We've been calling him that behind his back for years. Safe, predictable Patrick. He's nothing like the guys I usually go for. For starters, he's nice. Guys like him go for Kindergarten teachers who wear pastel-colored sweater sets and volunteer at soup kitchens on the weekends.

That's not me.

Not even close.

Patrick hadn't even known me and he agreed to take me home. I practically gave him a hand job in my driveway but instead of dragging me into the backseat—where I'd have gone willingly—he waited for me to finish embarrassing myself and said goodnight. He even waited for me to let myself in before he drove away. Three years later and I can still remember what it felt like to have his mouth on mine.

"I can't do that," I tell her shaking my head. I wish I had

the guts to make the first move but I don't. Not with Patrick. Not again. Because if he rejected me all over again, I'm not sure I'd recover.

"Okay," she says, attacking the problem from a different angle. "So, we're gonna have to force him to come to you."

"Force him?" I place a hand on my forehead and let out a sigh. "I can't believe we're even having this conversation," I say, letting out a sharp bark of laughter.

"Well, we are." Tess leans into the space between us. "Because that boy is too buttoned-up for his own good. He's never going to make a move on you..." She gave a mischievous grin. "Unless you push him into it."

"And how do you I suggest I do that?" I can't believe she's suggesting *any* of it. "Traipse around his apartment naked? Offer to loofa his back while he's taking a shower?"

"Not naked—" That grin of her turned downright evil. "half-naked should do nicely... and the loofa wouldn't hurt." She looks at me like I'm crazy for even considering passing up the opportunity.

"It'll never work," I tell her. "Patrick is different from most guys. He's not going to make a move on me, just because I make him horny. He's a gentleman." *A gorgeous, sexy as fuck gentleman.*

"He's into you," Tess says, shaking her head at me, refusing to let it go.

Now I know she's crazy. "He's really not, Tess." I laugh. "Trust me, I know."

"He was ready to take a bat to James' head." She says it like she was presenting key evidence in the trial of the century. "And he would've too if dickface Declan hadn't stopped him."

Dickface Declan. I smother another laugh while shaking my head. "He would've done the same thing for you," I say and the look on her face tells me she knows I'm right.

"Anyway, who cares if you're his type?" Tess raked a hand through her long, dark hair. "You wanna ride his disco stick—not marry him, right?"

I hold up a hand between us. "Please—don't say *disco stick* again. Ever," I say, my face scrunched up but she wasn't wrong. I'd been secretly drooling over Patrick since that night in his car... "And yes, I do," I say cautiously. "But he'll never fall for it."

"I beg to differ." Tess shakes her head at me like I'm a lost, little lamb.

"I *know* Patrick." *I know he doesn't want me.* "It will never work."

"Alright, Faraday..." Tess grinned at me. "Put your money where your mouth is."

The second I say yes, Patrick drags me upstairs to his apartment to show me the place and he's right. The spare bedroom is perfect.

It's large—taking up a third of the apartment's square footage—and bright. The interior walls are painted a lovely slate blue which offset the exposed brick of their exterior counterparts. Gorgeous hardwood peeked out from beneath the drop cloth he used to protect the floor while he painted. He's torn out the ceiling, and exposed the beams, the steep angle of the roof setting off a beautifully arched alcove. The wrought iron bed he picked up at a flea market a few weeks ago is set up across from an enormous bay window with the most fantastic view of the harbor I've ever seen. Patrick's room is little more than a cave by comparison.

"You only want $200 a month for *this*?" I shake my head, turning a slow circle. I catch the smell of fresh paint and the faint scent of sawdust. "That hardly seems fair, Patrick."

"Just until you get settled into your job," he says in a reasonable tone. "After that, we can renegotiate the rent."

I'm not convinced. "This is *your* room. You've been working on it for months," I say, shaking my head. "I can't just—"

Now he smiled. "See this?" he says, pointing toward the beautiful bay window I'd been admiring. "The light from this window is amazing. It's the perfect place to set up your easel."

My heart stutters in my chest. He was willing to give up this amazing room so I can have the perfect place to paint. "It's also the perfect place to set up a drafting table."

He shrugs. "It's worth giving it up if I can use the air conditioner," he says. "As it stands, I don't want to turn it on because I don't want to jack up the bar's electric bill. An extra two-hundred bucks a month will cover the difference."

What he's saying makes sense. Hearing it makes me feel better about taking advantage of him. Because I'm not taking advantage of him. We're helping each other out. I've almost managed to convince myself when he speaks up again.

"The only catch is that the bed stays." He looks at the bed

in the middle of the room, pulled away from the wall so he could paint. "It's too big for my room and it took me, Con *and* Declan to get it up here," he says with a laugh. "I don't think I can talk them into another move."

I look at the bed and think of my own pitiful super single. The same bed I've been sleeping in since I was fourteen years old. I'd gladly leave it on the curb.

I can feel myself caving. Who am I kidding? I know I'm going to say yes. I couldn't say no to Patrick if I tried. "Only if you're sure."

Knowing he's worn me down, Patrick gives me a satisfied smile. "We're friends—this is what friends do for each other, right?"

Friends. Right.

I push a bright smile onto my face and offer him my hand to shake. When he grins and takes it, I ignore the way my hearts flips over in my chest when our hands touch. "Right."

TEN

Patrick

Six months later....

My alarm goes off and I roll over, silencing it almost immediately. It's loud and I don't want to wake Cari.

Cari.

I groan, my hand going directly to my cock. As usual, it's rock hard, popping the mother of all tents in my flannel pants. It's not just morning wood either. This is a full-on, Stage 5, roommate-induced hard-on. I roll over onto my stomach and try to smother it but the added friction just makes it worse. "*Shit.*" I groan into my pillow. I can't deal with this right now.

I think about masturbating. These days, I'm doing it all the time. In bed when I know she's sleeping in her room. In the shower. In the living room when *she's* in the shower. The only place I haven't done it is in her room when she's not here because there's horny and then there's creepy and even though I'm dancing around that line, I haven't crossed it.

Not yet anyway.

Whatever. Jerking off isn't going to take care of the problem for long. In the long run, it isn't going to do anything but make my dick angry because it wants the real fucking thing and it knows the real thing is right down the hall.

I know it's useless, but I give it a try anyway, squeezing the head of my cock to catch the drops of the pre-cum beading on its tip before sliding my hand down the length of my shaft, working it in my fist until I'm panting, my free hand twisted in the bedsheet.

I don't know what I expected when I opened my big, fat mouth and offered her a place to live. I sure as fuck didn't expect our living arrangement to be clothing optional.

It's like I'm living at Sigma Pi all over again.

I can't close my eyes without seeing her. Walking around in the most pathetic excuse for a robe I've ever seen. Curled up on the couch next to me in a pair of my boxers, making me wonder if she's wearing panties underneath. Naked, her reflection thrown back at me by the mirror in the living room, hung at the perfect angle from her bedroom.

"Get a grip, perv," I mutter. *She's not giving you a free peep show. She's your friend and this is her home. You're the problem—not her.*

Because I'm obviously some sort of masochist, I let go of my cock without finishing the job. My dick jerks in protest but I ignore it. No, I can't close my eyes, so I stare at the ceiling, cock twitching until I get myself under some semblance of control.

These days, control is a tenuous thing.

Finally, I'm able to sit up without poking myself in the eye. Elbows braced on my knees, head hanging—my cock staring me in the face. Making me wonder if I should seek medical help. I mean, seriously—at what point does jerking-off become compulsive?

"Fuck me," I groan, standing up and glancing at the clock. It's 5AM. My meeting with Declan and a pair of potential clients isn't until ten. I consider going back to bed but I know what I'll end up doing if I fall into that trap. So, instead, I do what I do.

I run.

Ninety minutes and ten miles later, I let myself back into our apartment as quietly as possible. Cari doesn't have to be at work until 9:30 and she likes her sleep. So, imagine my surprise when the scent of fresh coffee hits me as soon as I open the front door. Reaching for the bottom of my sweatshirt, I yank it over my head and drop it in the dirty clothes basket by the door. Tomorrow is laundry day and I keep it there so Cari can sneak a few things in while she thinks I'm not looking. She hates doing laundry and it's not like I'm going to tell her to stop.

I head to the kitchen and sure enough, there's coffee. Thinking that Cari must've prepped the coffee pot and set the timer last night, I say a silent prayer of thanks and grab a mug from the cabinet and pour myself a cup. It's not even 7AM. Plenty of time to shower and go over my blueprints before I have to leave.

Turning, I step back into the hall, my gaze pulled in the

direction of Cari's room, caddy corner from the kitchen. I thought she'd be sleeping, the sun is barely up for fuck's sake, but she's not and the sight of her makes me bobble my coffee cup, hot liquid spilling over its rim, scalding the back of my hand.

She's painting. Carmel colored hair piled on top of her head in a messy knot, the hem of a worn T-shirt skimming the tops of her thighs, exposing bare, mile-long legs. Leaning close to her easel, she makes careful movements with a fine tipped brush. That's not what I'm looking at though. I'm looking at the way her perfectly formed ass cheeks peek out at me from a pair of tiny blue boy shorts that are definitely not doing their goddamn job.

You'd think a ten-mile beating would kill the monster in my pants, but no. It's alive and breathing and as hard as ever.

Move. Get the fuck out of here. Don't get caught letching out on your best friend, you psycho. Go.

MOVE YOUR ASS, FUCKFACE!

My brain is screaming at me, urging me to do the smart thing. The right thing. My dick, however, has different ideas. Ideas that involve picking her up and throwing her on the bed and ripping her panties off so I can throw her legs over my shoulders and bury my face in her pussy, eating her out until she's screaming my name and coming all over my face.

"Hey, you're back."

I look up from her ass to find her looking at me over her shoulder. "Yeah." Real smooth, Patrick. Real fucking smooth. "What are you doing?" Her door is open only halfway and I take a minute step to the left, trying to hide my traitorous hard-on in its shadow.

She laughs and wiggles her paintbrush at me. "Working on my novel."

Fuck me. Fuck me. Fuck me.

I can't tell if the mantra slamming around in my head is my brain freaking out or if it's my brain, switching sides. I clamp my mouth shut, so I don't say it out loud. Just in case.

"I made coffee," she says, dropping her hand, running the bristles of her brush absently along her thigh while she studies the canvas in front of her, trailing paint in its wake. It's a habit of hers. Which is why she stopped wearing pants when she paints. Her bare legs are covered in swipes of bright color and I wonder, for just a second, what paint tastes like.

I'm losing my mind.

"Got some," I say, holding my cup up as proof. "Thank you."

"It's just coffee, Patrick." She turns around fully and smiles. That's when I realize it's my shirt. Her full breasts swaying slightly as she moves, their tips pushing against the thin fabric. She's wearing my shirt.

"What do you think?" she says, stepping to the side to give me a look at the easel behind her and I try to look—I swear to Christ I do. But I can't focus. Can't think. All I see are vague shapes and colors. The same colors streaked across her thighs.

I'm not sure why—she takes my shit all the time—but for whatever reason, seeing her in my shirt right now and nothing else, except paint and panties, is nearly the death of me. It takes every ounce of restraint I have to keep my gaze trained on her face. I lift the coffee to my mouth and take a drink, not sure I'll be able to swallow it but God must love me because I manage it without choking. "It's good," I tell her, my voice sounds like it's being dragged through gravel. "I'm taking a shower." The second I hear it, I'm sure she does too. The need I have for her. The itch I've never scratched. The craving I keep denying.

"Alright," she says turning her back on me. "Save me some hot water. I have to get ready for work soon."

I know the perfect way to save time and hot water.

The thought forms in my head, tries to push itself out of my mouth but as usual, I lock it down. *She's your roommate. Your best friend. You think she'd be standing there in her underwear if she thought of you that way?*

"Don't I always?" I say, because that's who I am. The nice Gilroy. Not the serious one—the control freak who doesn't know how to smile and had his entire life planned before he was old enough to drink and certainly not the one who runs around sticking his dick in anything with a pulse. I'm Patrick Gilroy. Thoughtful. Considerate. Dependable.

Mr. Nice Guy. That's me.

ELEVEN

Patrick

I give in.

Stepping under the warm spray of water, I tell myself it's not a big deal. Masturbation is a normal human function. I'm a guy for fuck's sake—it's practically a behavioral requirement. We eat. We sleep. We jerk off. That's what we do.

"Okay, asshole," I say quietly, picking up the bottle of conditioner—Cari's—the one that smells like gardenias, and squirt some into my hand. "You win."

I feel like I'm fucking twelve, jerking it in my parent's shower, hoping like hell my mom doesn't walk in. I feel pathetic and kinda sad but soon, I'm too worked up to care. Leaning under the showerhead, water beating between my shoulder blades, I brace a hand against the wall in front of me while the other one tightens around my cock, pumping up and down along its swollen length. I think about ripping her panties off. Her paint splattered legs wrapped around my hips. Dragging my shirt over her head so I can see her perfect tits bounce when I ram my cock into her wet pussy, so deep my balls are pressed against her ass.

"*Cari...*" as soon as I say it, I force her out of my mind. I try thinking about someone else. Anyone but Cari. If anything, just to prove to myself that I can. That it's not her I want. It's the tits and ass she keeps parading in front of me like a goddamned naked marching band. It's not her. It's not. But my cock is calling me a liar because without the image of her in my head, I can't tip myself over the edge, no matter what my hand is doing.

That's when the bathroom door swings open.

Why didn't I lock the fucking door? I always lock the door.

"Patrick?"

That's the last rational thought I have before I hear her voice, practically in my ear, and I come, the orgasm barreling down on me so fast and hard I can't stop it. Can't stay quiet. "*Fuuuck,*" I groan, hot spurts of semen hitting the shower wall in front of me. Cari is standing inches away, nothing more than a shower curtain between us and I'm coming all over the place because she said my name.

Is it possible to drown yourself in the shower?

"Your phone—"

"Get out, Cari," I say, my hand still clamped around my dick while it jerks and twitches with its release. I can see her standing there, the shadowy outline of her on the other side of the curtain, not moving. I squeeze my eyes shut and shout. "*Get the fuck out.*"

She moves fast toward the door, mumbling something that sounds like *sorry*, making me feel like a total asshole. Like it's her fault I'm a sexual deviant.

I wait until I hear the door close behind her before I turn the water off.

Go after her.

The voice in my head sounds a hell of a lot like Conner which makes it easy to ignore. Conner is the last person I'm going to take advice from when it comes to Cari.

Stepping out of the shower, I grab my towel and give myself a quick rubdown. I came so hard my ears are ringing and my dick is still at half-mast, wanting more. Ignoring it, I tie the towel around my waist. My phone is on the bathroom counter and I pick it up. I don't remember bringing it into the bathroom with me. I open the door. I can hear her moving around the kitchen. Five missed calls from Declan. That's why she came into the bathroom. Because my phone was going apeshit and she was tired of listening to it.

My room is directly across from the bathroom but I'm having a hard time forcing myself through the doorway.

Stop being a little bitch. So, she caught you jerking it—who gives a fuck? What you should've done is pull back the shower curtain and ask her for help.

I dial my voicemail and wedge the phone against my ear so I can duck as quickly as possible across the hall. In my bedroom, I shut the door firmly behind me and this time I lock it. The first message from Declan is to tell me that our client meeting's been moved to noon. The other four were to tell me the same thing, four more times. If at all possible, Dec is even more tightly wound than I am.

My three-hour window just became a five-hour wasteland. I flop back on my bed. Listening to her move around the apartment, getting ready for work. I feel like I should apologize to her but I don't. How would I even do that? *Sorry I jerked off with your hair products and yelled at you while coming. My bad.* That's a boatload of nope.

Staring at the ceiling, I wait for Cari to leave.

TWELVE

Cari

I'm cutting it close. Instead of leaving the apartment at 8:45AM like I'm supposed to, I waited until the last possible moment. Loitering in the kitchen, fussing with my hair and make-up in the bathroom. Drinking a second cup of coffee—which I definitely did not need. I even turned on the television and watched the morning news. I'm waiting for Patrick to come out of his room. I'm not sure what I'm going to say to him if he does. I just know I need to see him.

These last six months have been torture. I know that's my fault—that if I was just honest with him, tell him what I want, instead of letting Tess talk me into what she's now calling *Operation: Get Gilroy*, I could either tear his clothes off and jump on his cock or accept the fact it's never going to happen. Either way, I'd be putting myself out of my own misery.

I was already up when he left for his morning run, the urge to paint pulling me awake long before the sun. It's like that sometimes. My fingers get itchy. I can't sleep. I get irritable and testy... or maybe I'm itchy and irritable because I'm living with Patrick Gilroy and I haven't had sex in six months. That's probably it but since sex seems to be off the table where Patrick is concerned, painting is the only outlet I've got.

By the time he comes back, I'm lost. Drifting in the half-dream, half-frantic state that painting puts me in. I hear him and know exactly what he's doing. Stripping his shirt off and dropping it into the laundry basket he's moved from his room to beside the front door in preparation for laundry day. Moving through the living room, he makes his way into the kitchen and pours himself a cup of coffee. Even in the *half here* state I'm in, I know exactly what Patrick is doing and I know the precise moment he realizes I'm awake and comes to stand in my doorway.

I know what he looks like without his shirt off but damn if I don't nearly swallow my tongue when I finally look at him. Perfect white teeth. Perfect brown hair. Perfect green eyes. Tall and lean. Smooth, sun-kissed skin—not a blemish or scar in sight. Broad shoulders that taper down, past tightly packed muscles into a pair of low slung track pants. I can smell him for here, clean sweat and sunshine. It makes my mouth water. Patrick isn't hot. He's beautiful. Probably the most beautiful thing I've ever seen. Too beautiful and clean to ever want anything to do with a girl like me.

That's when I catch him looking at my ass. The expression on his face is anything but clean. It was just for a second, so fast that I'm sure I imagined it. But I'm not imaging the rush of heat that shoots through me, pooling between my legs. I'm practically dripping wet and all he did was look at me.

I open my mouth to tell him I want him. That I've always wanted him, but that's not what I say. Like an idiot, I tell him I made coffee even though he's standing right in front of me with a cup of it in his hand and after a few minutes of small talk, he heads for the shower.

As soon as I hear the bathroom door snap closed, I drop my paintbrush and follow him down the hall. Pressing my ear against the door, I can see the shadow of him moving in the light that creeps under the door. I listen as he starts the shower before pulling back the curtain to step in. I imagine him running the bar of soap he uses across his shoulders. Over his chest. Down his tightly packed abs. That's when I hear it. I hear *him*.

A soft slapping sound so faint under the rush of water.

That's when he says my name.

Cari.

The throbbing in my pussy intensifies, pulsing in time with my knocking heart. With my ear pressed to the door, I listen. I can see him, his perfect body tense, his beautiful lips parted slightly, his chest heaving, his breath pushing out of his lungs in short, uneven gasps that keep time with the hand that's sliding up and down his gorgeous cock. I don't even know what it looks like but I know it's beautiful. Just like the rest of him.

Across the hall, his phone goes off. Loud. It sounds like a fucking air horn. Not once, not twice. Over and over until I'm sure he's going to hear it and stop what he's doing. I dart across the hall and silence it. Bringing it with me, I stand outside the door, hand on the knob. I don't want to just listen anymore and I don't want to rely on my imagination. I want to see Patrick. I want to see what he looks like when he comes.

In some sort of trance, I push the door open. I know he knows I'm in here, the bathroom door squeaks when you open it. But he doesn't stop.

"Patrick." My throat is burning, my hand gripping the hem of my shirt to keep from touching myself, the other reaching for the shower curtain. That's when he comes, saying something low and guttural, the hand braced against the shower wall above his head curled into a fist. He knows I'm in here but doesn't stop.

I lose my nerve. Looking down at the phone in my hand, I start babbling. Making excuses. "Your phone—"

"Get out, Cari," he barks at me. He sounds angry that I'm there. Like I'm intruding. Not like Patrick at all.

"I—"

"Get the fuck out."

I turn, tossing his phone on the bathroom counter and run, like the coward I am.

I slam my car door and hurry across the street, juggling my car keys, cell phone, and morning yogurt. Opening the gallery at 10AM is my responsibility, which means I have to be here by 9:30AM to make coffee and confirm Miranda's appointments for the day.

Hustling up the stairs, I shove my key into the lock and open the door. Noticing that the alarm is already turned off, I have a slight panic attack. I'm always the first one here and I know I set the alarm before I left last night.

Dumping my bag and yogurt on the floor at my feet, I clutch my keys and cell. Thanks to Patrick, my keys have a small can of mace attached to them and I have 911 on speed dial. I can hear him now. *I hate the idea of you closing that place by yourself. It's not safe.* He's gonna give me a big fat *I told you so* when I get home.

Inching my way around the stairwell wall, I expect to see paintings slashed out of their frames. Most of our artwork comes from local artists, struggling to make a name for themselves but we have more than a few pieces that come from well-established artists, any of which would be worth more than I make in a year.

I am so fired.

Poking my head into the gallery, I see what I see every morning. Beautiful art hanging on pristine white walls. Floor to ceiling windows, the strengthening summer sun streaming in through UV tint (to protect the paintings) to bounce off the flecks of pyrite in the dark granite floors.

I breathe a soft sigh of relief and stoop to retrieve my bag, sticking my yogurt into its side pocket before standing.

"Cari, can you please come in here?" Miranda's voice cuts through the silence and I have to slap a hand over my mouth to keep from yelping out loud. I look at the clock on the wall behind my desk. She never shows her face before noon. What the hell is she doing here?

I hurry to my desk and press the intercom button. "On my way," I tell her, kicking my bag under my desk. So much for breakfast.

Hurrying down the short hallway behind the main gallery, I pull up short in front of her office door and open it without knocking. "What's up, Miran..."

She's not alone and the person she's with causes the words to dry up in my mouth. I swallow, trying to force my throat to work properly. "I mean, what can I do for you, Ms. McIntyre?" In the six months I've worked here, Miranda and I have developed a good relationship. So good that I'd almost consider her a friend. We're on a first name basis, but never in front of clients. Or artists.

"Cari, I'd like to introduce you to Everett Chase," Miranda says, biting her lip to keep from laughing at me. "Chase, this is Cari Faraday, my personal assistant."

Everett Chase.

Everett. Fucking. Chase.

Suddenly, I'm feeling light-headed.

The man lounging in the chair in front of Miranda's desk stands slowly, offering me a hand. "It's a pleasure to meet you, Cari." He made no attempt to hide the amused smile on his face.

Take his hand, Cari and try not to mess this up.

I take his hand and give it a firm shake. I hate those women who shake hands like their wrists are broken. "The pleasure is mine, Mr. Chase," I say, thoroughly impressed with myself. I'm not fangirling. I'm forming rational, complete sentences. I almost sound like a normal person. "I'm a huge fan or your work."

Okay, I'm fangirling a *little bit.* He's gorgeous. Eyes that are almost too blue to be real. Reddish brown hair that curls around the collar of his expensive dress shirt, a pair of paint-splattered jeans and battered work boots that cost more than my car rounding out the casual wealth of his appearance. More than just gorgeous, he happens to be arguably the best contemporary artist in Boston. Certainly, its most famous.

I'm a painter too. The words force their way to the tip of my tongue and I have to grit my teeth to keep them from tumbling out. I'm not a painter. I don't want to be. I want to own my own gallery someday, like Miranda. Painting is just a hobby. That's all.

Chase's smile turns. He's not amused anymore. Now he's wondering if I'm full of shit, just trying to fluff his ego. "Oh? A fan?" Still holding my hand, he turns it over, studying my paint-stained cuticles. Bright blue eyes assess everything about me. I suddenly wish I was dressed in something a little less stuffy than black dress slacks and my white silk blouse. As if he's confirmed something, he looks up at me through thick, dark lashes. "Which of my paintings is your favorite?"

"Full Moon on Flowing Water," I say without hesitation. I'm sure he's heard it a thousand times. How great he is. How talented. All from brainless bimbos who see nothing more than a walking wallet with a pretty face to match. I'm embarrassed. Want to jerk my hand away from his but I don't. I just stand there and wait for the ridicule.

He shoots Miranda a quick look before letting go of my hand. "Points for originality," he says, reclaiming his seat. "But it's not my best work," he says, challenging me.

"Technically, no," I concede, clasping my hands behind my back to hide the fact that they're clenched into fists.

"But your use of light and texture are amazing. I saw it a few years ago when your personal collection was on loan to The Institute of Contemporary Art." I'm gushing, I know that, but I can't seem to stop myself. Instead, I seem intent on making it even worse. "When I looked at it, I felt like I was dreaming and awake at the same time. It was a... transformative experience." I sound ridiculous. Heat floods across my chest, collecting in the spot just below my collarbone. I turn away from Everett Chase's assessing gaze and focus on my boss. "Was there something you needed, Ms. McIntyre?" I say, trying to salvage what's left of my dignity.

"Yes," Miranda nods her head, fiddling with some papers on her desk before giving me a cool smile. "Can you please confirm today's appointments?"

Her request gives me pause. "Of course." What's going on? She's meeting with Everett Chase before opening hours and to top it off, calls me into her office to tell me to do something she knows I do every day without prompting. Completely confused, I give my head a short nod before making myself look at Miranda's guest. "It was nice to meet you, Mr. Chase."

"It's just Chase—no mister," he says, smirking at my formality. "And you're wrong. The pleasure was all mine, Cari."

I split a small smile between the two of them before turning and making my escape

.

THIRTEEN

Patrick

I noticed Cari's lunch on the counter about fifteen minutes after she blew out the door. Any other day I'd take a picture of it with my cell and send it to her and she'd text me back, calling herself a space-cadet or some shit like that. Then I'd go out of my way to take it to her, just so I can see her smile. But that was before she stood outside the shower and listened to me come while I was thinking about her.

Quit being such a twat. She doesn't know you were thinking about her. It's only weird because you're making it weird. Now man the fuck up and take Cari her goddamn lunch.

Swiping it off the counter, I set my coffee cup in the sink on my way out the door. The gallery is on my way to the jobsite where Declan and I are meeting prospective clients. Blueprints tucked under my arm, I use my free hand to dig my cell phone out of my pocket while I jog down the stairs. Who says guys can't multi-task?

"Call Declan," I say and a second later, the phone is ringing. I always like to make it to the job site at least thirty minutes before a meeting but this time I'll be lucky if I'm not late. Thankfully, I get Declan's voicemail. "Hey, Cari forgot her lunch again, so I'm gonna be a few minutes later than usual." Tucking my phone between my ear and shoulder, I fish out my truck keys and pop the lock on the diamond-plate toolbox in its bed so I can dump everything but Cari's lunch bag inside. "Tell the Beemans I'm on my way and they're gonna love their plans." Slamming the lid, I kill my cell and circle the truck. Climbing in, I toss it into the cup holder and start the car, hoping like hell Declan doesn't call me back. I can just hear him—*Let her starve a few times. Maybe then she'd stop forgetting her lunch.*

Usually, I just shrug it off with an *it's no big deal* because I don't want him or anyone to know that I'm not taking Cari her lunch because I'm afraid she'll starve. I'm taking it to her because, even after what happened this morning, I'll take any opportunity to see her I can get.

Because I'm a pathetic loser.

I make it to the gallery a few minutes before ten and park next to her car. These days she can afford a better car—the gallery commissions are padding her income nicely—but she's still driving the car she brought with her from Ohio. It's a complete rust bucket but it suits her and thanks to Tess, runs like a top.

I realize what I'm doing. I'm stalling. The thought of looking her in the eye after what she heard this morning has me jamming my key back into the ignition, ready to drive away. But I don't because I know the longer it takes me to look her in the eye, the harder it'll be for me to actually do it. I force myself out of the truck and up the stairs.

I can see her sitting at her desk, phone wedged between her ear and shoulder while she works on the computer. I wait for her to hang up the phone before I walk in. As soon as I do, her head comes up. Seeing me, she offers me a shy smile. Yup, she definitely knows what I was doing in the shower this morning. "What are you—"

Not sure I can manage actual words, I hold her lunch bag up.

"Shit," she says, the smile on her face edged with exasperation as she stands to round the desk I'm waiting in front of. "I'm so sorry—I was running late because..." Her voice catches, a flush rushing across the exposed part of her chest. "I really shouldn't paint before work," she says, catching her lower lip between her teeth. "I lose all track of time."

Seeing my opening, I kamikaze my way through it. "Look—Cari..." I run a hand over the top of my head, trying like hell to pretend I'm totally cool with the fact that she walked in on me jerking off, that it's no big deal, but before I get the words out, she's talking over me.

"I'm sorry, Patrick." She shakes her head. "It was inconsiderate of me to barge in like that. It won't happen again."

I stand there for a second, not sure what to say. She's acting like all of this is her fault. "I'm sorry too. I shouldn't have yelled at you like—"

"Cari, call Hector and tell him I need him to deliver the Randell watercolor to the Fletchers by—Patrick," I look over Cari's shoulder to see her boss standing a few feet away. "It's nice to see you again." Behind her is a man I've never seen before. Taking in his paint-splattered boots and expensive jeans, I peg him for an artist. A rich one.

I ignore the way she's looking at me, like she wants to eat me for breakfast. I think about Conner's offer a few months ago to fuck a payroll advance out of her for Cari and I have to clench my jaw for a minute to keep myself from laughing. Having gotten to know Cari's boss a bit, I have a feeling even Con wouldn't be able to keep up with her. "Morning, Miranda." I hold the paper bag I'm still holding up like a shield. "Sorry to interrupt, Cari forgot her lunch. Again," I say, teasing her just a bit because I like to watch the flush of heat creep across her chest to collect beneath her collarbone.

"Nonsense," Miranda says, shooing away my apology like it annoyed her. "You know you're welcome anytime." The way she says it, and the way she's looking at me heat the back of my neck. "Where are my manners?" She breaks eye contact with me and turns. "Patrick, this is my friend, Everett Chase—Chase, this is Cari's roommate, Patrick Gilroy."

I step forward, holding out my hand. "Nice to meet you," I say. The name is familiar. Probably one of the painters Cari talks about when she tells me about her workday.

"Patrick Gilroy?" Chase says, giving me a firm handshake before breaking contact. "The architect?"

I shoot Cari a quick look, wondering if she's been talking about me. "That's me."

Chase nods his head and smiles. "You do beautiful work—ever think about branching out into commercial design?"

It's not the first time someone has recognized my name and my work but for some reason, it catches me by surprise. "Eventually," I say, taking a step back. "My partner and I are really buried right now with residential projects." I offer him a quick smile before re-directing my attention to Cari. "Speaking of which, I've gotta run." I extend the bag to her and she takes it. "Pizza night?" We usually order pizza on Friday nights and clear the DVR which means watching reality television until my brain starts oozing out of my ears. After this morning, it's the last thing I want to do but in the interest of putting my embarrassment behind me, I'm going to try.

Cari takes the bag, catching her bottom lip between her teeth. "I've got a date," she says, shaking her head, watching from the corner of her eye as Miranda and her pet painter wander into the gallery and start talking about lighting and space. "Trevor is taking me to dinner."

"Cool," I say, even though it's anything but. I hate Trevor almost as much as I hated that douchey lawyer she was dating before she moved in. The one she caught banging his intern. To be fair though, I've hated every single one of her boyfriends.

Because none of them are me.

"I guess that means I don't have to watch *Reality Rapper Bachelor Housewives* until brain damage sets in."

She swats me with her lunch bag and laughs. "You love it, you're just afraid to admit." As soon as her boss is out of earshot, she takes a step closer. So close I can smell the gardenia-scented hair products she uses. The same hair products I used to jerk off this morning.

Despite the mortification currently making me want to disappear, I'm rock fucking hard before I have time to blink, the bulk of it pushing against the zipper of my jeans.

Don't look down, don't look down, don't look down...

"Look, are we okay?" she says, looking up at me. "Because I really am sorry about this morning and I don't want there to be any weirdness between us. You're my best—"

I smile. "No weirdness." If I have to hear her tell me I'm her best friend one more fucking time I'm going to put my head through the goddamned window. "But if I don't leave now," I say, backing myself out the door. "I'm going to be late for the Beemans and then Declan will probably murder me."

"Okay." She gives me a smile that looks relieved. Relieved that I'm not making this weird. That it's behind us. That I'm still good guy Patrick and I'm still her friend. "See you at home?"

"See you at home," I say, turning to let myself out. Jogging down the steps, I risk a look up. Cari's standing in the glass box of the gallery, paper bag clutched in her hand.

She's watching me walk away.

FOURTEEN

Patrick

"Hello—earth to Patrick?"

I look up to see Cari standing in front of me. As soon as she has my attention, she smiles. "Which one?" she says, jiggling the pair of hangers she's holding, one in each hand.

I look past them, at her. She's wearing her white silk robe and nothing underneath. Her nipples push against the pale, thin fabric and it hangs open just a bit, giving me a hint of soft, curving breast. I know that if I let my gaze dip just a bit lower, I'll catch a glimpse of her firm, tanned thighs. The dark, shadowy cleft between them.

"The black one," I say because I know it's her favorite, forcing my eyes to retrain themselves on the baseball game I'm pretending to watch. I love baseball—loved it since I was a kid. I haven't known Cari for half as long but right now, with her standing half-naked in front of me, it's no contest.

"Yeah?" She aims a slim, arched brow at the dress I chose. "You think it's fifth-date worthy?"

The dress in question is little more than a black lace tube that barely skimmed the tops of her thighs with straps so thin you have to squint just to see them. It's what she was wearing when I suggested she move in with me. Every time I see her in it all I can think about is helping her take it off.

"Yeah." I shrug like I don't care. "It looks good on you."

A slow smile spreads across her perfect face, lifting the corners of her full, lush mouth. "You think so?"

I shrug again. "Sure." I keep my eyes glued to the flat screen. All I can think about is what's going on under her robe while she's got me so deep in the friend-zone I'm helping her pick out dresses for her date with her douche de jour... what was his name? Tim? Travis? It didn't matter. It's their fifth date and I know what that means.

Someone's getting fucked tonight. It just isn't going to be me.

Choice made, she retreats to her room to finish getting ready. A few seconds later, old-school Madonna—*Lucky Star*—floats through the open door. She always listens to Madonna when she's getting ready for a date.

As soon as the music clicks on, I shift my gaze to the full-length mirror that hangs on the wall, to the right of the flat screen. From where I sit, I have a perfect view of Cari's bedroom... and she never closed her door.

I watch while she hooks the hanger of the dress she's decided against over the back of her closet door before tossing the other one on the bed.

The black one. The one I chose.

She unties her robe and I watch it slink down her arms to

pool at her bare feet. She's suddenly naked. Her breasts, full and firm, sway gently as she gathers up her long, caramel-colored hair and winds it into a loose bun at her nape. If she looks up or catches my reflection in the mirror, she'll know I'm watching her. Catch me perving out but I can't stop staring. For a second, I can almost taste her. Feel the hard bud of her nipple against my tongue.

All I can see is the smooth curve of her ass under my hands as I lift her hips to meet mine, her legs spread wide while the thick, blunt head of my cock rubs against the soft, wet folds of her pussy. Teasing her until she moans before driving into her in deft stroke, fast and hard...

She's going to catch me but I can't look away. My cock is throbbing, pushing against the unforgiving fabric of my shorts. There's no hiding it. If she looks now, she'll see.

She'll see that maybe I'm not such a nice guy after all.

Con was right. Asking Cari to move in was a mistake.

"Fuck you, Conner," I say under my breath, standing to limp my way into our tiny kitchen. Across the hall, I can see directly into Cari's room—no mirror required. Instead of letching, I turn my back on what's going on and reach into the fridge to pull out a beer. Twisting off the cap, I plink it into the trash before taking a long, hard swallow while I contemplate dumping the contents of the ice cube tray down the front of my pants.

Like it would help.

I take another, longer pull from the beer in my hand and drain it before tossing the empty in the trash.

Looks like another Friday night filled with MLB and masturbation.

It doesn't have to be that way, you know. Text Sara, she'd be over here, panties in hand, before you even hit send.

Thinking about Sara makes me feel guilty. After she gave me her number that night, I didn't call but she was more persistent than I gave her credit for. She showed up at Gilroy's night after night until I finally asked her out, out of some weird sense of obligation. We ended up dating for a few weeks before I broke it off. She was a nice girl and deserved better than me fucking her while I'm thinking about Cari.

Yeah? She made it pretty clear she isn't interested in better. She's interested in you.

"Hey, bring me one," Cari says, pushing all thoughts of Sara out of my head. Just the sound of her voice, soft and husky, is enough to make my cock twitch.

"Comin' up," I say, jerking the fridge open to grab two more beers, twisting the caps off before turning around. She's just shimmying into the dress, black lace and silk, sliding up long, lean thighs. I catch a glimpse of more lace. Cherry red this time, a thin strip of it strung between the cheeks of her tight, round ass. I can't imagine the one covering her pussy is much bigger. My cock isn't just twitching, it's throbbing and straining against the front of my cargos. There's no hiding the raging hard-on I've got going.

Shit. Please don't turn around.

I clear my throat to let her know I'm coming but the sound doesn't do much to hurry her along. It never does. As far as Cari's concerned, I'm about as anatomically correct as a Ken doll. "Here," I say, touching the frosty glass against her bare shoulder just as she hooks her arms into those uselessly thin straps. For a split second, I see myself slipping my finger beneath one of them, snapping it with the slightest crook.

"Thanks," she says, aiming a wide grin at me over her shoulder before taking the beer.

"You're welcome," I mutter, turning to leave. I have to get the hell out of here. Away from her.

"Zip me up?"

FIFTEEN

Patrick

Zip me up?

"Sure thing," I say, tilting my half-empty bottle in her direction and she takes it, setting both of them on her dresser.

Her hair's come undone from where she's put it up. It falls against her bare shoulders in soft, loose waves that smell like her—gardenias and vanilla, mixed with something darker. Deeper.

I'm losing my fucking mind.

I scoop it out of the way, the silk of it shifting through my fingers as I brush it over her shoulder, exposing her nape. My hands are shaking and my dick is doing push-ups inside my pants but I manage to grip the delicate tongue of the zipper, pinching the tail of it to anchor the dress in place while I drag it up, slow, so I don't snag the lace. She turns her head just a bit, giving me a glimpse of her perfectly angled jaw, the curve of her mouth. She seems to be waiting for me to say something, but what?

I'm gonna jerk off to this moment as soon as you leave.

I've been dying to fuck you ever since the night you kissed me in my car.

I've got an idea... cancel your date. We can order pizza and you can sit on my face.

I don't say any of those things. "There you go..." I say instead, feeling ten different kinds of lame. Mr. Nice Guy strikes again.

"Thanks..." She takes a step backward. It's a small step... not even a step, really. More of a sway. She swayed backward, grazing her tight, lace-clad ass across my erection. I know she can feel it, rock hard and hot between her ass cheeks. Hear the hissing intake of the breath I'm too stunned to swallow. I should step back. It was an accident. She didn't mean to—

And then she bends over.

Her ass is not grazing anymore. It's grinding against me. Massaging my cock in a lazy, circular motion that has me seeing stars. The friction between us is so sweet and hot the tip of my cock starts tingling. My balls tighten in anticipation. It's all I can think about. The feel of her ass pressed against my throbbing cock. That strip of cherry-red lace running right up the center of her. It's almost enough to have me coming right here, right now.

Before I know what I'm doing, I drop my hands to her hips, gathering black lace in my fists, ready to jerk it up, to drop to my knees and bury my face in her pussy to lap at all that smooth, dark honey I can smell between her thighs...

Someone's knocking. Probably been knocking for a while.

The thud of knuckles on wood sounds impatient. Like it didn't like being kept waiting.

My cock and I can totally relate.

Cari straightens her spine, flipping her hair over her shoulder. It falls, sliding across my face, a silken snare that cascades across my cheeks, shifting slowly, her face disappearing beneath the fall.

I'm still holding her hips, her ass snug against my hard as a rock dick. The hem of her skirt riding high against her thighs, the short length of it gripped tight in my fists. I have to let go. Problem is, I'm not sure I *can* let go.

The knocking again, fast and agitated, makes up my mind for me. I jerk my hands away and take a step back— that's when I realize why she bent over in the first place. She was pulling on her shoes. While I've been busy dry humping her, she'd been putting on her cherry red heels.

They matched her panties perfectly.

"Patrick..." she breathes my name, her sky-blue eyes wide. Trembling lips parted, gaze cloudy. Confused.

Fuck. Shit.

"Sorry." I go palms up, feeling like the biggest asshole alive. "That was totally uncalled for," I say, taking another step back and then another and another until I'm in the living room, heading for the door. I swing it open just as Tim/Travis, starts another flurry of impatient pounding.

I don't say anything, just fling the door open and let it hang while I bee-line my way to the kitchen. I snag a beer out of the fridge and twist the cap off before setting it aside.

Beer isn't gonna cut it. Not even close.

I rummage around in the cabinet above the fridge,

shoving bottles aside until I find what I want. Unscrewing the cap, I toss it in the sink before tipping the bottle of Jameson to my mouth. There's about a fourth left in the bottom of it and I'm guzzling like a man dying of thirst. The booze hits my empty gut like a nuke but I ignore the wildfire spreading through my abdomen and cut a glance at the douche in my living room. Another James clone—expensive watch. Expensive haircut. Trendy clothes. Probably drives a Porsche. There's been a steady parade through here since Cari moved in but none of them stuck until now.

I want to kill him almost as much as I wanted to kill James.

The front door is still hanging open but he's now standing by the coffee table, watching me. He looks a little scared of me and to tell the truth, I like the way that feels.

"Sorry, my manners are for shit—want some," I say, lifting the hem of my t-shirt to wipe at the rim of the whiskey bottle before holding it out to him.

"Ahh... no. Thanks anyway," Tim/Travis says, giving me a head shake along with a look that says he thinks I belong in a zoo. "Is Cari ready?" He looks down at his watch, "Our reservations are for..." He trails off when she walks into the room. "Damn, baby—you look hot."

"Thank you," she says, giving him a half-smile that doesn't quite reach her eyes. She hates it when they call her *baby*.

I take another dying-of-thirst guzzle, this one draining the bottle. Tossing it in the general direction of the trash can, it bounces off the rim and clatter onto the floor. I grin like an idiot for about two seconds before I catch her looking at me. Cari doesn't look confused anymore. She's clear-eyed and she's looking at me like she knows exactly what happened in her room. Like she did it on purpose.

Now I don't feel like grinning. Now I want to punch myself in the fucking face. Or maybe in the dick. That stupid thing still hasn't figured it out. She's just messing with us. Like that night in my car. Like every time she changes her clothes with her door open, or puts her hand on my leg while we're watching TV. This whole time, here I was, thinking it was my problem. That I was the one making things weird. Perverting everything. Taking advantage of our friendship and the fact that she had nowhere to go so I could be closer to her.

But I was wrong.

It's been the other way around this whole fucking time.

"Wow..." I laugh, bracing my hands on the kitchen counter and lean, letting my head hang between my shoulders for just a moment before I lift it, looking right at her. "Have fun," I say, cutting her a look that says something else entirely.

I watch Tim/Travis help her into her coat, shooting me quick looks like he's trying to hurry and get her out the door before I hulk out and rip his face off. So, maybe he's not as stupid as he looks.

Coat finally on, Tim/Travis guides her through the open front door. "See you later, man," he says, dropping his hand to her waist to push her along.

"God, I fucking hope not," I say out loud, lifting the beer I opened and didn't want to my mouth, draining it dry. I get the stink-eye from Tim/Travis and I give him a smile.

Fuck him. Fuck 'em both.

"Goodnight, Patrick," Cari says, reaching for the door to pull it closed behind them. I can feel her eyes on me. Watching me. She knows she's finally pushed me too far and is probably wondering if she's going to need to sleep with a can of mace and a steak knife from now on.

Probably wouldn't hurt.

As soon as she's gone, I head down the short hallway to my own bedroom. There, I change my clothes, pulling on a crisp, white cotton button-down and a clean pair of jeans. In the bathroom, I do a quick assessment. My dark brown hair is about 2 weeks past a haircut and I could use a shave. In the end, I settle for running my fingers through my hair and brushing my teeth before I head out the door.

If Cari wants to fifth-date fuck her latest douchebag, that's fine by me. I didn't need five dates. Hell, I don't even need one.

No more Mr. Nice Guy.

SIXTEEN

Cari

Have fun.

As soon as he said it, I knew Patrick figured it out. He knows I've been chipping away at his self-control on purpose and he's not happy about it. I want to tell Travis to leave. That I don't want to date him anymore. That I never really did. With him gone, I could explain things to Patrick. Apologize. Tell him how I feel. What I want.

Instead, I run like a scared rabbit.

For months, Tess and I have been working on getting Patrick into my bed. Curling up next to him on the couch while we binge-watch *Real Housewives.* Sneaking my panties into his laundry basket. That ridiculously thin excuse for a bathrobe. That was all her.

But hanging a mirror in the living room, directly across from my bedroom door? *Forgetting* to close it when I change my clothes? Asking him to help me into my dress and then bending over so I could grind my ass into his cock?

Those were my bright ideas...

Why am I going out of my way to help Tess with this

stupid bet?

Because this is one bet I want to lose.

I feel a hand land on my knee and I look up. We're stopped at a red light, cross traffic whizzing through the intersection. I can feel Trevor looking at me, so I tilt my head in his direction and smile back. "I'm thinking sushi," he says, giving my knee a squeeze before sliding it higher on my thigh. "How's that sound, baby?"

It sounds disgusting. Almost as disgusting as the prospect of listening to him call me *baby* all night. "I'm not a fan of sushi," I say, clenching my thighs together to slow the process of his wandering hand. "Why don't we just go for a burg—"

"I got us a table at Zen 88." His gaze dipping to my breasts while his tongue darts out to run along his lower lip. Zen 88 is a trendy, downtown sushi bar. He hadn't heard a thing I said. "After dinner, I thought we could go back to—"

The light turns green and I shift in my seat, pulling my leg from beneath his hand. "The light's green," I say, softening my rejection with a smile. As if to prove my point, the car behind us laid on its horn.

"Is there something wrong?" He shoots me a quick look while shifting the car into first. "You've been acting weird since I picked you up." He skips seconds and shifts into third to sling-shot around a minivan. "Did something happen with your roommate? You guys have a fight or something?"

"Patrick?" Saying his name caused my heart to knock against my ribcage and I suddenly feel his thick, hard cock pressed into the cleft of my ass, the size and heat of it causing my mouth to go dry.

"No," I say, forcing myself to smile at Trevor. "Nothing happened."

"Are you sure you're okay?" He's not buying it.

I look up to see Trevor staring at me, mild concern etched into his generically handsome face. We're at the restaurant and the valet has my door open, his hand dangling in my mid-air, offering to help me out of the car.

"Yes," I say, placing my hand in the valet's hand. "I'm just hungry is all." I smile again and climb out of the car.

SEVENTEEN

Patrick

The minute I come downstairs, I get catcalls and wolf-whistles. Gilroy's regulars giving me shit. It's still early in the night. Things don't start getting crazy until after ten but fuck if I'm sitting in my apartment until then.

"Look at this dandy," my Uncle Paddy calls out, flipping a pint off the bar while he takes in my button-down shirt and dark jeans—a far cry from my usual Gilroy's attire of cargo shorts and thrift-store T-shirt. The glass rolls from one hand to the other, as slick as can be, landing under the taps where he builds me a Guinness. "Here you go, *boyo*," he says, setting the pint in front of me before giving me a long, hard look. "On your way to church then?"

His remark has nothing to do with my shirt. My uncle's been running Gilroy's for almost twenty years now—he knows when someone comes into his bar looking for trouble. I just grin and raise my pint. "May the Saints preserve us," I say, mimicking his thick Irish brogue, earning myself a loud snort. "Conner around?"

"That altar boy of mine is in back." Paddy throws his towel over his shoulder before heading down the length of the bar to attend to another customer. I take my glass and head for the back of the bar.

"Nice shirt, asshole," Conner says, tucking a receipt between the pages of the book he's reading.

Gatsby. Always *Gatsby.*

He sets it aside while I slide into the booth across from him. I flip him the bird. "At least it's clean," I say and he laughs.

As soon as I'm settled, the waitress sidles up to the table. "Need another, Patrick," she says, eyeing the dregs left in my pint. Her name is Lisa and with her dyed black hair, candy-pink mouth and fake tits, she's about as *un*-Cari as it gets.

Another drink is the last thing I need but my nerve is a tenuous thing. My phone buzzes in my pocket and I pull it out.

It's Cari.

"How about a Jameson? Neat," I say, offering her a slight smile while I dump the call.

"Sure thing…" she smiles back before heading to the bar.

Conner leans back in the booth, watching the exchange, a slight smirk on his face. "Caught a look at Legs comin' through here a few minutes ago with her date…" he says as soon as Lisa's gone. "she did not look horrible."

I don't say anything. Just wait for him to say, *I told you so.*

Instead, he seems content to state the obvious. "It's been six months now."

"Yup," I say before swallowing the last of my pint. Six

months of being fucked with. Six months of letting myself get wound so tight I feel like I'm about to lose my mind half the time—and for what? Laughs? An ego boost?

"How's it going?" he asks, but he knows. Everyone knows.

"It's good," I lie through my teeth, wishing Lisa would hurry the fuck up with my drink. I have a feeling I need to be drunk for what's coming out of Conner's mouth next.

"You are a horrible fucking liar." Conner leans back and sighs like I'm a burden on his back and he's finally going to set me down.

I look at my watch. "It's getting late. Isn't it about time you start looking for your nightly bathroom hookup?"

"That happened forty-five minutes ago. Twice." Unfazed, Conner smiles. "Look, cousin. You know what you need to do, right?" he says. He's exactly five months older than me but if sexual experience were measured in years, he'd be a fucking dinosaur.

I shrug because as pissed as I am, I don't want to seem like I'm hanging on his every word. Which I am... I mean, I know what I *have* to do but maybe hearing Conner say the words will give me the kick in the ass I need to get the job done.

"You need to wake up your inner-asshole," he says, all sage advice and knowing smile.

Not really the advice I was expecting.

"I'm afraid the asshole gene skipped me over," I say, shaking my head. Inner-asshole? He might as well tell me to jump off the roof and fly.

Now Conner laughs at me. "Bullshit," he says, lifting his

own pint. "You're a Gilroy—that means you've got asshole in spades." He gives me a shit-eating grin. "You just have to stop giving a fuck."

"And how do you suggest I do that?" I say but I already know, don't I? It's why I came down here. Why I put on a clean shirt and brushed my teeth.

Conner must've been reading my mind because he laughed. "Take a look around this bar, man," he says, stretching his legs out in front of him under the table. "There isn't a woman in this place that would say no to me—you know why?"

"Because you're a sexual Sharknado?"

This earned me a laugh. "Fuck you," he finally says. "And yes, I am... but that's not why. It's because I'm an asshole and for some inexplicable reason, the vast majority of the female population love assholes. They love deluding themselves into thinking they'll be the one to change me. Fix me or some shit."

"Being an asshole isn't a superpower, cousin," I say but by now, he's got me half-convinced that it actually might be.

"If you do it the right way it is," he tells me. "It's time you use who you really are to get what you want. More to the point, *who* you want."

I shake my head again, spinning my empty pint between my fingers. Who I really am is miles and miles from the guy he's describing. Going upstairs to finish the Yankees game is starting to sound like a good idea. "I wouldn't even know where to start."

Seeming to know that I'm halfway buying his bullshit,

Conner goes in for the kill. "You know what Tess and Cari call you behind your back?" He leans back, head cocked like he can't look at me head-on and say it at the same time. "Predictable Patrick."

I feel my spine stiffen like he'd rabbit-punched me in the kidney.

Predictable Patrick.

Safe. Boring. Harmless.

That's what Cari thinks about me. It's how I feel and it makes me sick.

Conner lets out a rough sigh. "Look, cousin—" Before he can lay it on me, Lisa comes back with my Jameson, along with a water.

"Here ya go," she says setting the rocks glass on the table in front of me. Then she slides the water onto the table alongside it. "Paddy says to tell you it's holy water," she says with a shrug and I can't help but laugh. It's my uncle's way of telling me not to start trouble in his bar.

From the corner of my eye, I can see Conner watching Lisa with avid interest. I'm suddenly sure that instead of telling me what I need to do, he's going to show me. Before I can stop him, Conner reaches for Lisa's hand and pulls on it gently, giving her the same lopsided grin I've seen him give a hundred women—and watched it work every time. "Sit down for a minute, Lees, I want to tell you a secret…"

I'm not surprised when she does what he says because I've never met a woman who *wouldn't*. I watch while Lisa allows herself to be tugged down into the booth beside him, angling her shoulders so that they're pressed against the hard expanse of Conner's chest.

Watching him slip a tattooed arm around Lisa's waist, he leans in close to whisper something in her ear—something that makes her blush—was like watching myself. Or a much more adept version of myself. He's got his large, callused hand splayed across her abdomen, the tip of his work-roughened pinkie finger slipping inside the waistband of her shorts, making contact with bare flesh. That contact, coupled with whatever Conner is whispering in her ear is enough to loosen the lock Lisa has on her knees. They fall apart just a bit—enough to make it obvious that she's more than down for whatever it is my cousin is proposing.

I am no longer halfway convinced that being an asshole is a superpower.

I am a true believer.

I'm about ready to excuse myself from the table so they can have some obviously much-needed privacy when suddenly Conner leans back, unwinding his arm from her waist. Now I notice Lisa's got her eyes locked on me. She's looking at me like she's seeing me for the first time. Like I've got something she wants. She stands, skirting the table until she's standing right in front of me.

And she's holding out her hand.

I look at Connor and he's grinning at me—that dimple of his promising a boatload of sin. *Don't say I never gave you nothing, cousin*, I can practically hear him say it. He reaches across the table and palms my Jameson, offering me a silent toast before he drains the glass. In its place, he leaves a strip of foil-wrapped condoms.

I don't want to think about Cari anymore. I don't want

to want things I can't have and I don't want to worry about how this will make Lisa feel afterward or about what kind of guy this makes me.

I'm done thinking. Thinking is for nice guys and tonight—*right now*—that isn't me. I swipe the condoms off the table and shove them into my back pocket before I give Lisa my hand and let her take me to church.

EIGHTEEN

Patrick

Cari and I have one roommate rule—hard and fast.

No bringing home conquests. The moment Lisa takes my hand and pulls me out of the booth, I know I'm going to break that rule.

I could pull a *Gilroy* and fuck my uncle's cocktail waitress in the ladies' room, or I can treat her like an actual person with real feelings. I opt for the latter. I know, I know... not very *assholeish* of me.

Baby steps.

Somewhere between the booth where we left Conner and the bar my uncle is behind, I start leading her. Pulling Lisa through the growing crowd, we weave our way through a large throng of co-eds—girls drinking cranberry and Malibu and dudes choking down black & tans because ordering a Bud Light in an Irish pub is akin to pissing on a barstool.

I take Lisa's drink tray and toss it up on the bar as we

pass by. On impulse, I swipe an open bottle of Jameson from the well. "I'm taking my break, Paddy," Lisa calls over her shoulder as I pull her up the stairs leading to my apartment. She's slightly out of breath—whether it's because I've got her running the Boston Marathon or because I'm about five minutes away from getting into her pants, I don't know and I'm caring less and less.

"I want my waitress back in fifteen minutes, boyo," Uncle Paddy calls after me. I wave the bottle over my head and keep climbing. I can't be sure but I think I hear him say something that sounds like, *it's about feckin' time.*

I push the door open and drag Lisa inside after me, kicking the door shut. By now it's full on dark and I forgot to leave a light on when I left so as soon as I do, we're surrounded by dark, the only light that cuts through the gloom is the dim glow of a streetlamp. It's weak and watery, making it impossible to see her and I'm glad.

I lean into her, try to kiss her but end up catching her ear and she laughs softly. "Relax, Patrick..." she says against my neck, pushing my shoulders into the wall, not more than five feet from the door we just came through. "By the time I'm through with you, you won't even remember her name..."

I feel her hands, sure and practiced, working the buckle of my belt open—the clink of cool metal. The snap of warm leather. She tugs my zipper open, yanking my pants down low on my hips, giving herself enough room to slip both hands down the front of my jeans. One of them cradles my balls while the other wraps its fingers around my cock, a slow, teasing thumb brushes across the head. As soon as she gets her hands on me, her eyes flare for an instant before slipping to half-mast. "Your cousin wasn't kidding," she says softly against my neck, her tongue gliding up the rigid cords of my neck.

This isn't Lisa's first rodeo.

Pulling the speed pourer from the Jameson, I tip the open bottle against my mouth while pushing my hips against her hand, pumping myself into her grip. I don't ask her what she means by what she said. Truthfully, I don't give a shit. Eyes closed, I concentrate on the sensation of her hands on me rather than *who* has her hands shoved down the front of my pants.

She abandons my cock, her fast fingers working the button of my shirt open until it's laid open and her tongue quickly follows, licking its way across my pecs. I take another drink and whiskey hits my chin, running down my chest. She laps at it, running the flat of her tongue down my chest and abs, circling my navel. She's working herself lower and lower, lips and tongue against my hips while she sinks to her knees in front of me. I can feel her breath, hot and fast against my stomach and she yanks at my jeans, pulling them down until they're just under my ass, but she's still circling. Still waiting for me to tell her what I want. Like it isn't obvious.

WWCD? What Would Conner Do?

I cup my hand around the back of her head and guide her to my cock and like I waved a magic wand, she's got her lips wrapped around it, licking and sucking like her life depended on it. I take another drink because while Lisa is giving me the blowjob of a lifetime, all I can see is Cari. I look up from the shadowy head that's bobbing between my legs and find what I'm looking for in the watery half-light of the streetlamp. The full-length mirror I used to watch my roommate get dressed not more than an hour before.

Even though the angle isn't right and it's dark, I can still see her plain as day—that scrap of bright red lace stretched between her thighs. Her hair lifted away from her nape, exposing the slim column of her neck. My cock is rock hard in an instant. So hard it's almost painful.

"Her name is Cari," I say under my breath, whispering it into the bottle I'm drinking from. The mouth between my legs seems to take it as some sort of challenge and flips into high gear. For a second I can smell gardenias and suddenly I'm on the verge of coming. I feel my balls tightening under Lisa's expert fingers, her mouth a fast glide as she works me against the back of her throat...

Light peels across the wall I'm leaning against, pinching into my narrowed eyes. The bar noises from downstairs are suddenly amplified—college kids shouting drink orders and the loud clack of pool balls. I look up from Lisa's bobbing head to see Cari standing in the open doorway, watching us.

NINETEEN

Cari

Trevor presses his hand into the small of my back, steering me through the crowded restaurant, dodging wait staff and busboys while the hostess leads us to a table for two in the center of the room. As soon as she's gone, I flip open my menu and bury my head in it like it's made of sand. I don't want to be here. I don't want to be with Trevor.

"What looks good, baby," he says, glancing at me over the top of his menu.

None of it. I shrug my shoulders, closing my menu before laying it on the table between us. "I don't know. Sushi isn't really my thing."

Trevor laughs at me like I'm a three-year-old, faced with broccoli for the first time. "Crunch rolls are my favorite," he says, flicking his gaze over the menu. "Spicy tuna is good too." He says it like it's something dirty, lifting his gaze to pin it to my breasts.

I'm going to burn this dress as soon as I get home.

"Will you excuse me," I say, pushing away from the table to stand. "I need to freshen up." Not waiting for an answer, I swipe my clutch off the table and bolt across the restaurant, asking directions from a random waiter on the fly.

The bathroom is a unisex one stall. As soon as I push my way through, I bolt the door behind me. Shoulders sagging, I snap open my clutch and pull out my phone. Dialing with one hand, I use the other to turn on the tap while it rang.

Please answer. Please answer. Please answer.

The call was dumped into voicemail halfway through the second ring. "Hey, this is Patrick. I can't get to the phone right—"

I hang up without leaving a message. To be honest, I have no idea why I called him in the first place. What could I possibly say that would make this situation better?

Hey, I know I've been a giant cocktease for the past six months. Sorry about that.

Jesus.

Sticking my free hand under the spigot, I let cold water run through my fingers for a few seconds before pressing them to my chest. Not ready to give up, I shut off the tap before dialing a different number. This time the call is answered almost right away.

"Fuck," Tess says, grunting softly. In the background, I hear Poison's *Talk Dirty To Me* and the jangle of metal tools hitting concrete. "I thought you were on a date."

"Where are you?" I say cautiously even though I know. "Am I on speaker phone?" Tess works for Conner. He owns his own garage a few blocks away from Gilroy's.

"Competing in the Miss Universe pageant. Where do you think I am?" she says, delivering the last few words through gritted teeth. "I'm in the middle of dropping a transmission—" She grunts again, the sound followed by a satisfied sigh. "And yes, you're on speaker phone."

"Take me off." I can barely say what I need to say out loud, let alone broadcast it across the garage Tess works at on speakerphone.

"Con's not here," she says, reading my mind. "It's just me, Brett Michaels and a '57 Chevy—so spill."

I sigh, leaning against the bathroom sink and do what she says.

I spill.

To Tess's credit, she doesn't interrupt while I tell her what happened between Patrick and me. In fact, the only way I know the line is still open is because while I'm blabbering, Poison gives way to Skid Row. Even so, as soon as I run out of steam, I say, "Are you still listening?" It's only been a few minutes but as much as I'd like to, I can't stay in the bathroom forever.

"Yup." More tools clatter, one being exchanged for the other. "Let me see if I got this straight," she says, her words punctuated by the rasp of a socket wrench. "You've been spending the past six months whipping Patrick Gilroy into a sexual frenzy and when he finally snaps, you leave him and his raging hard-on to go on a date with Trevor?" Tools clang again, this time metal on metal. Finished with whatever she's doing, she's tossing them into her toolbox. "Is that what you did?"

"Yes." Hearing Tess say it makes me sound as horrible

and stupid as I feel. Tucking the phone between my shoulder and my ear, I wash my hands. "What should I do?"

"That depends," Tess says, blowing out a heavy sigh. "Do you still want to fuck him?"

That's Tess. As delicate as ever.

I think about this morning, my ear pressed against the bathroom door. Listening to him while he touched himself. The way he said my name, right before he came.

"Yes."

"So, order an Uber and get your ass back home." The Chevy's heavy hood slams shut. "And hope like hell he's still there."

I take Tess's advice. As soon as I hang up with her, I use the app on my cell to order a car. I wash my hands again. I'm stalling. I have fifteen minutes before the Uber arrives. About fourteen more than I needed to tell Trevor it's over.

Someone knocks on the bathroom door, the impatient rap telling me I've stalled long enough. I turn off the tap and dry my hands before tucking my clutch under my arm.

Time to face the music.

I visualize marching across the restaurant. Stopping in front of Trevor and telling him the truth. That while he's a nice enough guy, I don't have feelings for him. At least not the sort of feelings I'd need to take the next step.

As ready as I'll ever be, I pull the bathroom door open, apology poised for the person I kept waiting. "I'm so sorry I—"

It's Trevor. As soon as I open the door, he pushes me

back and slips inside, closing the door behind us both, His hands grab at the hem of my dress, trying to pull it up, mouth plastered to mine, tongue shoving past my lips and teeth. I jerk away and slap him, hard across the face. He stumbles back a few steps, looking confused. The confusion doesn't last. Now he looks angry.

"Jesus, Trevor," I say, scrubbing at my mouth with my knuckles. "What the hell do you think you're doing?"

"I got tired of waiting," he says, touching the corner of his mouth with his fingertips before pulling them away, checking for blood. There isn't any but that doesn't seem to matter. "Thought maybe you did too." His voice is soft, seductive but he's glaring at me like he wants to hit me back.

"You thought wrong," I say, inching for the door. Concern flows into panic when he matches my movements. He's not going to let me leave. Not without a fight. "I called an Uber. I'm going home and I don't want to see you anymore."

I take another sidestep for the door and he follows suit, close enough to reach out and grab me if he wants to. And he wants to. I can see it in his eyes.

"It was just a misunderstanding, baby," he says, shaking his head. "I'm sorry. No need to overreact."

Overreact my ass. "I'm leaving, Trevor." I put as much force into my tone as I can muster while my hands curl themselves into fists. "And just so you know, I hate it when you call me *baby*."

He smiles at me again. "Okay, *Cari.* If that's what you want." His face goes soft, the smile does too. "At least let me drive you home."

Fuck. No.

Before I can put my refusal into words, there's another knock. "Is everything okay in there?" A female voice, unsure yet determined.

I dart toward the door and yank it open to find a waitress on the other side, her gaze bouncing between my face and Trevor's before settling on mine. "Are you okay?" She sounds concerned.

"I'm fine," I say, nudging her out of the doorway so I can slip into the hall. "I've called an Uber. Can you wait with me until it gets here?"

She looks over my shoulder at Trevor, her eyes narrow slightly. "Absolutely."

"James says hi, by the way," Trevor sneers at me and my shoulders stiffen. Trevor knows James. Six months later and I can still see his face, angry and cold because I finally, after nearly a year of being his doormat, told him no. It makes me wonder what would've happened if I'd let Trevor take me somewhere private.

We leave Trevor in the bathroom, the two of us weaving ourselves between tables and booths, moving toward the exit as fast as possible. "So, your boyfriend is kind of a dick," the waitress says behind me and I can't help but laugh.

"He is *not* my boyfriend."

I'm settled into the back of the Uber and halfway home when my cell phone rings. Thinking it's Trevor, I dig it out of my clutch to tell him to fuck off but it's not Trevor. It's

Conner.

"Hello?"

"Hey, Legs, sorry to interrupt your date but our boy's in pretty bad shape." Connor's usual lazy drawl sounded strange. Almost urgent.

"Patrick? What happened?" I sit up, pressing my shoulders forward. I can hear Gilroy's Friday night crowd, a dull roar in the background. It can get pretty crazy sometimes, especially when Connor is there to lead the charge. "Is he okay?"

"Depends on your definition of okay," he says. "He's pretty wasted. My dad cut him off and sent him home. He took a tumble down the stairs." There's a pause, the sound cut off like Conner's covered the mouthpiece with his hand.

"Conner?"

And then there's sound again. "Think you can come home?"

"I'm on my way."

TWENTY

Patrick

"Hey, roomie... you're home early."

As soon as I say it, Lisa pulls her mouth off my cock and looks over her shoulder.

When she sees Cari, she scrambles to her feet out the door before I can say, *thanks for the blowjob*.

I take another swig from the bottle, grinning around its rim before letting it fall away from my mouth. The bottom clunks against the wall I'm leaning on and the booze inside it makes a sloshing noise. It's the only sound I hear aside from the cacophony of noise that drifts up from the bar downstairs. Cari's got her eyes nailed to the spot on the wall just left of my face. Her cheeks are stained red and for some reason, I look at her shoes. That's when I remember that my pants are yanked down around my hips and my johnson is still on full display. "Well... this is awkward." Looking down, I see candy-pink lipstick smeared all over my cock. I know I should be embarrassed. Probably even ashamed but I'm neither. I just keep grinning.

She doesn't say anything, she just shifts herself out of the doorway and shuts it softly before turning the lock. She clicks on a lamp while I stay where I am, shoulders pressed against the wall the only thing holding me upright while I watch her move across the room, tossing her purse on the coffee table before disappearing into the bathroom. I hear the hinges on our linen cabinet squeak a second before the quiet rush of water. She's back in less than a minute, wet washcloth in her hand.

"Are you okay?" She sounds half-pissed, half-concerned, an odd combination that has me laughing. She's looking at me like she's taking inventory. Like she thought something was wrong.

"Well, if you'd waited another five minutes before storming the castle," I say, pulling that cocky grin on like a mask. "I'd be a damn sight better."

She scoffs and nods, glaring at me like she's trying to figure out what the hell is wrong with me. "I'll have my things out by the end of the week," she finally says, tossing the washcloth at me, hitting me square in the chest. It sticks there for a moment before it falls, hooking itself around the semi I've still got going. She doesn't wait to see if I use it, she just turns away and leaves me standing there.

Her words are like a bucket of ice water tossed in my face. One second, I'm half-plowed and feeling pretty full of myself. The next I'm stone sober and I've got a cold, wet towel hanging off the end of my dick.

The bottle of Jameson slips through my fingers and I barely take the time to clean up before I'm pushing myself back into my pants. I see myself going downstairs. Getting drunk with Conner while he talks some wasted co-ed into letting us do body shots off her tits on one of the pool tables. Maybe I can even talk Lisa into finishing what she started. The night is salvageable. She wants to move out—let her. Like I give a fuck.

But I don't. Because I do.

About two seconds after I wrangle my cock back into my pants, I storm after her. She's in her bedroom and this time her door is shut.

Like throwing gasoline on a fire, I pound on the door with the side of my fist. "So, *now* you close the goddamn door," I say on a laugh, my voice slightly raised. "Too little too late, sweetheart."

I can hear her on the other side and for a second, I think she's going to ignore me. Or maybe call the cops. Instead, she throws the door open, cutting me down with an ice blue glare.

"What the hell is that supposed to mean?" she says, her cheeks flushed. She's wearing that fucking robe again. And pretty much nothing else.

"You know *exactly* what I'm talking about, Cari," I say, barging into her room. I turn on her and she takes a step back, pressing her shoulders against the doorframe. She's looking me in the eye and I realize she's still wearing the heels.

"You don't close your bedroom door—not *ever*." I take a half step, throwing up a hand, bracing it against the frame, hemming her in so she can't run away. "Do you know I can see you? That every time you change your clothes, every time you get out of the shower, I *sit on the couch* and watch you in the living room mirror?"

"I—" She starts to deny it but then the flush blooming across her chest spreads, the heat of it collecting under her collarbone before inching lower, into the soft valley between her breasts. "Of course I know, Patrick—" She says it softly, the tip of her tongue licking her lips like her mouth has suddenly gone dry. "Why do you think I hung it there in the first place?"

There it is. Confirmation that she's been playing me since the day she moved in and it's all I need to hear.

Keeping her hemmed in, gaze locked on hers, I use my free hand to tug at the hastily knotted belt keeping her robe closed.

She doesn't try to stop me.

"Did you fuck him?" I say, finally managing to pull it loose. The slinky length of it slips through my fingers and lands on the floor between us.

She's looking at me, eyes wide and blue enough to drown me. "Who?" The word skates across my bare chest on a warm breath that shoots down my spine. My cock is rock hard again in the space of about five seconds and all she had to do was breathe.

I slide a hand into the open space between the silk of her robe and the silk of her skin. My fingertips glide over trembling flesh and it's hard to tell which is softer. "Tim/Travis," I say it easy, like I couldn't care less. The truth is, the thought of that asshole putting hands on her makes me want to kill something. "You know, Mr. 5th date." I finally drop my other arm to circle her waist with my hands, popping her hips off the wall, feathering my thumbs across her belly button. "Did you fuck him?"

She furrows her brow for a moment, her blue eyes glazed and cloudy. "His name is Trevor."

Her breathing has gone ragged. Each pump of her chest pushes her breasts against the robe. Her nipples are stiff and swollen. Begging for relief. Begging for me.

I can feel the corner of my mouth lift in that trademark Gilroy grin again. It's new to me but fits perfectly. "Answer the question, Cari." I lower my head to her breast, drawing the hard, swollen tip of it into my mouth, sucking her hard through the silk, grazing her nipple with my teeth.

"I didn't," she shudders out on a broken sigh, her fingers threading through my hair. "I didn't." she arches into me, pushing her breast against my mouth. "I wouldn't... not after..."

I wouldn't... not after...

I don't want that to matter. Not now. Not after she's all but admitted to turning me inside out, on a daily basis, for nothing more than sport. Instead of answering her, confessing to her that I love her, that I've loved her for as long as I've known her, I don't say anything at all. The time for pretty words and true confessions is long gone.

I wrap a hand around her hip, the long fingers of my hand gripping her while my thumb slides up the middle of her. "So, when you asked me to zip you into your dress..." The scrap of lace between her legs is wet. I crook my thumb, jerking it to the side to give myself access to the slippery warmth beneath it. "That was just more of you driving me crazy." I whisper it, finding her center with the pad of my thumb while my other hand cups one of her breasts, its tight peak pressed against my palm. It's not a question and I don't phrase it like one.

I start to move my thumb in slow, lazy circles against her clit and she whimpered, eyes closed. "Patrick, I didn't—"

"*Shhh...*" I dip my head to the breast I'm cupping, grazing her nipple with my teeth before drawing it into my mouth for a slow, hard suck. I keep at it—teasing and sucking until I can feel her thighs start to shake under my hands and her chest heave beneath my mouth.

When I have her on the brink of coming, I stop. "I want the truth, Cari. Not excuses." Take a step back. "Turn around," I say, putting some weight into my command.

The sudden absence of sensation opens her eyes. She's looking at me like she has no idea who I am.

That makes two of us.

She levers herself off the wall and does what I tell her. Arms folded and pressed into the wall, she pillows her face against them while I position her hips, angling them off the wall so that her tight, round ass is pressed firmly against my cock. "Spread your legs." I lean into her, whispering it in her ear, while I trail my fingertips along the inside of her thigh. Again, she does what I tell her.

A guy could get used to this.

"Earlier, when you bent over to put on your shoes." I say it calmly, each word brushing my lips against her ear. "That cock massage you gave me with this..." I grip her ass with both hands, thumbs feathering against the thin strip of cherry red lace nestled between her cheeks. "That was on purpose."

Her spine goes stiff. "Patrick—"

I deepen the pressure of my thumbs, pushing just enough to loosen her knees. "That was on purpose," I say again, making it clear I'm not interested in apologies.

"Yes..." She moans the word, the sound jerking my cock like it's on a leash. "I—"

"To play with me." If she has an explanation, I don't want to hear it. We're past that now. "To push me."

"Yes." She whispers the word but I'm only half listening, too busy to care.

"Is that what you were doing, Cari?" I hook that strip of cherry-red lace with my finger and pull it to the side even farther. "Were you trying to push me?"

"Yes..."

"What did you think would happen?" I cup her wet, throbbing pussy in the palm of my hand, the tip of my middle finger pressing against her clit, giving her slow, lazy circles. "That once I figured it out, I'd just keep my hands to myself. Let you keep twisting me in knots." She starts to rock against the pressure of my hand, the motion grinding her ass against me.

She shudders, moaning softly, fucking herself with my hand. "No—"

The feel of her. The sound she makes when I touch her is enough to push me over the edge if I let it. I fight for control, hiding behind the calm, cool exterior I use to conceal the way I really feel. What I really want. "This whole time…" I slip two fingers between the soft folds of her, barely breaching her entrance, nothing more than a promise of relief. "It was just a game. A joke." Their way eased by her arousal, I fuck my fingers into her, fast and deep. "Is that what I am to you, a joke?"

She's shaking her head, whimpering, her hips moving against my hand. "No…"

Pulling halfway out, I give her short, shallow strokes, each one grazing her clit, while I use my free hand to gather her hair and pull it away from her face. Her eyes are squeezed shut, lips parted slightly, panting with need.

Pulling my fingers free, I can feel the hot, tight walls of her pussy tightening, trying to stop my withdrawal. "Open your eyes, Cari," I say, raising my glossy fingers to my mouth. She does as I say and opens her eyes, lids heavy with arousal. She watches as I put my fingers into my mouth and suck them clean. She tastes just like I imagined she would. Warm and wet. Dark and sweet.

I want more.

I drop to my knees behind her to cup her ass in my hands, dipping my thumbs under her cheeks to spread and lift her toward my mouth to drag my tongue up the center of her. She cries out again, moving against my hands, seeking the pressure of my mouth. I pull my face away and she whimpers. "I want you to come all over my face, Cari," I say, hooking my fingers around the lace at her hips and jerk her panties down around her knees. "Tell me that's what you want."

"Yes…" The word trails off into a shuddering gasp when I bury my face in her, licking and sucking at her pussy lips, the taste of her almost enough to pull me apart. Pushing my tongue deep, I find her clit. Tongue pressed against it, I start to suck her off—hard, relentless pulls against tender flesh. She bucks against my mouth, pushing herself against my face, her hips rocking against the suction created by my lips and tongue. *"Patrick... oh, god..."* Each breath a gasping sob. *"Patrick, please. I can't—"*

She starts to quiver against my mouth, her swollen clit throbbing on my tongue, begging me incoherently. I don't stop, fingers digging into her ass to hold her against the unyielding pressure of my mouth. She lets out a shuddering moan that sounds like my name as a sudden shot of honey coats my throat. I keep sucking, wringing out every drop of sweetness she has to give me until she's limp and still.

When I finally moved from between her thighs, she's sagging against the wall, caramel-colored hair falling across her face, breath ragged, body slicked in a sweat. She looks spent. Completely satisfied. I like that I'm the one who did that to her. That I'm the one who made her come.

Standing, I turn her around so that she's facing me, tendrils of hair curving around her breasts. I work my pants down around my hips again. "Take your panties off," I tell her, licking at the sweat-salted tips of her breasts and she arches into my mouth just before I break away again. Reaching into my pocket, I tear off one of the condoms Conner gave me—*God bless him*—and I rip it open to roll it on.

She doesn't say anything. She just watches me while she steps out of her panties.

I reach for her, fitting my hands under her ass. Lifting her, stepping into the widened cradle of her thighs. She wraps her legs around my hips, eagerly pulling me close until the tip of my cock finds the slick, wet center of her. I look down—watch as her soft, wet folds split around the blunt, swollen head of my shaft. I rock against her hips, pushing myself deeper and deeper with each thrust. "Fuck, Cari," I groan against her neck. "Jesus, you're so fucking tight." The walls of her pussy squeeze around my cock and it feels so good I'm almost blinded by it. Unable to stop myself, knowing I have to get inside her, I grit my teeth and stroke into her with a deep, hard thrust that brings us hip to hip and has her letting out a shattered moan.

I don't move. I can't move. Not if I want this to last so I kiss her the way she kissed me that night in my car. My tongue licking and swirling inside her mouth. I kiss her until I can feel her drowning until she's lost to everyone but me. One arm anchored under her ass, I lift a hand to her breast. Caressing it, rolling its tight, swollen nipple between my fingers, squeezing until she cries out.

"Patrick, please..." Eyes closed, bottom lip caught between her teeth, she grinds her hips against me, urging me to move but I don't.

Angling her farther off the wall, hands wrapped around her waist, I lift her up the length of my cock until just the tip is still buried inside her. "You want to come on my cock?" I say, lowering her just enough to make her moan. "If that's what you want, you just have to ask."

One of her hands slips off my shoulder and down my torso to find the place where we're joined, her fingertips grazing the base of my cock as she finds her clit so she can stroke herself. "Please, Patrick... please let me..."

She lets her eyes slip closed on a shuddering sigh.

That sigh breaks something inside me. I'm no longer able

to hide behind the calm, and there's nothing reasonable about what I want to do to her. I want to fuck her for hours. Days. Make her come over and over, licking and sucking every inch of her until she's completely wrecked.

Hands still wrapped around her waist, I slam her down the length of my shaft so hard and fast her eyes fly open, the fingers gripping my shoulder rake into my skin, the pain of it so thin and sweet I can feel my balls contract, getting ready to release. I fight the sensation off with a vicious growl. I'm not ready to let this end. Not yet.

Instead, I do what she wants. I fuck her like it's my job.

I pound into her, my hips pound against the soft cradle of her thighs with deep, hard thrusts that bang her shoulders into the wall I have her pinned against with each spine-shattering stroke.

I step into her to bury my face in her throat with a groan, slipping my arm between her back and the wall to cushion her from the blows. "Is this it," I rasp against her neck, using my free hand to angle her hips so that each of my thrusts rubs the base of my cock against the clit she's fingering. The smell of her—salty and sweet. Dark and warm—beg me to take a taste. "Is this what you want?" I lave my tongue along the column of her throat, but it's not enough. I bare my teeth to the hammering pulse at the base of her neck, grazing and nipping against her skin but that's not enough either.

"Yes... oh god, Patrick..." She's sobbing now, ankles locked around my hips. Nails clawing into my shoulders while her other hand pushes up between us to squeeze her own breast. "I'm coming, I'm..."

She shatters around me, her pussy bearing down on my cock, gripping it like a fist. I keep fucking her through her orgasm, my hips pounding against hers, hard and fast. Her hands latch on to my shoulders again, her cherry-red heels digging into my ass like spurs, urging me to take what I want. To use her the way she used me.

My own orgasm hits me like a speeding train, my balls tightening and tingling while stars explode in front of my eyes. She cries out again, the inner walls of her pussy tightening, pulling me deeper. I crush her against me, pinning her between my chest and wall, her arms and legs wrapped around me. Hair tangled and wild. Breath ragged and harsh.

The euphoria doesn't last. Within seconds, I remember how I got here. How she played me. How she pushed me. Years of games and frustration—of being jerked around like a puppet—for nothing more than her own personal amusement.

I'm a chump.

The thought has me stepping back. 24-hours ago I would have done just about anything to be where I am now. And now, I just want to disappear.

I'm hurt. And that makes me angry... it also makes me a little dangerous.

We looked at each other, long and hard, for a few seconds. Assessing one another carefully. She must know I'm angry, can probably see it written all over my face. "Will you at least let me explain?" she says, pushing her long, thick tangle of hair out of her eyes.

I shake my head. I didn't want to hear an explanation

while I was fucking her and I sure as hell wasn't in the mood for one now. "That's not necessary," I say, jerking the condom off my cock before zipping up my pants for the second time in one night. "I think I understand perfectly." I drop the condom, unceremoniously, into the wastepaper basket by her door.

She watches me, arms crossed over her chest—whether it's to hide herself from me or because she's angry, I don't know. "I'm sorry."

"No, you're not." I bend down to retrieve her robe and toss it at her. "You're just sorry you got caught," I say before I walk out. The last thing I hear before I leave is her bedroom door as it quietly clicks shut.

TWENTY-ONE

Patrick

I find Conner where I left him, only this time he isn't alone. Hemmed into the booth by a trio of co-eds—two blondes and a redhead—he saw me coming. By the time I slid into the booth across from him, my cousin wears the kind of grin that would make the Cheshire Cat wonder what he'd been up to.

"It worked," he says, taking in my misbuttoned shirt, undone belt and generally disheveled appearance. "Fuck me, it actually worked."

"What worked?" I say, scanning the crowded bar for Lisa. I spot her over by the pool tables, slinging drinks. When she sees me, she cuts me a quick smile—one that says she's embarrassed about what happened but not so embarrassed that she wouldn't give it another go. The blonde sitting next to me slides across the booth, inching a bit closer—so close her smooth, bare thigh is pressed against me and I can smell pop princess perfume. She's been looking at me, practically licking her chops, since I sat down. I try out my Gilroy grin again, letting her have it. She responds by putting her hand on my knee.

Will wonders never cease?

"You banged Legs." Conner says it proudly—like I've just birthed him a son and I look at him, suddenly putting it all together.

Lisa and the handsy blonde forgotten, I lean across the table. "What did you do, Conner?" I ask, even though I've already guessed. He's the reason Cari walked in on Lisa and me. He'd somehow gotten her to come home early from her date.

He leans away from me and laughs. "Me?" he says, green eyes round with feigned innocence. "I'm sure I have no idea what you're talking about."

"You guys look alike," the girl sitting to Conner's left says, flipping her bleach-blonde hair over a self-tanned shoulder. "Are you twins?"

"No—he's my clone. Bought one of those self-cloning kits off Amazon." I say before Conner has the chance, and the blonde's face crumples slightly like she's trying to figure out if I'm joking or not—my guess is she's not attending college on an academic scholarship.

Before she can ask, Conner reaches into his pocket, pulling out a wad of bills, peeling several off. "How about you go pay our tab so we can get out of here," He drops the money into the redhead's open hand with a grin. "Go back to your place." Conner never takes them home.

"Are you coming too?" Suddenly the blonde sitting next to me is practically in my lap, her hand wrapped around the inside of my thigh.

I maneuver myself away from her, sliding out of the booth so she can join her friends. "Maybe I'll try to swing by later," I say, holding out a hand to help her up and she pouts prettily at my answer.

"Try hard," she says, trailing her fingertip over my shoulder as she wandered toward the bar with her friends.

As soon as they're gone, I turn on Conner again. "What did you do—" I advance on him, cocking my head. "and don't tell me nothing."

"I may have called her and told her you fell down the stairs to your apartment." He says it fast like he's ripping off a bandage.

"Are you for real?" I don't know if I want to laugh or choke the shit out of him.

Conner shrugged. "Look—that girl has been leading you around by your balls for *years* and since you let her move in, it's been fucking unbearable to watch. I had to do something."

"So, you decide to *Parent Trap* us?" I say it like I'm mad but I'm not—not really. How can I be? Conner interfered but considering my face had been buried between Cari's legs less than an hour ago, I'm having a hard time being angry.

"I sure the fuck did," he says, without an ounce of remorse. "You two have been dancing around each other for so long I was starting to get dizzy."

"How'd you even know it'd work?" I say, shaking my head.

"Are you kidding me?" he says, looking at me like I'm a mentally challenged toddler. "Let me let you in on a little secret—men and women: not so different as they would like us to believe. They want what they can't have, the same as we do."

"I don't know... she was pissed. Still is," I say, thinking for the first time that maybe this wasn't what I wanted—it certainly wasn't *how* I'd wanted it. "She's moving out."

Now Conner smirked. "She say that before or after you fucked her?"

I glare and he laughs, shaking his head.

"You want her to move out?" he says, laughing again as soon as he finishes the question. The look on my face must've answered his question just fine. "Okay. Do you love her or is it just about the sex?"

Love or sex? For Conner it'd never been an issue—love never factors into the equation. The only thing he loves *is* sex.

I look behind me to find all three girls waiting for him by the front door, ready to go. "Your groupies are waiting," I say, avoiding the question.

He shrugs, a cocky half-smile resting comfortably on his face. "They're not going anywhere."

I've been lusting after Cari for so long, maybe I've confused the two. Maybe I don't know what I want anymore. All I know is that as hurt and angry as I am, I can still taste her. Still smell her and I'm not ready to walk away from that... but she's been playing me for months— hell, *years*.

It's time to give her a taste of her own medicine.

"I don't know, cousin..." I say, signaling Lisa to bring me a beer. "But we're gonna find out."

TWENTY-TWO

Cari

W hat the hell just happened?

He left me here. Walked out the front door while I brace myself against the wall, naked and slightly dizzy from the absolute best fuck of my life. I can't follow him, even if I wanted to. I'm pretty sure my knees would buckle before I took my first step.

Waiting until my breathing returned to normal, I brace a hand against the wall while reaching down with the other to pull off one heel and then the other. Flat on the ground again, I feel a little bit better.

I don't know what to do. The rash, impulsive me wants to throw on some clothes and charge downstairs. Hound him until he listens to reason. Until he lets me explain. The rational, prudent me—the me I should've been listening to all along—is telling me to let him go. He's angry and he has every right to be. Just give him some space. Let him cool off.

Is that what I am to you, Cari? A joke?

No. Nothing about what just happened was even remotely funny.

Totally unexpected? Yes. Ridiculously hot? Hell, yes.

So hot I want to do it again.

I instantly reject the idea. Less than thirty minutes ago, I walked in on him getting a blowjob in our living room and what do I do? I let him fuck me. What self-respecting woman does that? And I didn't just *let* him—I begged him to.

Please fuck me, Patrick…

The memory heats my cheeks, the warm flush streaking lower to pool, hot and heavy between my thighs. Incredibly, I'm not ashamed of the way I behaved. What I let him do to me. I'm ashamed that I'm *not* ashamed if that makes any kind of sense.

I decide to listen to rational me. I'm not chasing after Patrick Gilroy. If he wants to talk, he knows where to find me.

I think about a shower. I need one. I smell like Patrick. And sex. Instead of heading for the bathroom, I decide to go to bed. I'm about to crawl between the sheets when I hear my cell chime from the living room, signaling a text. Retrieving it from my purse, I carry it back to my room. It's a text from Trevor.

Trevor: CALL ME.

I'd rather jump naked into the harbor.

The texts keep rolling in, one after another.

Trevor: CALL ME.
Trevor: CALL ME.
Trevor: CALL ME.
Trevor: CALL ME.
Trevor: CALL ME.

James says hi.
It's what he said to me as I was leaving the restaurant.
James says hi.
I tap out a response.

Me: Tell James I said fuck off.
That goes 2x for you.

I get a response almost immediately.

Trevor: Yur going to be sorry you said that.

Whatever. Not wanting to deal with it, I set my phone to silent and resolve to call my provider in the morning and have Trevor's number blocked from my contact list. If that doesn't work, I'll change *my* number.

I plug my phone into its charger before tossing it onto my nightstand. Laying down, I slip beneath the blankets and settle in, listening to the dull roar of Friday night college revelry going on downstairs. On a typical Friday night, I'd be down there, shooting pool with Tess and Patrick, taking bets on which co-ed would crack first and follow Conner into the ladies' room.

No doubt Patrick is down there and if he is with Conner, there's no telling what they're doing. Or who they were doing it to. I push the thought out of my head. Who Patrick fucks is none of my business. I think about the scene I walked in on, Lisa the cocktail waitress on her knees in front of him. Patrick's jeans open and jerked down around his hips. Her mouth on his cock. The way he looked at me when he saw me standing there. Like he wished it was me. Me on my knees in from of him. My mouth he was fucking.

Like he hated me for it.

I wake up way earlier than I want to. Reaching for my phone, I see it's barely 7AM on a Saturday. Also, I have a waiting text message. Thankfully, it's not from Trevor.

Tess: So...

I scowl at my phone for a few moments before tapping out a response.

Me: So what?

Tess: Quit being a dick.
You and PP—did it happen?

PP. Predictable Patrick. I look over the foot of my bed, at the wall Patrick'd had me pushed against last night, his face buried between my legs. I can still feel him pressed against me. Moving inside me... not even Nostradamus could've predicted that.

Me: yes

Tess: OMG!! FINALLY!!

I want details. Scratch that.
I deserve details! Plus, you
owe me lunch. I can take m
break around 2.

The last thing I want to do is go into detail with anyone about what happened last night. Any other guy—sure. But this isn't any other guy. This is Patrick.

Me: K. Meet me downstairs?

Tess: c u @ 2
I won the bet!!

I set my phone back down and get out of bed because if I lay here for one more second, thinking about him, I'm going to go crazy. I reach for my robe, actually tried to put it on before I remembered what had happened to it. I lifted it to my nose and breathed deeply. It smells like him. Like us.

Hanging the shredded robe on its hook, I pull on a pair of boxers I stole from Patrick's laundry a few weeks ago. They were blue plaid, worn thin and soft. I don't even know why I'd taken them other than the fact that they were *his.*

Adding a baggy white T-shirt before throwing my hair into a quick ponytail, I finally gather the courage to open my bedroom door. The apartment is quiet, Patrick's bedroom door firmly shut. He'd been drunk last night. Drunk enough to bring one of Gilroy's cocktail waitresses up here for a quickie.

I want to be mad at him for it but I can't—not really. I'm

the one who'd pushed him after all. Maybe if I'd just been honest about what I wanted instead of agreeing to play Tess's head games, things would've happened differently.

Or maybe they wouldn't have happened at all.

Irrational me rears her ugly head, urging me to justify the damage I'd done. The delicious ache between my legs helped convince me that irrational me is right. I got what I was after. Sure, Patrick was angry but he'd get over it. I just have to find a way to apologize and set things right.

In the kitchen, I make coffee before poking around in the fridge for a few minutes. Finally finding a yogurt, I shut the fridge just as I hear the front door to our apartment open. A quick glance over my shoulder tells me that Patrick isn't hungover and he isn't sleeping. Despite tying one on last night and everything that happened after, he looked normal—like he did every morning.

He looks fantastic.

"Morning," he says, stopping just inside the door to kick off his running shoes.

Knowing he left after what happened, I expected to catch him doing the walk of shame in last night's rumpled clothes, I'm surprised to see him in workout clothes, like it was any other Saturday morning. "Good morning," I say in a voice that's surprisingly steady considering I suddenly can't get the image of the two of us pressed against my bedroom wall out of my head.

Moving across the living room in my direction, he snags the hem of his fitted tank and drags it up over his head, tossing it into the basket of dirty clothes he has parked by the coffee table. It's all a part of his Saturday routine.

Workout. Laundry. ESPN until his eyes glaze over.

Predictable Patrick.

"You're up early for a Saturday," he says, giving me that same easy, gorgeous smile he'd given me yesterday morning and every morning since the day I moved in. "I didn't wake you, did I?"

Last night he'd been angry. Unwilling to talk about what happened. Unwilling to let me explain. Less than twelve hours later, it's like it never happened.

I want to ask him when he came home—*if* he came home—last night but I don't. I'm not his girlfriend. We fucked, once. One mind-blowing, earth-shattering time. Who he was with and where he went afterward is none of my business. Instead, I turn around, yanking open the silverware drawer for a spoon. "No—" I say, my face hot. Had I dreamt it? Had he been so drunk last night that he doesn't remember what happened? Thinking about it, the ache between my thighs grew warm and heavy. "Tess texted me."

"Oh." He laughs while squeezing into our tiny kitchen, his smooth, muscular chest bare and slick with sweat, brushing past me on his way to the fridge. "I bet she's chomping at the bit to know what happened last night."

I drop my spoon and it clatters to the floor. "*What*?" I say, cutting him a sharp look. He's got his head stuck in the refrigerator. All I can see is a set of tight abs and a pair of navy track pants slung low on well-defined hips. A baseball scholarship in college and working construction with his cousin Declan has paid off. The result is a body that would make any woman weak in the knees.

Myself included.

"Tess," he says, straightening away from the fridge with a bottle of water. "She texted you to get the down and dirty about Trevor, right?" He leans against the counter behind me, cracking the lid on the water to take a drink.

"Yeah," I say, turning my back on him to focus on my breakfast. The faster I eat, the faster I can go back to my room and hide. Yanking the foil lid off my yogurt, I fold it neatly and throw it in the trash before bending over to retrieve my spoon off the floor. "She wants to have..."

Patrick isn't leaning against the counter anymore. He's standing right behind me, so close I can feel his rapidly growing erection against the curve of my ass.

I stand up slowly, agonizingly aware that this is almost exactly what'd happened between us last night. What I'd done to start all this...

Only now *he's* doing it to me.

His hand skims across my hips, fingertips brushing the hem of my shirt. "Are you gonna tell her?" I can feel his breath against the nape of my neck, slow and even.

Oh. My. God...

I take a deep breath, fighting to stay calm. "Tell her what?" I say, my hand clenched around the handle of the spoon so tight I can feel the imprint of it on my skin.

"Are you gonna tell her what happened?" His large, callused hand slips under my shirt, his fingers doing a relaxed slide up my ribcage while his hips do a slow grind against my backside.

"Nothing happened with Trevor. I told you—"

"That's not what I'm talking about." Laughter brushes

against my ear a moment before he presses his mouth against the underside of my jaw. "And you know it."

Any hope that he'd been too drunk to remember what happened between us—and *why*—is gone, leaving me with the overwhelming and unexplainable urge to explain myself. To apologize.

"Patrick..." I don't know what I'm going to say but it doesn't matter. The second his hand closes over my bare breast, my mind shuts off completely.

Totally blank.

"Yes, Cari?" he says, the words brushing his mouth against my nape. He fondles me under my shirt, cupping my breast, rolling my swollen nipple between his fingers— tugging and pinching—exerting just enough pressure so that when his other hand slips into the waistband of my boxers, I widened my stance without even thinking, giving him room to do whatever he wants to me.

"Patrick," I try again, squeezing my eyes shut, forcing myself to focus even though the last thing I want to do right now is think. "I think we need to—"

His long fingers skim the damp seam of my pussy, teasing me. "Why aren't you wearing panties?" he whispers in my ear and I have to swallow hard against the moan that his hands are building up inside me.

"I don't..." I swallow again, my head kicking back against his shoulder when the fingers plucking at my nipple squeezes even harder, the sensation shooting through my belly, straight to my clit. "We should talk." I pushed the words out even though I'm afraid that once I do, he'll stop touching me. I think I might die if Patrick stopped now.

"We are talking," he says in that same calm, measured tone he'd used on me last night. "Where are your panties?" His fingers roll and tug at my nipple while his tongue traces the line of my neck. "Tell me, Cari…" he says when I don't answer right way.

"You…" I manage to say despite the fact I can't breathe. "you took them off last night."

"Oh yeah…" Patrick's fingers slide into me and my back arches, urging him to stroke me even deeper. "I remember now." He skims his teeth against my jaw and that moan I've been fighting shudders out of me when he pulls his fingers out to work the drenched length of them against my swollen clit. "You're wet," he groans against my throat, his hand tightening on my breast. "Have you been thinking about me? The way I made you come on my tongue?"

"Yes…" My brain is completely scrambled. I push myself against him, working my hips against the maddeningly slow ride his juice-slicked fingers are giving me. I can feel the rigid length of him, pushing against my ass and suddenly, his fingers aren't enough.

I want him inside me. Now.

I try to push his hands away so I can turn around and rip what's left of his clothes off but he tightens his hold on me, keeping my back pressed firmly against his chest. "Is this it?" he says, his voice hoarse and tight, like he's fighting for control. "You want to come on my cock again?" he grinds himself into the cleft of my ass, pushing against me through our clothes.

"Yes…" I don't even know what I'm saying, what I'm

agreeing to but it hardly matters. Not if it means he'll stop playing with me and get serious.

His tongue skates along the long line of my throat, coasting toward my ear. "You want me to jerk these shorts down around your ankles?" He slides his fingers inside me again, slow and deep. "Bend you over the counter and pound my cock into this sweet pussy of yours?"

Something about his calm and reasonable tone, coupled with the filthy things he's saying in my ear send another lightning bolt of arousal shooting through me, flooding my pussy. "Yes..." My breath stutters out of me as his fingers find my center again. They move in slow, feather-light circles that increase in pressure until my knees are loose and unreliable and my breath is hitching in and out of me in ragged pants.

"Patrick..." I can feel it build. My legs start to tremble. The quivering sensation that begins in my belly—a vibration that spreads slowly but doesn't overtake me. And then I know. He's punishing me for what I did to him. All those months of teasing I subjected him to. "I'm sorry... I'm sorry for everything."

"It's a little late for that," he says in my ear, confirming my suspicions. "It's going to take more than a simple apology to make it up to me." His mouth slides around to the back of my neck. "A lot more."

And then, just like that, everything stops. As suddenly as it started, it's over and he's walking away from me. "I'm meeting Conner later," he calls over his shoulder like the last three minutes never happened. He strolls down the hall, disappearing into the bathroom, leaving me stunned and shaking in the middle of the kitchen.

TWENTY-THREE

Cari

He's obviously pissed and if there's anything I've learned in our three years of friendship, it's that a pissed off Gilroy is not a thing to be messed with. I should just walk away. From him. From this whole mess. Last night, I said I was moving out—another stupid, impulsive mistake—but standing here, strung out from the feel of him all over me—*inside me*—it seems like the only sane thing to do. I should just leave. What I did was horrible and cruel but he got his revenge. That made us even.

But I don't want to be *even* and I can't walk away. Not from this.

Not from him.

I stand in the middle of our tiny kitchen for a few moments, waiting for my legs to stop shaking and then I go after him, barging into our shared bathroom, the door rebounding off the sink so hard it slammed shut again.

"Wow," he says, his voice bouncing off the shower stall walls. "You've developed a habit of walking in on me while I'm jerking off."

His taunt should shame me but it doesn't. It just makes me angry. And the anger makes me reckless. "You can't just *do* that, Patrick," I yell at the shower curtain.

"I can't hear you," he shouts over the sound of the shower. I'm not sure but I think he's laughing at me.

Incensed, I rip the shower curtain open. "*I said—*" I'm still yelling but I'm unprepared for the sight of a fully naked and very wet Patrick and I almost swallow my tongue. Jesus, he's beautiful. The kind of beautiful that makes you feel a little desperate. Like you can't even *hope* to measure up. Like you'd be willing to do just about anything to prove that you do.

"You can't..." I take a deep breath and try again. "You *can't* do that to people."

Despite what he said to me, he's washing his hair, water and soap runs down his chest. Slushes off tightly packed abs. Splits around the base of his thick, hard cock to coast down long, muscular legs...

I'm trying not to look but *seriously*?

"Hello... my eyes are up here, Cari." This time I'm sure he's laughing at me. I can hear it in his voice.

Mortified, I force my eyes back to his face.

He finishes rinsing his hair and drops his hands. "Do what?" He's using it again. That calm, reasonable tone that makes me crazy. He's looking at me like I *am* crazy.

"You know what." I say it through clenched teeth, my cheeks hot.

He's not laughing anymore. "Oh... you mean tease you?" he says, the corner of his mouth lifting in a grin that's totally void of humor. "Touch you." His hand slides down his well-defined chest, taking my gaze with it, to wrap around his cock. "Make you wet..." He starts to work his hand in a slow, even rhythm, gripping the head before sliding his fist all the way to its base. "Make you want things... and then just walk away."

That's exactly what I'd been doing to him for months now. Hearing him say it jerks the indignation right out of me. "You're right." I manage to push the words out against a throat that suddenly feels like it's full of sand. I lick my lips, trying to find my voice. "What I did was shitty and I'm sorr—"

"Stop. Apologizing." He bites the demand in half, his reasonable tone taking on a dangerous edge.

"Then what?" I whisper, my throat horse, eyes glued to his hand, watching him. "What do you want from me?"

He doesn't answer me, just throws me a question of his own. "Do you know how many times I've thought about you while doing this?" Something about his voice pulls my gaze back to his face and I find him watching me, his hooded, green stare nailed to my mouth. "You, in that goddamned robe..." His voice is thick, chest pumping, quick and hard. "That fucking dress..." His hand is still moving, flexing and sliding around his cock while his gaze dips to my breasts, their tight, swollen tips pushing against the thin cotton of my T-shirt.

That's the last coherent thought I have. Before I can think about what I'm doing and why, I grip the hem of my shirt and drag it over my head, exposing myself to him.

I cup one of my breasts, rolling and pinching its nipple

between my fingers, the sensation of my hand and his eyes on me, watching me touch myself, slams into my gut with the force of a freefall.

Catching my bottom lip between my teeth, I slide my other hand beneath the waistband of my boxers. "I'm guessing you've thought about me as much as I've thought about you..." that last word gets caught in my throat as I skim my fingers along the seam of my pussy, pushing inside just enough to get them wet—mimicking what he'd done to me in the kitchen. He's watching me, his own hand gone still and fallen to his side.

I stop touching myself too. "To be honest, it feels better when you do it," I say, holding his stare for a few seconds before I turn and walk out.

I barely get the door open before I hear him behind me, ripping the shower curtain off the wall, scrambling across the slick tile floor of the bathroom, careened after me.

Thank god.

He catches me in the hallway outside my bedroom and we go down hard, Patrick's wet, muscular body covering me, his hips wedged between my legs. I can feel the stiff length of him against the back of my thigh, his breathing hot and ragged against the side of my face, his wet, muscular chest plastered against my back. "I thought I made it clear last night," he says, dropping his shoulder and bending his elbow a bit to bring his mouth closer to my ear while he grinds his rigid cock against the thin cotton barrier between us. "You shouldn't push me, Cari."

I suddenly realize that even though we've been friends for years, I don't know Patrick Gilroy at all. I know the boy scout. The nice guy. The Patrick who's nursed me through a dozen break-ups. The friend who always lets me have the last slice of pizza when we order in. The roommate who tolerates my obsession with reality television. This is not that Patrick.

This is someone else entirely.

"The only thing I learned last night," I say, pushing myself against the hard length of him, practically begging him to fuck me. "Is that I like what happens when I push you."

I've lost my mind completely and he confirms it when he rears up, cursing—the sound of it low and harsh against the back of his throat—as he grabs onto the waistband of my boxers and jerks them down.

Before I can take my next breath, his fingers are thrusting into me so fast and deep it steals my breath, scatters stars across my field of vision.

He covers me again, breathing harsh and uneven against my neck. "I don't think you understand," he says, seemingly calm despite the ragged breath that skates down my spine, his erection bobbing between my legs with each deep, lazy stroke. "You're not calling the shots anymore." The tip of his blunt, calloused fingers graze the sensitive spot deep in the center of me, again and again, and I whimper in response, pushing back against his hand. I want more. Need more. "I am." He keeps fucking me with his fingers. His hand. The maddeningly reasonable tone of his voice. "Got it?"

No, this isn't the Patrick I know at all.

Cheek pressed against the floor, eyes squeezed shut, I

nod. My legs start to shake again, the warm heaviness in my belly pressing lower with every stroke he gives me. I'm close to coming for the second time in less than ten minutes and I'm not sure I can take it.

"Say the words, Cari," he whispers in my ear, his fingers buried deep inside me, their calloused tips crooked slightly while I move my hips, stroking myself along the blunt length of them. "Say, *I understand, Patrick.*"

Not caring anymore, so desperate to get off I'm on the verge of crying, I push my hips off the floor, making room for my hand between them and the floor. "I understand, Patrick." I moan it out, pressing my fingers against my clit.

He chuckles softly in my ear and the sound of it would make me angry if I wasn't dangling off a cliff. "Good girl."

He pulls his fingers out, the wet suction sound of it heats my chest even as I let out a frustrated groan, the orgasm spinning away from me. I press and circle my fingers against my clit, harder and faster, trying to catch it.

"No, you don't." He flips me over, grabbing my wrist to pull my fingers from between my legs, holding it high above my head. "That's against the rules."

Rules? I lift my head off the floor, my gaze pulled downward to land on his rigid cock. It's only inches from where I want it, the rock-hard heat of it scorching the inside of my thigh. I force myself to lay flat, meeting his gaze.

I let out a strangled scream, tears prickling the back of my eyelids. "I hate you," I say it through clenched teeth and I mean it. I hate him.

He grins down at me. Hand still clamped around my wrist, he lifts my hand between us, its fingers still wet and glistening with my own juices. "If you say so," he says, slipping my fingers into his mouth, sucking them clean.

I can feel the head of his cock, twitching against the junction of my thighs. I close my eyes, my concentration centered on the feeling of his tongue on my skin, even if it's just my fingers. Lifting my hips off the floor, I run the slick seam of my pussy against the head of his cock. "Please…"

"If you still want to move out, then move out." He drops my hand and reaches back, fingers digging into my upper thigh, stopping me cold. I can see it. How angry he is. The hard set of his jaw. The hurt I caused him, still fresh in his eyes when he looks at me. "Go ahead—I'm not going to stop you. I'll even help you pack," he tells me, leaning hard on the arm planted on the floor so he can lean closer. "But if you stay, I'm gonna fuck you." The movement pushed the head of his cock against my entrance, stealing my breath. "Whenever I want. As much as I want. However I want. Understand?"

Again, like a complete idiot, I nod.

"New roommate rule:" he says, dipping his head to my chest. "You don't come without my say so."

His tongue touches my nipple, circling sensitive flesh before drawing it into his mouth, sucking and nipping at it with his teeth until I'm panting again, each draw his mouth makes on my breast bumping the head of his cock against my slick, wet center.

I moan.

Patrick lifts his head and gives me a crooked grin before he levers himself off the ground and away from me. "Now, if you don't mind," He turns his back on me, heading toward the bathroom. "I'm going to finish my shower."

TWENTY-FOUR

Patrick

I leave Cari in the hall and head back to the bathroom, locking the door behind me. The shower is still running and its curtain is laying on the floor. The spring rod it hangs on is floating in the tub. I fish it out and hang the curtain back up before stepping back under the spray to finish showering. I want to jerk off so bad it's making me dizzy. Scratch that—I want out of this shower. I want to bury myself balls deep in Cari's quivering pussy. I want to pound myself into the center of her so hard and fast she won't walk right for a week. I want her screaming my name so loud the whole damn neighborhood will know who's fucking her.

Instead, I stay where I am. The shower is ice cold but I force myself to stay put until my hard-on is gone and my dick is practically shriveled in on itself.

If this is what it takes to be an asshole, I'm not sure I can manage it.

Out of the shower, I sling a towel around my hips and

duck across the hall into my own room as quickly as possible—but not so quick that I don't notice her bedroom door is closed.

I'd had a plan—a simple one. Give as good as I'd been getting. Make her feel all the things I'd been feeling for the past six months—hell, the past three *years*—while keeping my own response in check.

Usually something I'm good at.

The only thing I learned is that I like what happens when I push you.

That's all it took. All she had to say before I was yanking down her pants and finger fucking her in the hallway.

The guy I'd been 24 hours ago would never do something like that. He wouldn't have let things get so out of hand. He wouldn't have tackled her like a sexually deranged linebacker. He wouldn't have taken her to the brink of coming and then left her there without delivering.

And he wouldn't have felt so good about it either.

I rub my hair dry and get dressed—cargos and a random t-shirt—before I realize I still haven't shaved. Not wanting to risk another visit to the bathroom, I make a beeline for the living room. Stopping only long enough to pull on a pair of shoes and snag my laundry basket, I head out the door.

When I leave, her bedroom door is still shut.

I don't go far. Heading downstairs I round the bar to see Declan behind it, building a round of Black and Tans for a bunch of rowdy locals in the back of the bar, watching the Sox game.

He gives me a chin jerk and tosses me a key as I walk

past the bar before reverting his attention to the pints he's working under the taps. Carrying my load of clothes down the hall, I use the key he tossed me to unlock the office where we keep a stackable washer and dryer. Adding soap to my load of clothes, I set the dial before locking the office on my way out.

When I get back, Lisa is standing at the bar, waiting for her order. When she sees me, she smiles and I smile back as I slide onto a worn leather stool. "Hi, Patrick," she says, looking at me through her lashes while Declan sets the last of her order on her tray.

"Hey," I say, gaze straight ahead as she walks past to deliver the round.

"Con told me but I was sure he was full of shit," Declan says as soon as she's out of earshot.

"What?" I look up to catch his expression. He's either amused or concerned. With Dec, it's hard to tell.

He sets a pint of Harps in front of me and shakes his head. "She's more trouble than she's worth," he says, whipping the towel off his shoulder to wipe down the bar between us. "Trust me, you don't want to go there."

I think he's talking about Cari and I feel my jaw flex, the muscles in my neck going tight. I've known Cari for years but that didn't mean I know about every guy she's been with. The thought of her and Declan together makes me want to hurt something. Namely him.

Before I can say anything, he continues. "I dated her for a few months in high school," he says, shaking his head. "She's crazy. Like, bag-full-of-cats crazy."

He's talking about Lisa. I pick up my beer to cover up the

fact that I'd been three seconds away from committing assault over just the *thought* of Cari with someone else and even though it was a simple misunderstanding, I can't quite shake the anger that's clawed its way into my gut.

I shrug, already done with the conversation. "It was over before it even started," I say setting my pint on the napkin he tossed in front of me. "And I'm not looking for a do-over."

"Really?" Declan says, arching an eyebrow at me. "Does she know that?"

"She'll get the picture." I lean back on my stool, elbows resting on the edge of the bar, gaze glued to the muted television behind him. "Eventually."

"Yeah?" Declan looked at me for a second before letting out a low laugh. "You heard the part about her being nuts, right?"

I think he might be right and it feels strange not to care. Before I can tell him to drop it, light streaks across the dark Mahogany bar as someone comes through the door, drawing his attention. Ready to call out a friendly greeting to his new customer, Declan sees who it is and tenses, his fingers tightening around the towel in his hand before he drops his gaze, the greeting never uttered. Curiosity getting the better of me, I shoot a quick look past my shoulder to see who has my control freak, over-achieving cousin polishing rocks glasses like his life depends on it.

It's Tess. She shoots me an *I-know-your-secret* look as she strides past the bar before bouncing it up, letting her gaze skim past Declan, barely acknowledging his presence before landing it on the Sox game going on over his head.

Ouch.

"What are you doing here, anyway?" I say, lifting my pint and draining it. I set it on the bar and nudge it forward. After our construction business took off, Declan rarely worked weekends. Matter of fact he only works Thursdays and that's just so he can keep Conner's bathroom conquests to an absolute minimum. The thought of Conner left alone to tend bar on Ladies' Night was as awe-inspiring as it was frightening.

"Con's backed up at the garage and Da's taken Mom away for the weekend." He looks relieved that I'm not peppering him with questions about what I just witnessed. "It's their anniversary." He sets a fresh pint in from of me. A reward for minding my own business.

I lift the pint and shake my head. "You should've told me. It's my—"

I hear her before I see her and I can't stop myself from looking in her direction as she steps off the stairs and into the bar. She's wearing her loose sundress; the one I tease her about looking like a blue potato sack. It's about as sexy as a hospital johnny but the sight of her in it jerks at my cock like a divining rod. Because I know what's underneath it.

She looks directly at me. Challenging me, like she knows exactly what I'm thinking and I have to force myself not to look away. To give as good as I get without dragging her back upstairs to finish what I started this morning.

She passes by, giving Declan a wave on her way to the table where Tess is waiting for her.

"Hey."

I look over the bar to see Declan watching me watch her.

"What?" I gulp half my pint down in a few swallows.

"What's going on with you?" Now there's no question about it. He's concerned.

"Nothin'," I say, contemplating the Jameson in the well behind the bar. Maybe if I get drunk enough, I'll manage to put my cock into a booze-induced coma.

Right—because it worked so well last night.

"You sure?" Declan looks at the pint in front of me like he's sorry he poured it. "Because you fucked the cocktail waitress last night. That's not like you."

I didn't fuck Lisa but I don't correct him. Let him think what he wants. "Maybe I'm just tired of letting Con have all the fun," I say with a shrug, already tired of this conversation.

Declan shakes his head at me. "You're too smart to pull that shit and I'm too smart to buy it."

"How's the wedding planning coming along?" I swivel in my stool, looking directly at Tess for a second before turning back to Declan. "Mind if I bring a date?"

"You're too smart for that too." Declan's jaw sets, his hand going tight around the towel again.

I scoff, aiming another look over my shoulder, letting him think I was checking Tess out when the only thing I can see is Cari. "Smart is overrated."

Growing up, Conner and I used our fists on each other plenty and I've had to pull Con and Declan apart more than once before things got too bloody, but me and Declan? We've never come to blows.

I have a feeling that's about to change.

He must feel it too because he loosens his grip on the towel and blows out a sigh. "Look, I'm just worried about you. That's it."

"Keep your worry." I drain the pint and push my empty across the bar. "Give me a Jameson."

Declan snatches my empty glass off the bar and drops it in the sink. "What the fuck did Conner do to you last night?" He's not looking at me when he asks, so I don't answer.

He's also not pouring me a Jameson.

Before I can reach across the bar and help myself, the door behind me flies open again. This time ushering in a swirl of moderately expensive perfume and the fast click of knock-off stilettos. This time I don't have to turn around to see who it is.

Jessica.

"I don't care *who's* in the hospital," she says in a tone that shrivels my balls. "I have a cake tasting scheduled for 2:45." Out of the corner of my eye, I catch sight of her leaning across the bar, pouty lips puckered, smudging lipstick across Declan's cheek. She's fake—every inch of her from her bleach blonde hair, right down to her bogus shoes. The door knocker of a diamond sparkling on her finger is the only thing real in between. I let out a sound that would've been a laugh if it didn't feel so sharp and nasty against the back of my throat.

"I don't want excuses," she hisses in the phone, tossing her long hair over her shoulder. "I *want* a wedding cake and there better be someone there to sell me one." She jabs her finger at her phone, silencing the apologies of whoever she'd been verbally abusing, before giving Declan her full attention. "What are you still doing here?" She says, rubbing her thumb against his cheek, smearing lipstick across his face. "My parents are meeting us for dinner at six."

I look at my watch. It's not even noon.

"Hey, Jess," I say, calling her *Jess* because she hates it and I'm just drunk enough to not give a shit. Our brewing fight forgotten, Declan shoots me a warning look before producing a glass with a few fingers of Jameson in its bottom. Probably in hopes of bribing me into keeping my mouth shut.

"I have zero time for your shit, Conner," she says to me, narrowed eyes taking in my three-day beard, ratty t-shirt and cargos. I give a fleeting thought to correcting her but I kinda like the fact that someone who's seen me a thousand times and is standing right next to me has mistaken me for Conner. I lift my glass and down the whiskey, muttering "fuck off," into the bottom of it between swallows.

Acting like she didn't hear me, she turns toward Declan again, giving him a *what are you doing just standing there look.* "Well? Let's go."

Declan sighs. "I can't just *go,* Jessica," he says to her, gesturing around the bar. "I'm working."

"No, you're not," she says. "You're standing here, talking to your brother."

"I'm the only one behind the bar," Declan says in the kind of tone you'd use to reason with cranky toddlers. "That means I'm working."

Jessica scoffs before letting her gaze float around the bar, her face hardening almost instantly. "What is she doing here?" she says turning toward him again, voice raising an octave.

I turn on my bar stool and look at Tess. She focused on Cari, not to pay attention to the fight that's brewing a few yards away. Cari's got her hand clamped around her wrist like she's holding her in her seat. I whip around, mouth open but Declan shoots me a glare and pours me another Jameson. Instead of talking, I drink.

Declan sighs again. This time it's the long-suffering sigh of someone who's had this argument a thousand times and doesn't want to have it even one more time. "She's eating lunch in a public place, Jessica," he snaps at her, jerking the towel off his shoulder again. "and we've known her since we were kids—"

I'm about five seconds away from picking her up and dumping her ass on the sidewalk. Instead, I reach across the bar and yank the soggy towel out of Declan's hand. "Get the hell out of here," I say before draining my glass. "And take your screech owl with you." I slam my glass on the bar and stand.

Jessica's eyes narrow again at the insult but she's smart enough to let it go. "Let's go," she says, smiling now that she's gotten her way.

Declan gives me a *fuck no* look. "You've been drinking."

Jessica scoffs. "Shocker," she mutters before turning and making a beeline for the table Cari and Tess are huddled around. I want to follow her and do what I can to shield Tess from the river of shit that's about to be unleashed. Instead, I walk around the bar, ducking under the pass through.

"Get her out of here, Declan," Standing beside him, I hold out my hand, gesturing for the apron he's wearing but he's not paying any attention to me. Instead, he's looking across the bar, zeroed in on whatever's going on between his fiancé and his brother's best friend.

"Dec," I say, nudging him in the arm. "I'm serious. Just give me the keys and get her the fuck out of here."

Making up his mind, Declan looks at me and nods, reluctantly fishing the office key from the front pocket of his jeans. "Are you sure?" he says, finally reaching around to untie his apron.

No matter what Jessica thinks, he knows I'm not his brother and that other than occasional weekday shift, I have zero experience behind the bar. I am in no way ready for a Saturday night shift.

The fact that I'm sorta drunk is a secondary concern, and we both know it.

I just smile. "What are brothers for?"

TWENTY-FIVE

Cari

Tess is staring at me, her mouth open, while I quietly recount how I spent last night and this morning. "Patrick said that?" She leans across the table, placing the flat of her hands on its surface to push herself forward. "That he was going to... and that you were..." She leans back in her seat, looking genuinely confused. "We're talking about Patrick *Gilroy*, right? The guy who spent forty-five minutes last Sunday, helping Mrs. McGintey wrangle that bastard dog of hers? The guy who coaches baseball and volunteers at the library? *That* Patrick?"

"That's him," I say, doing my best not to look over my shoulder. If I do, I'll see Patrick sitting at the bar. Watching me. Thinking about him, the warn ache between my thighs starts to throb, making me irritable. Making me wish I'd defied Patrick's orders and made myself come before I came down here and tried to interact with polite society. "And could you keep your voice down—we're in enemy territory."

"Sorry," Tess says, taking it down a few notches while sitting back in her seat. "It's just..." she shakes her head, shooting a quick glance over my shoulder. "That's not what I expected."

"Oh, yeah?" I say, flipping the menu open even though I've read it a thousand times. "What did you expect, exactly?" I can't keep the hostile tone out of my voice. I know it's not Tess's fault things have gone so wrong between Patrick and me but blaming her is easier than blaming myself. This was all her stupid idea to begin with, wasn't it?

"I don't know..." she says with a shrug, seemingly oblivious to my current mood. "But I *didn't* expect Predictable Patrick to go all *50 Shades* on you." She falls silent and leans back. "What you're describing isn't anything like the sex Sara clued me in on."

The second Tess says the name of Patrick's ex-girlfriend, I nearly choke on my own tongue. "What?" I manage to croak out, too loud. I aim a quick look over my shoulder. Patrick is still sitting at the bar talking to Declan. "You asked Sara what he was like in bed?" I hissed at her. "Are you nuts?"

"Relax," Tess sighs, rolling her eyes like I'm the crazy one. "I made it sound like I was interested in taking a run at him," she laughed at the thought, shaking her head like Sara was an idiot for buying it. "She wasn't too happy with the thought but she told me what I wanted to know."

I held out for about two seconds before curiosity got the better of me. "And?"

Before she had a chance to spill, Lisa appears with our

drinks.

"Here you go," she says, syrupy sweet. Too sweet. "What can I get you girls to eat?"

I listen while Tess orders, a double bacon cheeseburger, chicken wings and a basket of onion rings. She's five-foot-nothing, and wouldn't weigh a hundred pounds after being fished out of the Mystic. Where she puts it, I don't know.

Unfazed, Lisa scribbles on her pad before looking at me. I can't be sure but her eyes seem to narrow just a bit. "Same," I say, smiling while I hand her my menu like I didn't catch her with Patrick's cock in her throat less than twelve hours ago. Like I didn't want to punch her in the fucking mouth and drag her down the street by her goddamned hair. "Thanks."

She takes the menu and nods, that sugar sweet tone smeared across her face in the form of a smile. Tess watches her go, slim, dark brow arched. "Was that weird?" she says, looking at me. "She was acting weird, right?"

"I caught her going down on Patrick last night," I say, waving a hand in Lisa's direction. Right now, I didn't give a shit about Lisa. "What did Sara say?"

"*What the fuck,*" Tess hisses at me, slapping her hand on the table with a laugh. "What the hell did you do to him last night?"

Her question sends another rush of heat through me. I can still feel his mouth between my legs. His tongue, thrusting into my pussy. Lips sucking my clit. "What. Did. Sara. Say?"

She considers me for a few seconds like she's thinking about leaving me hanging. "That he was gentle. Sweet.

Generous. Considerate—all different words for the same thing." Tess grins at me. "Boring."

"Of course," I mutter, pulling the wrapper off my straw, sticking it in my drink.

"What's that supposed to mean," she says, dark brows arched over her wide hazel eyes.

"Nothing," I shake my head. How can I explain to her that Sara's description of Patrick's bedroom behavior all but confirms that as far as he's concerned, I'm not girlfriend material. I'm not the girl you bring flowers to and put on a pedestal, treat gently and say sweet things to. I'm the girl you take standing up. Finger fuck in the hallway. And the kitchen. Laugh at when she all but begs you to fuck her.

You asked for it. And fuck if I didn't love every second of it. What does that say about me?

Tess must've picked up on my tone because she narrows her eyes at me. "Wait—are you mad?"

I shake my head—I'm not sure what I am right now. "*He's* mad. At me. He wants me to move out."

Tess grins at me. "Revenge sex can be pretty hot," she says, shifting back in her seat. "Truthfully, I didn't think Mr. Predictable had it in him."

"Quit calling him that," I raise my voice, drawing the attention of a couple of regulars, playing pool. I drop my voice to a harsh whisper. "Did you hear what I just said? He wants me to *move out.*"

"That's not what he said, exactly." Tess pursed her lips. "Sounds like he's leaving it up to you."

If you stay, I'm gonna fuck you. Whenever I want. As much as I want. However I want.

My pussy clenched tight at the memory, forcing me to clamp my thighs together. "I know," I say, pushing my drink away. "but he's angry, Tess. I'm not sure it's a good idea for me to stay."

Tess starts to respond but closes her mouth when Lisa makes another appearance, this time with food. "Here ya go," she says, moving to set a plate in front of Tess before lifting it back up. "Oops." She sets the plate in front of me instead. "Your wings are coming right up." Lisa smiles, showcasing the candy pink lipstick smeared across her teeth.

"Thank you," I tell her, looking at the burger she placed in front of me then at the burger she put in front of Tess. They were the same, so why is she being so specific about who got what?

As soon as she's gone, Tess lifts the bun on her burger and adds mustard. "Are you afraid he's going to hurt you?" she says, her expression caught between concern and disbelief. "Because I've known Cap'n a long time and he'd never—"

I didn't even have to think about it. "No." Patrick had almost beaten James to death with a bat for grabbing my arm. There was no possible way he would hurt me. "That's not what I'm worried about... I'm just not sure our friendship is repairable."

"Did you try apologizing to him?"

"Yes," I bark the word. "Every time I even look like I'm going to say the word *sorry*, he—"

"Gives you a mind-blowing orgasm?" Tess says baldly, chomping on an onion ring while shaking her head. "What an asshole."

"Shut-up," I grumble at her and she laughs. I'd told her a sanitized version of this morning's episode. I didn't tell her about being so frustrated and desperate for release that I'd started finger fucking myself in front of Patrick or that he'd stopped me.

If I don't stop thinking about him, my pussy is going to chew my leg off. I force myself to focus on the conversation. "He won't listen." I sigh and push my plate away. There's no way in hell I'm eating food Lisa touched. Not ever again. "What we did was mean. It was wrong and..."

"We?" Tess says before taking a bite of her burger.

"Yes, *we —* " I hiss, looking over my shoulder toward the bar again to find Lisa watching me. Now I'm positive she's spit in it. "This whole thing was your idea, Tess. Patrick *hates* me."

"What do you care?" she picks up the bottle of ketchup and squirts a blob onto her plate. "I mean, really? You got what you wanted. You've scratched your Gilroy-sized itch and now it's done," she says, dipping another onion ring into the ketchup before popping it into her mouth. "On to the next, right?"

That's what I'd thought. What I'd fooled myself into believing but, no. Not on to the next. There was no *next*.

There was only Patrick.

Tess must've seen it on my face because her burger hit her plate with a resounding *plop*. "You forgot to mention that part while you were offering up your feeble protest about Operation: Get Gilroy," she says, using air quotes around the word *protest*.

I'd forgotten how observant she was. How easily she can read people. "What part?" I reach across the table to snag one of her onion rings off her plate.

"The *you're in love with him* part," she hisses at me. "I never would've suggested any of it if I'd known you have actual feelings for him."

"What?" I scoff at her like she's crazy. "I'm not in love with Patrick," I say. "I'm just having my doubts that fucking him was worth ruining a friendship over."

"Uh-huh. Right," she says, slapping my hand away from her plate when I reach for another onion ring. "Eat your own."

"I can't," I say, looking at my plate. "I think Lisa spit in my food."

She looks at me like I'm crazy but, something catches her attention behind me and her face drains of color. I turn to look, my stomach dropping to my feet the second I do. Declan's fiancé, Jessica breezes in, talking loudly on her cell, knock-off Coach bag swinging from the crook of her arm.

"I wish you would've told me about you and Dec before I agreed to be one of her bridesmaids." I turn in my seat to find Tess staring at the TV screen directly above Declan's head. "I would've said no. I might've even spit on her."

My words draw her attention and she smiles like nothing's wrong. "Are you kidding? If you're not there, who will give me the down and dirty on how much of a train wreck it turns out to be?"

"You know the only reason she asked me is because I'm a

blonde and can pull off the dress, right?"

"That's not why she asked you." Tess shakes her head. "She asked you because you're my friend," she says, getting ready to scoot her chair away from the table. "I have to use the—"

I reach across the table and close a hand around Tess' wrist. "You have every right to be here," I say, stealing a quick glance over my shoulder. Declan and Jessica are arguing and Patrick is looking at us. He's pissed and for once in recent history, it isn't at me. Before I can blink, he's out of his seat, tossing back his shot before snagging the bar towel out of Declan's hand. Whatever he's saying, it looks like Jessica is temporarily mollified.

I turn back to Tess and smile. "See? Everything's—"

"Christ," Tess mutters under her breath, eyes locked on something over my shoulder. "Fuck my life."

Before I can turn in my seat and see for myself, a shadow falls across our table and I look up to find Jessica standing over us. "Cari," she says, a plastic smile fixed on her face. "I'm so glad I caught you—we're having a little girl's day next weekend. Declan's ordered a limo to pick up all my bridesmaids and take us to Anton's for dress fittings."

Just then, Lisa pushes in, a basket of hot wings in each hand. "I'm sorry it took so long, the fryer is acting up," she says, wedging the baskets between the condiment caddy and the napkin holder. "Is there something wrong with your burger?" She looks at me, seemingly confused.

Uhh, I'm pretty sure you poisoned it.

I shake my head, forcing a smile. "Nope."

As soon as Lisa is gone, I look up and catch Jessica

looking at the food spread across the table, nose scrunched in disgust. "I ordered you a size six," she says, shifting her gaze to take in my baggy sundress. I fight a smile because I know it's impossible for her to get a read on my current weight. "I hope that's going to work for you."

I reach over and snag one of Tess's onion rings and stuff it into my mouth. "Should be fine," I say around the food in my mouth, being gross on purpose. "And if not, that's what fittings are for, *amiright*?"

Unamused, Jessica fakes a laugh before turning her attention to the real reason she came over here. "Hello, Tess," she says, looking at the grease stains on Tess' hands. "On your lunch break?"

"Yup," Tess answers, fishing in the basket of wings for a drumstick. Finding one, she pulls it out and starts to chew.

Finding her opening, Jessica goes in for the kill. "I don't know how I'd manage a job *and* planning a wedding." The plastic smile turns nasty. "I'm so lucky to have someone like Declan to take care of me."

I feel my fingers curling inward, hooking themselves into claws but before I can launch myself at Jessica and show her what she can do with her size six, Declan appears, closing his hand around his fiancé's elbow. "Let's go," he says, pulling her away from the table. "Sorry to interrupt your lunch." He's looking at me but he's talking to Tess, I can tell. Tess doesn't even look at him.

"Don't forget, next Saturday," Jessica says, pulling out of Declan's grasp to loop her arm through his. "It's going to be so much fun."

Declan looks like he's going to be sick but he manages to

turn her around and pilot Jessica toward the exit, but before he passes through the door, he looks back at our table and I see it etched plainly on his face.

Regret.

TWENTY-SIX

Patrick

As soon as Declan leaves, I stop drinking. I'm going to have enough trouble getting through the next couple of hours without adding booze on top of everything else I'm feeling. I scoop some ice into a pint and added club soda and lime. If I don't sober up soon, I'll make some coffee.

Cari and Tess are still here, both of them leaning into the table, talking quietly. Tess looks a bit shaken—a confrontation with Jessica could do that to anyone—but she's recovering quickly. Just in case, I called Conner.

"Gilroy's Garage," he barks into the phone, music blaring in the background.

"Hey—it's Patrick," I say, keeping my voice low. "How slammed are you?"

He laughs like it's a stupid question. "At the rate I'm going, I'll get caught up by Christmas. And that's *if* Tess gets her ass back here and finishes the tranny rebuild and two oil changes she started yesterday."

I watch Lisa saunter over to their table and rip their check off her pad, talking while she slides it onto the table. I'm not sure I want to know what's coming out of her mouth. "Any chance you can give Tess the afternoon off?"

Conner sighs into the phone and I hear a sharp metal clang like he'd just slammed a socket wrench into the heavy metal table he uses for rebuilds. "What did that cocksucking brother of mine do this time?"

I tell him about Jessica coming in and stirring everyone up before dragging Declan out by his balls. "He left you alone?" Conner says, angrily.

"I'm not a fucking idiot, Con—I know how to use the bottle opener and make change," I say, an unrecognizable edge sneaking into my tone. "I didn't call about me, I called about Tess."

"Doesn't change the fact that he's a pussy-whipped, dumb-ass, piece of fucking …" he mutters under his breath before letting the insult trail off. "How is she?" he says and I know he's not asking about this brother's fiancé.

"You know Tess," I say, hitting the volume button on the TV above the bar, trying to drown out the sound of my voice. "She looks fine, but …"

"Yeah." Another sigh, followed by another clang. "Fuck it. Let me call her, tell her I'm closing up early to help you with the bar. Give her the night off."

"Alright, man—thanks," I say, quickly, watching Cari carry her check up to the bar. I hang up right before she stops in front of me. "Need something?" I say, wiping the bar down in front of her even though it was spotless.

She doesn't say anything, just flashes her check before

holding it out for me to take. As soon as I take it, she reaches into her purse for her wallet.

"Something wrong with your food," I say, keying in the total while behind her, Tess's phone goes off. She answers it, looking momentarily confused before the expression gives way to one caught between gratitude and annoyance.

"I'm pretty sure your girlfriend spit in it," Cari says, fishing her debit card from her wallet.

I started to say Lisa wouldn't do something like that but then I remember what Declan said about her. That she's crazy. Instead of defending her, I take the card out of Cari's hand and run it for half the amount. Behind her, Tess finishes her conversation and gets up, heading for the door. She leaves without saying goodbye and I don't try to stop her. She knows I called Conner and she's pissed. A few seconds later, I watch her pass by the window, on her way back to the garage. She flips me the bird as she passes by.

"I don't have a girlfriend," I say ripping off her receipt before slapping it and a pen onto the bar between us. I meet her gaze, my hand still settled on top of her receipt, not letting her take it just yet.

She narrows her eyes at me for a second, an angry flush crawling across her chest. The birthmark on her chest is darker than I've ever seen it. The deep wine color can only mean one thing. Cari's pissed. Between having my fingers inside her, her taste in my mouth and watching her finger fuck herself, my cock's been hard all day. Knowing she's angry at me pushes me across the line.

"Thanks for coming," I say, giving the last word some weight, just to see how far I can push her. I think it might be my new favorite thing. Seeing how far I can push her.

Cari goes a little pale, the blood rushing from her head to her chest. She opens her mouth but before she can say a word, the side door closest to the bar—the one that requires a key—opens, letting Conner in. And he has someone in tow.

Seeing us in what looks like the start of pretty good row, Conner jerks his thumb over his shoulder. "This guy's looking for you, Legs," he says, stepping out of the way so the guy behind him can step up.

"I've got a delivery for Cari Faraday," he says, reading the name off the clipboard in his hand. "That you?"

"Yes," Cari says, regaining a semblance of composure. She blots her hands on the skirt of her dress before reaching for the package. It's large, two feet by three, thin with hard angles, poking through its plain brown paper wrapping. The delivery guy hands it over and she sets it on a barstool, leaning it against the bar.

"Don't keep me guessing, Legs," Conner says, rounding the bar, pulling on an apron while he walked. "Open it."

She blushes, her birthmark glowing bright red, gaze darting between the two of us like she's trying to figure out which one of us is playing a trick on her. Finally, her curiosity gets the better of her and she reaches out, ripping the paper away from the package.

"Oh…" The word flows out on a sigh, soft and feathery, filled with reverent disbelief. Her hand flies to her mouth, fingers trembling just a bit against a mouth that slowly spreads into a smile. I want to vault over the bar to get a look at what it is but I plant my feet firmly and wait for

Conner to do his job.

"Come on," he says, giving her an impatient gesture. "Let's see it."

She lifts the package and turns it, smiling and still a little breathless. When I see what it is, it's like a fist slamming into my gut.

It's that painting. The one she went nuts over when it was on exhibit at the museum a few years ago. She must've dragged me there a dozen times to stare at it. The artist is local... I finally make the connection. It's from that guy I met yesterday at the gallery. Everett Chase.

Early thirties. Successful. Wealthy.

Just her type.

Knowing that I feel the fist in my gut start to twist at my insides. Tucked into the corner of the frame is a small white envelope with her name printed across the front in small, neat letters.

She plucks it from the frame and lifts the flap to pull the card free. I watch her big blue eyes scan the card, her cheeks so flushed, I immediately look at the spot below her collarbone. It's as red as an apple.

Someone clears their throat and we all look up to see the delivery guy still standing by the door, clipboard in hand. "I'm supposed to deliver your answer."

Cari looks down at the card, re-reading the note before bouncing a quick look up at me. Our eyes connect and hold for a few moments before she looks away, tucking the card back in its envelope.

Picking up the painting, she turns, reaching out for the clipboard to sign for the delivery. "Tell him I said yes," she says, handing back the clipboard before heading upstairs without a backward glance.

TWENTY-SEVEN

Patrick

I tell myself I'm not going to follow her. I don't have any real claim on her. So, I fucked her last night. Big deal. She's a big girl. She can do what she wants, with whoever she wants. If she wants to go out with some rich artist, I can't stop her. It's not like I own her.

You don't come unless I say so.

She hasn't been gone more than fifteen minutes before I'm ripping off my apron and throwing it under the bar.

"Gonna go help her pick out her shoes?" Conner calls after me, laughing at me when I throw the pass-thru up with a loud bang. "Maybe curl her hair?"

I flip him the bird before charging up the stairs.

Stepping into the living room, I slam the door behind me. The apartment looks normal. Worn leather couch, curb-find coffee table. Big-screen TV. Dinette set shoved into the corner, hardly used for more than a catch-all. It all looks like it did yesterday, which is wrong because everything is different now. Everything.

I stalk across the living room headed for Cari's room when I see the note card, tossed onto the coffee table. Her name is printed across the stark white envelope in heavy block strokes. I pick it up and turn it over, sliding the card from its sleeve. Reading it, I feel a little lightheaded.

Cari —
It was nice meeting you at the galley yesterday.
So nice, I'd like to do it again, maybe with food this time. Dinner? If it's a yes, I'll send a car at 7pm.
I hope it's a yes.

          E. Chase

I read the note again. And then again, because I like torturing myself before I slide it back into its envelope. I want to wad it up in my fist. Then, I want to go find Mr. E. Chase and jam it down his fucking throat.

I want to do all sorts of crazy, violent things that would probably land me on the evening news and possibly end with some sort of sentencing hearing.

Yeah, I want to. I really, really want to. But I don't. Instead, I toss the card back on the coffee table where she left it.

Her door is open like it always is and I lean against the frame, arms folded over my chest, watching her while she flips through her closet. The painting that accompanied the dinner invitation is leaning against the bed like she didn't know what else to do with it.

It's worth about twenty grand and I want to put my foot through it.

She's wearing nothing but a towel and a frown. Her hair piled on top of her head, the nape of her neck damp. She knows I'm here and she's ignoring me. Or at least trying to. Like I'm going to let that happen.

"Guess I just missed the shower show, huh?" I say leaning against the doorframe. The thought of her in the shower, her skin wet and warm, makes me hard. So hard that I'm having a hard time breathing.

She scowls but doesn't look at me. The birthmark on her chest is better than a mood ring. It's a deep wine color. That means she's pissed and Cari's not the silent type when she's angry. I'm inclined to wait her out.

It doesn't take long. After a few minutes, she sighs, flicking me a glance. "What are you doing here?" she says, clearly annoyed. "I have a date." She's finished apologizing for what she did. For reasons I can't even begin to understand, knowing that makes me even harder.

"I figured," I say, careful to keep my tone casual. "That's why I'm here—I mean, it's my job to help you get ready isn't it?" I give her a one-shoulder shrug. "Help you pick out a dress. Help you zip it up. Smile and wave goodbye when your *douche de jour* comes to pick you up."

She glares at me and now I'm not just hard. My cock is throbbing. "Fuck you, Patrick," she says, ripping hangers down the rod so fast she can't possibly be considering half the shit she's pretending to look at. "I tried apologizing. I tried explaining—you don't want to listen. You just want to make me—"

"Wet? Come?" I say like I'm being helpful. "Scream my name so loud the whole neighborhood knows who's fucking you?" I give her a grin while her hand stalls on the parade of hangers and she pulls a dress out of her closet.

Not just a dress. The dress.

My dress.

I don't feel good anymore. I don't feel calm and reasonable. I feel like I'm going to blackout. "Don't." The warning comes out, rough and guttural, rumbling in my chest like I'm some sort of wild animal.

She hesitates for a moment before she turns and tosses it onto her bed with the rest of her maybes. "I'll wear what I want, Patrick Gilroy." She's looking at me, her lips parted slightly, cheeks flushed with color.

Even keel has always been my default. I'm not easily riled. My whole life I've been the nice guy. Flexible, rational, go-with-the-flow Patrick. But that was before. Before I had her and now that I have, there's no going back. She's done something to me. Cari's broken something inside me that can't be repaired. Something that can't be fixed, no matter how hard I try.

That's the only explanation I have for what I do next.

TWENTY-EIGHT

Cari

I had no intention of wearing that dress. The dress. The one I was wearing when I finally pushed Patrick too far. I was flipping through my closet, ignoring him while trying to find something that looked professional but not matronly. Feminine but not sexy. Because I'm not even sure why I said yes other than the fact that Patrick was standing there, watching with such a passive, accepting look on his face that I wanted to do something—*anything*—to wipe it off.

This dress definitely does not fit the look I'm going for but seeing it, touching it, makes me remember how it felt to have Patrick pressed against me. His hands fisted in its skirt, pulling it up my hips. His warm, slightly uneven breath skate across the back of my neck.

And thinking about it makes me wet, the dull ache in my pussy starting to throb.

"Don't."

I hear it in his voice. It's not a request and it's not a

suggestion. It's a warning.

One I have no intention of heeding.

"I'll wear what I want, Patrick Gilroy," I say tossing the dress on my bed with the others, meeting his gaze, challenging him. He's got that look again. The same look he had in the shower this morning when I barged in on him. When he was... I lower my gaze, letting it slide down the length of him until I find what I'm looking for. He's hard, the length of his cock pushing against the zipper of his cargos. And he's making no attempt to hide it.

I'm remembering the way it felt to have Patrick move inside me, his hips pounding against mine. His mouth, sucking my swollen nipples through the silk of my robe.

That fucking robe.

I'm mesmerized. That's why I don't see him move.

One second, he's leaning against my doorframe and the next he's in front of me, snatching the dress off the bed and tossing it at me. I catch it, holding the lace and silk against me, eyes wide with surprised confusion. And then he's standing over me, so close the steady pump of his chest brushed against me with every breath he takes. I take a step back, bumping into the wall, less than an inch from where I was standing.

"Go ahead," he says his tone easy, reaching up to trail a finger across the top of my breasts. "Put it on." He leans into me, pressing a tender kiss to the scorching hot spot below my collarbone before lifting his head, lips brushing against my ear. "See what happens."

"Stop," I whisper.

"Are you sure that's what you really want, Cari?" He

seems to know it isn't because I feel the curve of his mouth lift into a smile before it moves lower to press a soft kiss against the pulse that's hammering against the skin of my throat. "If it is, all you have to do is say it again. Tell me to stop, I'll stop. Walk right out the door."

I open my mouth to say exactly that. I'll tell him to stop and he'll go away. I know he will. He's different than I've ever seen him but I know he'd never force himself on me. If I tell him to stop, he will... "I hate you," I whisper instead, my eyes fluttering closed. "I hate you, Patrick Gilroy."

"So you keep saying..." He laughs, warm breath skating down my neck, the tips of his fingers sliding along the inside of my thighs until he finds the edge of the towel. "Let's see how much, shall we?" He grips the towel and gives it a tug and I let it go, a soft whimper catching at the back of my throat. Dropping it on the floor, he reaches up to brush the pad of his thumb against my nipple, growling low in his throat when it stiffens under his touch. His other hand touches the inside of my thigh, his fingers slipping into their juncture. "Open your legs."

I want to tell him no. That he can't just tell me what to do. Issue orders and expect me to follow them. But I don't say anything. I just do what he tells me. Because I don't want to tell him no. I want him to touch me.

He cups my pussy, the heel of his hand pressing against the top of my mound while his fingers slide along its swollen, wet seam, his touch instantly bringing me to the edge. "Yeah... *fuck*," he says, his voice rough and uneven, breaking over the last word as he slips a finger inside, pushing deep, its way eased by my arousal. "Yeah, you hate me alright," He replaces the heel of his hand with the pad of his thumb, giving my clit soft, feathery strokes that have me moaning his name. "It's hurtful, really, all this animosity. I'm just trying to help."

"I don't need your… *oh, god.*" He adds a finger, thrusting into me, stroking my clit until I'm breathless. "I don't need your help," I say, opening my legs wider, begging for more.

"You sure about that?" he says, his tongue tracing the line of my throat, his fingers working in and out of me, slowly, like he has all the time in the world. "You're a mess. What kind of friend would I be if I let you go out in public like this?"

My knees nearly give way at his words. "I can do it myself," I say, risking a move to reach out and wrap a hand around his arm, digging my fingernails into his skin because I'm dizzy, my breath coming quick and shallow. "I don't need you to make me come." My hips call me a liar, bucking against the pressure of his fingers inside me. "I can do it myself."

He makes an odd noise in the back of his throat, his hand closing over my breast, pinching its nipple hard enough to make me gasp. "But you didn't." He says it against my mouth, his tongue licking along my lower lip, his fingers moving inside me, slow and languid, drawing me closer and closer to orgasm with each thrust. His lips skim along my jawline while his hand slips up, along my shoulder to cradle the base of my skull.

"No." I whisper it, my pulse banging against my throat, that tight, heavy feeling gathering in my belly, my orgasm growing inside me.

"Why not?" he says, catching my lower lip between his teeth, biting just hard enough to send a sharp, stinging pain rocketing down my spine, straight to my pussy where it mingled with pleasure, pushing it higher. Making it sweeter.

"*Oh*... I told you." I grip his wrist, the one between my shaking thighs, holding him inside me because I'm so close, *so fucking close*, and if he denies me again, I'm going to die. "It feels better when you do it."

"Jesus, Cari," he groans, low and guttural, the hand at the base of my skull tightening in my hair, grabbing it by the roots before crushing his mouth against mine. He consumes me, his tongue swirling and rubbing, licking and sucking until I can't breathe or see or feel anything but his mouth on mine. His finger inside me. His hand in my hair. The soft fabric of his T-shirt brushing against my swollen nipples.

He adds a third finger, filling me, stretching me with each stroke, touching the place deep inside me that has me spinning higher and higher while his thumb works my clit so perfectly that I'm delirious, writhing against him. Panting into his open mouth. Clawing at his skin, my hips pumping to meet each thrust, pushing against the rock-hard length of his cock. I want it inside me, thrusting and pounding into my pussy. I move my hands to his waist, my trembling fingers fumbling with the button of his pants, trying to tear them off. "Please..." I'm whimpering, desperate to get him inside me. "Please, I need—"

His hand tightens in my hair, giving me a quick jerk, hard enough to make me gasp. "No." He breaks our kiss to press his face to my neck, his breath harsh and uneven against my feverish skin. "This isn't how it's supposed to be." He sounds angry, his hand in my hair pulling my head back, baring my neck, the thrill of it shoots straight down my spine when I feel his teeth graze the soft skin of my throat. "What the fuck are you doing to me?"

I don't know what to say and I'm too far gone to think right now. "I need…" I whimper. "Please, Patrick…"

"You need me to make you come?" he says in my ear, his thumb rolling over my clit, the pressure of it so exquisitely relentless it boards on cruel.

"Yes."

"Say it." His fingers stroke me, filling me until my knees give and the only thing keeping me from sliding to the floor is the hand in my hair and his hand between my legs.

I moan. "I want…" the thought spins away from me. "Please..."

He pushes his erection against the inside of my thigh, the head of it straining against my belly, "Not until you say it, Cari."

"Oh, my god—" I can feel tears forming behind my closed lids. Need and frustration tearing down the last of my defenses.

"Say it," he growls at me, his mouth against mine. "I want to hear you say it. Say, *I need you to make me come, Patrick.*"

"I—" I gasp, his teeth closing over my bottom lip, nipping so hard I almost give in to the orgasm threatening to tear me in half. "I need you to make me come, Patrick."

The hand between my legs push deeper, his fingers

buried, his palm cups my pussy, the tips of them stroking the spot that makes me forget my own name. "Come for me, Cari," he says quietly, his voice tight and straining.

Like his words flip a switch, I give in. "*Patrick.*" I scream his name, coming so hard, bolts of light and shadow streaking across my vision while my pussy clamping down on his fingers like a fist, heaving and shuddering as my orgasm rockets through my body.

His hands loosen in my hair, the hand running down the length of my bare back. "*Shhh…*" He keeps fucking me, gently now, my tender flesh quivering around his fingers, his lips pressed against the hammering pulse at my neck while his other hand glides slowly along my spine. "*Shhh…*"

For a moment, I feel cherished. Special. The way I imagined being with Patrick would make me feel and I smile.

He slides his fingers free, cupping my pussy for a moment before sighing, his warm breath against my bare skin stirring something inside me. Lifting his head, Patrick straightens himself enough to look me in the eye, the rigid length of him pressed against my thigh.

Moving his hand from between my legs, he lifts it to my mouth slowly and I catch the scent of my arousal in the air between us. Gaze locked on mine, Patrick touches his glossy fingers to my lips and they part, letting him push them into my mouth. The taste of my juices on his skin against my tongue sends a flush of heat radiating from my belly, stiffening my nipples.

"That's what your hate tastes like," he tells me, his tone

measured. Calm.

He steps away from me, putting enough distance between us so he can bend down and pick up my towel to clean his hand. "You should finish getting ready. You don't want to be late." He drops the towel in my hamper and starts to walk away. "Sure you don't need any help?"

I shake my head, my chest tightening painfully. "I think you've helped enough."

"Okay." He laughs, holding up what he has in his hand. My dress. "But if you try to leave the building in this dress, I'll rip it the fuck off you before you clear the stairs," he tells me, tossing the dress on the bed before walking out the door.

TWENTY-NINE

Patrick

I expect Conner to talk shit when I come back downstairs but he doesn't. He just looks up from the taps where he's drawing a round of domestic pitchers and gives me a look. "Got it all worked out?" he says, lining the bar with pitchers. In the back of the bar, I can see a large party—local guys, wearing baseball jerseys from some park league.

"Yup," I say even though my dick is hard enough to cut glass. Walking over to the bar sink, I start washing glasses, getting ready for tonight. It's Saturday and we're gonna get slammed. After washing and drying every glass I can find, I stock the well and garnish stations. Keeping myself busy so I don't have to talk to Conner about what happened upstairs.

He thinks I went upstairs to fuck Cari. If I'm honest, that exactly what I went up there to do. I wanted to fuck her. To claim every inch of her. To ruin her for every other guy on the planet.

That's what I wanted to do—it was what I was *going* to do. But then she pulled that goddamned dress out of the closet. Acted like she was actually considering wearing it again, even after what happened last night, and I lost it.

I was too keyed up. Too angry. Too dangerous. I'd been angry last night and a part of me fucked her to get even with her. To prove she wanted me just as much as I wanted her. To punish her for making a fool of me. To make her feel just as out of control as I do. As angry as I was then, it's nothing compared to how I'm feeling now. That's why I didn't fuck her.

Because this isn't me. None of it. I'm not this guy. The guy who takes his fingers out of a girl's pussy and pushes them into her mouth so she can taste just how much she wants me. Who keeps going, even after she says no—no matter how wet she is or how hard her nipples are for me. I'm not this guy. I'm not.

I'm totally fucked up and Cari Faraday is the reason why.

She comes downstairs a few hours later. The baseball team at the back of the bar has been joined by a couple dozen tourists, and a handful of college bros, getting a jump on their Saturday night. I'm wiping down tables, my back to her but I don't need to see her to know she's there. Moving on to wipe down the next table, I turn, angling myself so I can see her.

She's standing at the base of the stairs, ignoring me even though I know she's just as aware of me as I am of her. She makes a show of checking her phone and slipping it into the little black purse she's carrying before letting her gaze flicker over me for a moment. The second our eyes connect, a flush rushes over her skin and she looks away.

She's wearing a dress—but not *the* dress. It's white, the top of it snug, sculpted over her breasts, the V of it plunging between them just enough to give the hint of cleavage before flaring out over her hips, caressing the perfect curve of her ass, the hem of it skimming her knees. She's wearing the same heels as last night. The red ones. The only pair she owns. It's one of the outfits she wears when she works gallery openings for Miranda. It's professional and feminine. Completely appropriate and suitable.

I want to bend her over the nearest table, lift that completely appropriate skirt and fuck her so hard she can't walk. Pull her hair and come all over her ass.

What the fuck is happening to me?

"Lookin' good," Conner calls out from behind the bar, shooting me an evil grin before he refocuses on her, making her blush. "Come have a drink with me, Legs, before Prince Charming sweeps in and takes you away from all this." He's been calling her *Legs* since the day he met her and every time he does, she blushes. Before last night it annoyed me. Right now, I want to punch Conner in the throat. And that motherfucker knows it.

I ignore them, just keep wiping, staying as far away from her as possible, while she laughs and approaches the bar to have a seat. From the corner of my eye, I watch Conner mix her a vodka soda while they talk. Whatever he's saying to her has her laughing. It feels like forever since I made her laugh.

You don't want to make her laugh. You want to make her come.

I grit my teeth and keep wiping.

A large group of college kids push through the door, loud and raucous, heading straight for the bar. Conner ignores them, focused on whatever Cari is saying to him. He's trying to force me back behind the bar.

Well, fuck you.

After a few minutes, Conner motions at me with his hand. "Come take care of these fuckers, I'm busy," he says, openly challenging me.

I consider telling him to fuck off but I don't. I toss the bar rag over my shoulder and approach from the other side, still keeping as far away from Cari as possible until I'm behind the bar. The group starts calling out drink orders and I fill them, focusing on pouring liquor over ice and working the taps until they're moving away from the bar, drinks in hand to play pool or throw darts.

"Hey," Lisa says in my ear, coming out of nowhere, her hand sliding down my back before anchoring itself to my hip. "Call me crazy but it feels like you've been avoiding me." She's been trying to get my attention all day long. Standing too close. Following me into the office when I went in to switch out my laundry.

"I've never worked a Saturday night before—just don't want to fuck it up," I tell her, brushing her hand off my hip.

Not getting the hint, she reattaches herself, lifting herself on her tiptoes to set her chin on my shoulder. "We never got a chance to finish what we started last night."

I want to push her away and tell her it's not going to happen—ever—but I don't. Instead, I move away from her under the pretense of drawing myself a pint. "Yeah, about that—I was drunk." I shake my head, trying to keep my voice low because I don't want to embarrass her. "You're a nice girl—"

She follows me to the taps, standing so close I can feel her lips brush against my ear. "You know what they say about nice girls..." She reaches down to wrap her hand around my cock, rubbing her thumb across the head. "We swallow."

I flip the tap off and grab her by her wrist. "It's not going to happen. Ever," I tell her, jerking her hand off my dick. "So, don't touch me." I expect her to start screaming about how I'm hurting her but she doesn't. She just turns and leans into me, pressing her rock-hard nipples against my arm like being grabbed is turning her on.

Jesus. I'm beginning to think Declan was right about this girl.

I let go of her. "Stay away from me," I say through gritted teeth. "What happened was a mistake. Not one I'm looking to repeat."

Something flashes in her eyes and for a second, I think I'm going to have a problem, but then it's gone and she smiles. "Okay," she says, moving away from me, her cocktail tray tucked under her arm. I stand there for a few seconds. At least I found the cure for the perpetual hard-on I've been sporting for the past 24-hours.

When I turn around, I find Cari staring at me.

She watched the whole fucking thing.

THIRTY

Cari

I sneak another look at my phone. It's eight minutes until seven. At least eight more minutes of sitting here, pretending I don't care that Patrick is completely ignoring me while some crazy-ass cocktail waitress is practically jerking him off behind the bar. While I'm pretending, I sip my vodka soda and fantasize about smashing my rapidly emptying glass against her stupid face.

"Want another one?"

I look up to find Conner standing in front of me, a bottle of Kettle One in one hand, the mixer gun in the other. I do want another one. I want another six. A gallon of the stuff. Enough vodka to blind me sounded good right now. Instead, I shake my head, placing a hand over my glass. "No, the last thing I need is showing up for a date with Everett Chase, half in the bag."

Conner motioned my hand away from my glass, giving me a shot of club soda from the gun without the vodka.

"Am I supposed to know who that is?"

"Not unless you're an art nerd like me." I laugh and shake my head. From the corner of my eye, I can see Patrick on the other side of the bar, talking to Crazypants. They're standing close together and he has her by the wrist while she eyefucks him. I get a sudden flash of Patrick hovering above me in the hallway, his hand gripping me by the wrist to lift my fingers to his mouth. Drawing them into his mouth to lick them clean of my juices.

I'm so lost in my own head that it takes me a moment to realize that whatever was happening between Patrick and Crazypants is over and he's looking at me. Caught me watching him get his cock massaged by the same girl who had her mouth on it less than 24-hours ago. Then the asshole winks at me.

He. Winks.

Heat floods my chest and I tear my gaze away, forcing myself to focus on Conner. "What was that?" I say, smiling up at him.

"I said…" Conner laughs, tossing a look down the bar where Patrick is popping the tops on a round of long-necks. "This guy any better than the usual dickbags you go for?" he says, tossing a lime wedge into my glass.

I should be insulted but I can't seem to muster the indignation. He's right. My usual taste in guys is bad. Slicked back hair and expensive suits bad. Guys who just want something pretty hanging off their arm. Guys who treat me like I'm stupid with nothing important to say. Instead of getting angry, I shrug, unable to stop myself from looking down the bar where Patrick fields the steady stream of drink orders that come his way. "He's an artist," I say, tearing my gaze away from Patrick, focusing it on his cousin instead. "Miranda's hosting a show for him in a few months. Some benefit thing. For combat vets."

"Vets? So, he's not a complete asshole," Conner says, nodding his head. "And he gives a shit about something other than himself." He shrugs. "I could get behind that."

"Could?" I say, laughing a little while chasing the lime wedge around with the short red straw in my glass.

"Yeah—*could*," he says setting a pair of shot glasses on the bar. "If you weren't going out with him just to fuck with my cousin."

His accusation stiffened my spine. "Excuse me?"

"You heard me just fine." He lifted a bottle of Jameson from the well in front of him and poured a shot into each of the glasses in front of him. "I don't know what your game's been these past six months, but it's not funny anymore. He deserves better."

His words sting like he slapped me in the face. "And I don't?" I blurt out before I can shut myself up.

"Cap'n is a nice guy. He—"

I laugh because I just can't help it. "Trust me—your cousin isn't as nice as he pretends to be."

Conner narrowed his gaze on me for a second before he seemed to make up his mind about something. "You're right. He's not nice. He's repressed." He tossed back one of the shots, not even flinching at the burn. "You want to know why he never made a move on you? That's why," he says, refilling the glass he just emptied. "He's afraid of who he really is and what he really wants because it's *not* nice.

It's not polite. It's dirty and it's messy, so he ignores it and pretends those things about himself don't exist." He leans across the bar and drops his voice. "His feelings for you make it hard for him but he could handle you working him up, day in and day out—all he had to do was pretend it was all in his head. What he can't handle is knowing you were doing it on purpose, just to fuck with him like he's some kinda nutless chump."

"That's—" I'm shaking my head, staring at Conner, my throat seizes up, hand wrapped around the glass in front of me like it's the only thing keeping me from falling off my stool. Before I can formulate a response, he starts talking again.

"Look, I like you, Legs. I like you a lot," he says. "That's why I'm telling you all this. One of you is gonna have to pull your head out of your ass and be honest about how you feel and what you want and I can almost promise, it's not going to be him because there's *still waters* and then there's where Cap'n likes to hang his hat."

He's right. I know he is, but I don't have a clue on how to fix it. "How do you propose I do that, Conner?" I'm not angry anymore. I'm asking for help from someone who seems to know Patrick better than he knows himself. "I've tried apologizing. I've tried explaining. He won't listen to me."

"Fuck if I know, Legs, I'm just a grease-monkey who can't keep his dick in his pants but I'll tell you this much—" He lifts the shot glass again, this time clinking it against my glass of club soda before tossing it back. "You broke it. You bought it."

THIRTY-ONE

Patrick

The car shows up for Cari at seven o'clock sharp, the driver pushing through the door to stand just inside the bar, searching for someone in the sea of frat bros and college girls who looks dignified enough to warrant a chauffeured car. As soon as he sees Cari, he straightens his posture and nods at her while she slides out of her seat and makes her way toward him.

I'm in the middle of building a round of black & tans, using every ounce of focus I have to ignore the fact that I can still feel the way her pussy clamped down on my fingers while she rode my hand. Her nails digging into my bicep, her eyes wide and glazed with lust when I pulled her hair. The way she moaned my name and reached for my cock like it was the only thing in the world that could satisfy her. The way she came for me when I told her to.

Fuck. Me.

Rounding the bar, I meet her a few steps from the door. "Let me help you with that," I say, reaching for her red cashmere wrap. Taking it from her, I drape it around her shoulders, using my grip on it to pull her close. My mouth hovers over hers for a moment, my gaze focused on her lips, slightly parted. I brush the pad of my thumb over her strawberry birthmark, the edge of it peeking out from the neckline of her dress. It's warm, I can feel the blood rushing across her chest to gather there and I smile because I know it's because of me. How close I am. "Do you have your cell phone?" I ask like I'm her fucking mother or something and she looks at me like I'm nuts.

"What?" She sounds confused, looking over my shoulder at the guy here to drive her to her date. "Yes."

"And it's charged?" I let my thumb skim lower, running along the swell of her breast, dipping into her cleavage. "We both know you don't keep it charged."

"Yes," she says softly, her pupils dilating, breath catching in her throat. "It's charged... I have to go, Patrick."

I ignore her, sweeping my thumb over the thin fabric of her dress, my cock jerking when I feel her nipple go hard. "Money, just in case?"

She nods her head, her eyes slipping closed for a moment, her tongue running lightly along her lower lip. I want to take her lower lip between my teeth. Bite and nibble and lick and taste my way over every fucking inch of her.

I lean even closer, bringing my mouth to her ear while my thumb draws lazy circles against her nipple. "Are you wearing panties?" I whisper in her ear before my teeth close over its lobe while I pinch her nipple between my thumb and forefinger, rolling it beneath the fabric of her dress.

She gasps, the shuddering breath of it skates across my neck and I can feel her nod, the top of her head brushing across my jawline. "Yes."

I know people are watching us but I don't care. She's leaving to go on a date with another guy but before she does, I'm going to remind her that she's mine. That she belongs to me. "Are they wet?"

She tries to jerk back, put space between us but I tighten my grip on her wrap, pulling her close enough to feel the hard length of my cock pressing against her belly. "You better answer me, Cari," I tell her, fighting to keep my voice level. "Because if you don't, I'm going to have to check for myself—right here, in front of this whole fucking bar. Are. They. Wet?"

I can feel her turn her head, looking around the knot of people we're standing in. It's barely seven o'clock on a Saturday but Gilroy's is already half packed, people milling around us, giving us quick, knowing looks. "You wouldn't—" she says before cutting herself off like she's no longer sure who I am and what I'd be willing to do to her in public. "Yes."

Smart girl to answer me because what she's thinking about me is right. I've gone off the deep-end when it comes to her and right now, I'm not drowning. I'm doing the fucking backstroke. Enjoying every second of my temporary insanity. "For me?"

"Yes," she says, shifting the hold she has on her purse, the back of her hand grazing my cock.

I groan softly. I'm about five seconds away from telling

the guy behind me to fuck off, drag her upstairs like a Neanderthal and fuck the shit out of her. It takes me a moment to gain a semblance of composure but when I do, I take a step back and look her right in the eye. "I'm going to fuck you when you come home," I say like I'm asking her to pick up milk on the way home, not even trying to whisper. "Have a good time," I tell her grinning at the way her eyes widen slightly before I let her go.

I walk back to the bar and make my way behind it. When I do, I look at the spot I left her standing in. She's already gone.

I spend the next few hours on auto-pilot, slinging drinks and breaking up fights while doing my best to dodge Lisa's groping hands. I'm not sure how much clearer I can be about regretting what happened between us but at this point, I'm over being nice about it. Every time she touches me, I brush her off and tell her to get back to work. She just smiles at me and saunters away for a while before circling back around to cop a feel.

While I'm dealing with Lisa, Conner pulls his Houdini act with progressive frequency. I try not to pay attention to how many girls he goes through or how often he disappears. It's not hard to do, really, all I can think about is Cari. What she's doing. If she's having a good time. If this Chase guy took her to a nice place. If he opened her car door for her. If he helped her take off her wrap when they got where they were going. If he's treating her how she deserved to be treated.

Because I can't seem to get the job done.

I'm not even mad at her anymore—not really. Not when I'm like this. Not when she's nowhere near me. Right now, I just want her to come home. I want her to walk through the door, so I can take her upstairs and help her out of her dress. I want her to curl up on the couch next to me in one of my T-shirts and force me to watch some shitty reality show about fucked-up, D-list celebrities or rich, bored housewives. I want to be with her. Like we were before— only *not* like before. I want to kiss her like I have the right. Touch her without wondering when she's going to finally catch a clue and start laughing. I want to sleep next to her without worrying that this is all some long, elaborate joke.

And that's the problem, isn't it? I don't trust her—this. Whatever *this* is. What's happening between us, I don't trust that it's real. I don't think it's going to last because, let's face it—no matter how much I want to be, I'm not the kind of guy a girl like Cari Faraday ends up with. I'm not rich. I'm not famous. I don't drive a Porsche. I'm not good enough for her. Every time she apologizes for the colossal mindfuck she pulled on me, it makes me feel like a puppy she just kicked through the uprights. Like some pathetic loser, she feels bad for. Like I'm some kind of pity-fuck.

That's what pisses me off.

"Hey, can I get a Guinness?"

I look up, to find Sara standing in front of me, looking like she did the last time I saw her. She's a cute girl—light brown hair, warm brown eyes. Nice. She was just finishing up her student teaching when we split. I wonder if she's finished and if she's getting ready to move back to wherever she came from for college and for a split second, I wish I felt for her, what I feel for Cari. "Sure you don't want a whiskey sour?" I tease her, forcing a smile onto my face. We broke up four months ago and she hasn't been back to Gilroy's since, even though we swore we'd still be friends.

She laughs, jostled slightly by the crowd shouting drink orders behind her. "You remembered," she says playful and flirty, making me wonder why she's here. It can't be a coincidence that my ex-girlfriend pops up the day after Cari and I finally hook up. I automatically shoot a glance down the length of the bar, looking for Conner. This is the kind of thing that meddling asshole would set up, all in the name of *helping me*.

He's MIA. Shocker.

"Come on," I say, shoveling ice into a pint glass, filling it with Jameson before giving the drink a cursory squirt of sweet and sour from the mixer gun. "It's the official drink of Gilroy's college girls." I give it a twist and set a straw into it before passing it over the bar.

From the corner of my eye, I catch sight of Tess, making her way down the bar to stand next to me, the top of her head not even level with my shoulder. She showed up around nine and climbed behind the bar. I'm not sure if Conner called her in or if she was walking by and saw me drowning and decided to jump in and lend a hand and I don't care. Right now, she's my favorite person.

"Hey, Sara," she says giving my ex a quick smile while flipping the tap over a pitcher, filling it with some shitty IPA that tastes like lemon-scented floor cleaner. "Where the fuck is Con?" she says to me, obviously irritated.

"Who knows," I say, giving Sara an apologetic smile. "It's been a clusterfuck of a night," I tell her, lining up a long row of rocks glasses so I can fill them with ice.

Tess rights the pitcher and flips the tap before passing it across the bar with a stack of frosted pints, exchanging it for cash. "Fuck this." She drops the cash in the register, slamming it shut before turning toward me again. "Boost me up, Cap'n," she says, tugging on my sleeve and I do what she says because it's Tess and to be honest, she kinda scares me.

Closing my hands around her waist, I lift her up until her boots hit the bar. I keep a hand wrapped around her ankle because I'm afraid she's going to launch herself into the crowd while I use the other to speed pour well whiskey over the ice I just shoveled.

Glancing in Sara's direction, I find her where I left her, drink in hand, a weird look on her face, bouncing it between Tess and me. "What are you doing here?" I know I sound like an asshole but I don't really have time to be nice about it. I add sweet and sour, running the gun down the row of glasses.

"I'm here with Alisha," she practically shouts, stirring her drink before taking a drink. Alisha is the blonde Con has a near miss with the night I met Sara. "Your cousin called her. Asked her to come in."

Sounds like Conner. Fucking dick has girls lining up and he calls in a pinch-hitter while we're in the weeds. Before I even open my mouth, Tess reaches down to grab a handful of hair, giving it a yank.

"Fuck," I shout, glaring up at her while she smiles down

at me, all sweet and proper. There's nothing sweet and proper about Tess.

"I thought you liked it rough," she says, giving me another sweet smile that makes me want to shove her off the bar. Any hope Cari didn't tell Tess that I've been acting like a sexual deviant for the past 24-hours has gone out the window. I can feel Sara's stare burrow into the side of my face.

"Tess…" I'm shaking my head at her, warning her to keep her mouth shut, but the grip she has on my hair makes it painful.

She laughs at me and unlatches her hand from my head. "Let me go," she says and again, I do as I'm told. A second later she's scrambling off the bar, disappearing into the crowd. With her tiny tank top and grease-stained overalls that put her tattoos and piercings on full display and her scuffed Doc Martin's, she looks like Punk rock Tinkerbell— if Tinkerbell could rebuild a transmission and kick your ass.

Probably at the same time.

Sara's still staring at me. Both hands-free, I start handing out the whiskey sours, exchanging them for money until I'm out of drinks. "Look, it's nice to see you but—"

"Are you guys hooking up?" Sara blurts out, casting a quick look over her shoulder.

"Seriously?" I say, starting on a round of Malibu and cranberries. "Me and Tess?" I shake my head. "No—she's just an asshole. She says shit like that all the time." I can't look at her, so I concentrate on counting out pours of coconut rum. "Hangs out with Conner too much."

"She asked me about you." Sara shrugs. Even though I'm only paying half attention to her, I can see she's jealous. A blind guy would be able to see it. "About how you are—sexually."

What the shit?

"I'm not hooking up with Tess," I say, shoving drinks into hands, dropping money into my apron. "She's like family."

Sara gives me a funny look. "That's not what—"

"*Fuck, woman.*"

I look past Sara, watching the crowd of bros part like the Red Sea, eyes wide, mouths hanging open, somewhere between laughter and sheer terror. Here comes Tess, dragging Con through the middle of them by his ear. "I'm just about the only *woman* in this dump you *haven't* fucked," she shouts back, pulling him along behind her, taking the long way around the bar. "Matter of fact, your dick called. He's tired and would like a break."

"Tessie, are you jealous?" he tosses back, his quip followed by a howl. "*OWW!* It's not detachable—shit!"

She huffs a lank of dark hair out of her eyes and keeps walking. "Wanna bet?"

"If you want a ride, all you have to do is say so. I'll let you jump the line." He's laughing because he's a total dick and just fucked-up enough to find this situation amusing, despite the fact that he's in serious danger of losing an ear.

As soon as they're back behind the bar, Tess lets go to drill her finger into his chest. "I'd rather lick the sludge off these bar mats than get *Gilroyed*—thanks anyway."

Con grins at her, rubbing his ear. It's bright red and looks about two inches lower on his head than it did before Tess got her hands on him. "One of these days you're gonna have to admit that you want me, Tessie," he says, reaching for her to press a wet, noisy kiss to the side of her face. If there's anything Conner loves more than pussy, it's getting Tess riled up. The fact that he's managed to obtain both in one night has him practically giddy.

"Gross," she says, pushing him away while wiping at her face, trying to fight the smile that's threatening to break loose. "Who knows where your mouth has been."

"I can show you if you want," he says, reaching for her again and the whole bar laughs at the show the two of them are putting on.

"One Gilroy under my belt is quite enough, thanks," she says loudly before motioning for me to lift her onto the bar again. Fitting her fingers into her mouth, she lets out an ear-splitting whistle. Like Pavlov's dogs, every single drunk in the place stops and looks up at her. "College girl specials." She points at a spot down the bar. "Beer," she says pointing at the area in front of the taps. "Everything else." She jerks her thumb in the opposite direction before stopping cold, her gaze zeroing in on someone standing by the door. "And you—" she says, pointing at a stunned and angry-looking Declan. "If you're finished with your cake tasting, I'd appreciate it if you'd get your ass back behind the bar and start washing glasses."

THIRTY-TWO

Cari

As far as dates go, this one has been as close to perfect as I've ever had. When Chase's driver stopped the car in the middle of the warehouse district, I thought maybe he was lost. Or maybe he wasn't Chase's driver at all. Every episode of *The First 48* I've ever seen flashed in front of my eyes. Just when I was getting ready to dig my phone out of my purse, my door opened and there was Chase. Behind him, parked on a dimly lit side street was a food truck.

"I hope you like tacos," he said, reaching out to help me from the car, still holding my hand when he took a step back to give me a head to toe look, coupled with a low whistle. "God, please tell me you like tacos."

Laughing, I nod, pulling my hand free under the pretense of shutting the car door. "I do indeed."

"In that case, we'll name our first-born Everett." Chase grins at me, offering me his arm.

"Everett?" I say, playing along because

Everett *fucking* Chase is flirting with me and I'm going to *like it* whether I like it or not. "You don't strike me as the kind of guy who longs for a junior."

"It's a *have to*, not a *want to*," he says, rolling his eyes for effect. "Family name."

Giving in, I take his arm, letting him guide me toward the back of the food truck's lengthy line. "But what if it's a girl?" I say, arching a brow at him.

"We're young and hip enough to pull off naming our daughter Everett," he assures me grinning like he's got it all figured out. "It's our son who's going to have a hard time."

I feel my phone vibrate inside my purse and I clutch it tighter, holding it against my thigh. "Don't tell me Harold is a family name too," I say, forcing myself not to think about who's texting me. Or hoping that it's Patrick.

"I wish," Chase says, shaking his head gravely. "Gertrude—after my grandfather."

I laugh, wishing I felt a flutter in my stomach when he presses his hand against the small of my back. "We'll call him Gertie for short."

In my purse, my phone vibrates again. And again. Loudly.

"Do you need to get that?" Chase says, genuine concern etched into his face. And what a face. Is it possible he's gotten better-looking since yesterday morning? His reddish-brown hair is tousled around his spectacular face. Brilliant blue eyes, framed with thick lashes that crinkle at their corners when he smiles. Large, calloused hands with paint-stained cuticles. He's smart and funny. He talks to me like I'm an actual person. He's the darling of Boston's art scene for fuck's sake. If I had a checklist titled PERFECT BOYFRIEND, he'd tick every damn box.

And it's all completely wasted on me. Because Conner is right. The only reason I said yes to Chase was to get under Patrick's skin.

"No," I shake my head, strangling my purse in my grip. "It's probably just my roommate." As soon as I say it, my chest flushes so fast and hot, color creeps up my neck.

"The architect," Chase says, reminding me that they met. "I wasn't kidding yesterday—he's making quite the name for himself. You guys known each other long?"

Something that feels like pride swells in my chest. "Going on four years," I say with a shrug, trying to pretend that none of it mattered to me—the fact that Everett Chase was impressed by Patrick. My Patrick. "We've only been roommates for the past six months though."

New Roommate Rule: you don't come unless I say so.

Like it was on a timer, my phone buzzes in my purse.

"Trust me?" Chase says, splitting a look between me and the food truck looming in front of us. Somehow, we'd made it to the front of the line without me noticing.

"With my life?" I say, smiling.

"Let's save something for date #2," he says, laughing. "With your food choice."

I look at the menu painted on the side of the truck. It all looks good to me. "Yes."

He nods, pressing his hand into the small of my back again. "So, go grab us a table and check your phone."

Leaving him to order, I hurry toward a rickety-looking

card table flanked with a couple of folding chairs, digging my phone from my purse while I walk. Sitting down, I swipe at the screen. I have nearly a dozen unanswered texts.

None of them are from Patrick.

Tess: Declan is here.

Here can only be Gilroy's. It's the only place the two of them ever cross paths. Declan doesn't even show his face at Con's garage unless he knows Tess isn't there.

Tess: Holy shit. I'm freaking out.

Tess: Did I die? Am I in hell?

Tess: I am trapped behind the bar with him. I can't deal.

But Declan left early, didn't he? He had some kind of wedding appointment to take care of with Jessica. Why would he go back?

Tess: Do you think I'm small enough to drown myself in the bar sink?

Tess: I hate you. While you're off fancying it up with some art douche, I'm dying.

Tess: I. AM. DYING.

Tess: Help me.

I give up trying to make sense of what I'm reading and call her. While I'm listening to the phone ring, another text comes through but Tess answers before I can check it.

"Hey," she says, all breezy and calm. "I was hoping you'd call." In the background, I can hear the three-ring circus that is Saturday night at Gilroy's.

"Is he still there?" I say, giving Chase a thumbs-up when he holds up a couple of ice-cold beers.

"Of course," she says, laughing while I listen to her scoop ice.

"Are you okay," I ask, even though I know the answer to the question. To anyone else, she'd sound perfectly normal. Flirty, even, but I can hear how strung-out she is. She's two breaths away from a full-fledged panic attack.

"Not really," she laughs again. "Did you get the picture I sent you?" Almost immediately I hear the rumble of a deep voice.

Who are you talking to?

My mouth drops open. Declan. Talking directly to Tess. Why does all the good stuff happen when I'm not around?

"None of your fucking business," Tess snaps back, her tone muffled by the hand I know she's put over the phone.

I'm picking up your slack while you're sexting dirty pictures to your fucking boyfriend. That makes it my business, Tesla.

Holy. Shitballs. He just called her Tesla. No one called her Tesla. Not even her dad. Not even Conner.

"Don't hit him," I screech, hoping like hell she's still listening, even if she's not talking to me anymore.

"Just go back to washing glasses and mopping up beer," she snipes back. "Nobody asked you for your opinion."

Why are you being so difficult?

"Why are you being such a nosy bitch?" The phone jostles in her hand. "Are you still there?" She's talking to me, her voice silky smooth.

"You called him a bitch," I squeak out, trying like hell not to laugh.

"I sure the fuck did, sweetheart," she says, sounding smug. And better. More like Tess. "Will I see you tonight?"

She's asking if I'm going to make it an early night or if I'm going to draw this sham of a date out just to screw with Patrick. "I'm not sure."

"Check your phone before you say no."

My stomach rolls over. I can imagine what kind of photo Tess managed to snap. Patrick, sucking tequila out of a college girl's bellybutton. Licking salt off her tits. Using his tongue to dig a lime wedge out of her— "Okay," I say, giving myself a mental slap in the face. "Do you want me to come home?"

"Yes," she says, following it with a long, heavy sigh. "No."

"I'll be home in a few hours," I tell her, looking at the clock on my phone. "No committing murder until I'm there to help you move the body."

In the background, I can hear the low rumble of Declan's voice. Apparently, being called a nosy bitch only keeps him silent for so long.

"No promises," she grumbles.

I laugh. "I love you."

She sighs, her voice shaky for just a moment. "I love you too."

I hit end and stare at the screen for a few moments before I swipe at the screen, searching my unread texts.

Tess: Oh, and BTW—this is happening.

The text is accompanied by a picture like Tess promised and it's a thousand times worse than Patrick licking salt off some bimbo's tits. It's of Patrick, smiling, looking sexy as fuck, leaning against the bar, talking to a girl. Not just a girl. His ex, Sara.

"Give me a hand?"

I look up to see Chase standing a few feet away juggling takeout boxes and beers.

"Sure," I say, closing the picture on my phone before tossing it onto the table. Standing, I take the beers and one of the boxes. I sit back down while he rounds the table to take the chair across from me.

Whatever's in this box smells delicious. I open it and instantly feel my stomach bulge. "Geez, did you enter us into an eating contest of some sort?"

"I suppose I should tell you before we set the wedding date," Chase says, opening his own container to stare lovingly at the food in front of him. "I'm a food truck junkie." He gives me a sad shrug while pulling his fork from its plastic sleeve. "Don't ask me to choose."

I laugh around the beer bottle I have pressed to my mouth. "I knew you were too good to be true," I tease back but my heart's not in it.

"Everything okay with your roommate?" he says, lifting a taco from the heap of food in front of him and biting it nearly in half.

"What?" I say, sinking my fork into what looks like a tamale. "Oh—yeah. It wasn't Patrick. It was my friend, Tess." I swear to God I sound disappointed. "Guy trouble."

He shakes his head at me, his face scrunched up in disgust. "Fucking guys."

Why does he have to be perfect?

Because God hates me, that's why.

"I know, right?" I take a bite because I don't want to talk about it anymore. As soon as the tamale hits my tongue, I swear my eyes roll back in my head. "Is this heaven?"

Chase grins at me over the taco he's inhaling. "Welcome to paradise, Ms. Faraday."

THIRTY-THREE

Cari

After eating our weight in tacos and tamales, Chase and I walk—making me wish I opted for a pair of low wedge sandals instead of heels—and while we walk, we talk.

"What's your plan, Faraday?" he asks, taking me by the elbow to pull me away from a questionable pile of *something* on the sidewalk in front of us. "You can't want to work for Miranda for the rest of your life."

"I like Miranda," I tell him, shrugging because the subject makes me uncomfortable. "She's a great boss."

"I like Mandy too," he says, leading me around a corner, down what looks like an alley. For the first time since we started walking, it occurs to me that we aren't just wandering aimlessly. He's taking me somewhere. "But you're not a secretary." He shrugs and smiles like he's figured everything out. "So, what's your plan?"

"I've never heard anyone call her Mandy before." I laugh. "It sounds weird."

"Mandy and I've known each other since we were kids." Chase shrugs, but I can tell he's choosing his words carefully. "And you're avoiding the question."

He's right, I am. Why? It's not like what I want to do with my life is some sort of secret. "I want to own my own gallery someday," I tell him, my tone firm and sure. "I want to help artists get discovered."

He gives me an odd look. Like he thinks I'm full of shit. "I thought you were a painter."

"Now you sound like Patrick," I tell him, rolling my eyes. "I'll tell you the same thing I've told him a million times— it's just a hobby." I shrug, avoiding his gaze. "I'm not good enough to make a real go of it."

Chase stops walking. "Who says?"

Now he really sounds like Patrick. "Where are you taking me?" I dodge the question because, over the past few months, the things I want have started to change and to be honest, that scares me a little. "Are you the kind of guy who plies girls with tacos and beer and then ax murders them in a dark alley?"

He lets it go and starts walking again. "Seriously?" he laughs at me, leading me farther down the alley, a light at the end of it growing brighter the closer we get. "I would never ax murder the future mother of my children."

I point a finger at him and laugh. "But you *do* ax murder girls—that's what I'm hearing here."

"What can I say?" He smiles. "The tacos and beer slows 'em down." Laughing, he keeps walking, pulling me along in his wake. "So, how long has it been?" he says, shooting me a knowing smile.

"How long has what been?" We're close enough to the end of the alley that I can see people standing in line, waiting behind a red velvet rope. "Where are you taking me?"

He ignored my last question and answered the first. "How long have you been in love with your roommate?"

I almost choke, inhaling hard enough that air got stuck in my lungs. Coughing, I cleared my throat. "What?" I shake my head hard, hand pressed to my chest. "Why does everyone keep asking me that? I'm not in love in love with Patrick."

Chase gives me a long, sideways look—one that makes me feel odd. Open. Like he can see things inside me that I can't. Then he shrugs and smiles. "Sorry, my mistake," he says, stopping a few yards from the entrance of what looks like a dilapidated warehouse.

The door is open and I can see movement inside. People in fancy clothes, walking the perimeter of the space. Splashes of color decorate the walls, illuminated by strategically placed lighting, waiters with trays of champagne weaving through the crowd. He fed me tacos and brought me to a gallery opening. "No," I say, slumping against the wall. "I'm sorry... I didn't mean to snap at you. Things between Patrick and I are complicated right now."

"When I saw the way he was looking at you yesterday, I knew he was crazy about you," he explained, leaning against the wall beside me. "I assumed the feeling was mutual."

Crazy. I can't think of a better word to describe the way Patrick and I have been behaving these past 24-hours. "I never noticed."

Chase opens his mouth to say something but before he can get a word out, someone interrupts him.

"Cari?"

The sound of his voice stiffens my spine and I turn to see James standing on the pavement a few yards away, a beautiful blonde draped over his arm. She looks vapid. Dim. Like an expensive, beautifully dressed pet, waiting for her commands.

That used to be me. That's what people see when they look at me.

I feel my stomach twist and it must show on my face because Chase steps closer, blocking my view of James and his date. "Are you okay?" he says, eyebrows lowered, jaw suddenly tight.

"I'm fine," I say with a smile because there's no way in hell I'm going to cause a scene. Not here. Not one that involves Chase. I angle myself around him to find James closer than before. "Hello, James."

James says hi.

The idea that he followed me here pops into my head. But that's crazy, right? It's been months since we broke up and I haven't heard a single word from him. As crazy as it is, I nearly cry with relief when I feel Chase slip an arm around my waist, pulling me close. He doesn't know what's going on but whatever it is, he's not going to let me handle it alone.

"I thought that was you…" James's eyes flick over Chase's hand on my waist and he smirks for a second before aiming a smile at me. "It's nice to see you again."

I don't say anything. Instead, I give the blonde on his arm a polite smile. "I'm Cari," I say, offering her a hand.

"Mimi," she purrs, slipping a limp hand into mine while giving Chase a long look. "Hello, Chase."

Chase's hand tightens on my waist. "Mimi," he says before focusing his attention on James. "If you'll excuse us, Cari and I were in the middle of a private conversation. Perhaps we'll see you inside."

I have to roll my lips over my teeth to keep from laughing out loud. James looks like Chase just took a shit on his shoes. Before he can say anything, Chase uses the hand on my waist to usher me away.

"Ex-boyfriend?" He says softly, leading me toward the open door where a large man in a tuxedo is checking names against the list on his clipboard.

"Unfortunately." I cast a quick glance over my shoulder to see James watching us. The look on his face tells me his being here is not an accident. "Ex-girlfriend?"

"Fuck no." Chase laughs out loud this time. "Despite her best efforts... she's just a model. I've used her a few times."

I want to ask what *used* means but I don't. It's none of my business.

He stops us in front of the man at the door. "See the blonde in blue and the shifty-looking shit with her?"

The man flicks a glance over Chase's shoulder, watching as James and his date cue up in line. "Yes, sir."

"They don't get in." Chase taps a finger on the man's clipboard. "I don't give a shit what that thing says."

The man gives him a conspirator smirk. "Yes, sir."

Chase claps a hand on the man's shoulder. "Thanks,

Emilio." He grins at me, slipping his hand off my waist to offer me his arm. "Great—now that that's over with, let's go drink champagne and look at some shitty, over-priced art."

I take his arm, looking around while I shake my head. "You can't say things like that," I whisper. "Someone will hear you."

"Who cares?" He laughs at me, pulling me through the door, totally circumventing the line of people waiting to get in. "I can say anything I want—it's my shitty, over-priced art we're gonna look at."

THIRTY-FOUR

Patrick

The crowd starts to die when we call last-call around midnight. Technically we don't close until 2AM but if there's one thing the four of us agree on, it's that this night needs to be over already. As soon as Tess's boots hit the bar and she makes the announcement, blowing kisses at frat boys when they flip her off for cutting them off and flipping off drunk girls as they stumble out the door, toward the cavalcade of Ubers waiting to drive them back to their sorority houses.

"You're a charmer," I tell her, grinning up at her when she plants her hands on my shoulders as I help her off the bar.

She blows out a hard breath that ruffles the dark hair that falls into her eyes. "It's why all the boys want me." She gives me a wink, making me laugh even though laughing is the last thing I feel like doing. It's after midnight and Cari still isn't home from her date.

What did you think was going to happen? She basically got

asked out by the man of her dreams. Did you really think you stood a chance?

Behind me, Declan is cashing out the waitresses. I can feel Lisa standing close. Too close. She's practically breathing down my neck. On impulse, I grab Tess by the hand and pull her down the bar. Leaning over her, I brace a hand against one of the wells. "Put your arm around my waist," I tell her quietly and because Tess is a trooper, she does it, no questions asked.

Well, almost.

She pushes up onto the toes of her boots, bringing her mouth as close to my ear as she can manage, considering there's almost a foot and a half height difference between us. "Are you gonna kiss me?" she whispers. "Because if you kiss me, I'm probably gonna throw up in your mouth."

I turn into her, pressing my mouth to her ear, trying not to laugh. "Kiss you? Please—I'd rather eat dog shit."

Tess tossed her head back and laughs, the sound of it loud and deep. When Tess laughs, she goes for broke and everyone in the room stops to listen. "So, I guess that means you're not taking me up to your swingin' bachelor pad to give me the honor of sucking your dick?" Her hand slips off my waist and onto my ass, her fingers digging in hard enough to make me jump. I know she's doing it for Lisa's benefit but it feels wrong. Really, really wrong. Like, getting groped by my sister wrong.

"Cari told you?" I want to slam my head against the bar.

"She told me everything." She shakes her head, grinning at me like a loon.

"I had a momentary lapse in judgment." An embarrassed

flush creeps up my neck. "I blame Conner. And Jameson." And Cari. I blame her too. I look over my shoulder to find everyone watching us. Sara. The waitresses and Declan.

As soon as I look, everyone snaps into action. Declan gets busy with pulling cash and receipts from the drawer while the waitresses walk away, mouths hidden behind their hands while they whisper. Thankfully, they take Lisa with them.

"Goodnight, ladies," Tess says, lifting her hand off my ass to flutter it in a girly wave that is so *un*Tess it makes me snort.

As soon as they're out the door, I laugh and push myself away from her. "You're an asshole." I hear the cash register slam shut a second before I see Declan move out from behind the bar, heading down the hall toward the back office. The door slams shut a few seconds later. "What crawled up his ass," I mutter.

"I did," Tess says, grinning ear-to-ear.

I laugh out loud, shaking my head while collecting empties off the bar. "You shouldn't poke at him," I told her. "He came in on his night off to help us out."

"His night off? Are you serious? *I don't even work here,*" she says, scoffing loudly. "I came in because Con wouldn't answer his phone and I wanted to tell him I cleared the deck at the garage and what do I find? You, drowning in a sea of Malibu and IPA and our loveable manwhore, turning tricks in the bathroom." She throws up her hands before settling them on her hips.

"I didn't ask you to stay," I remind her, even though I should be kissing her ass because she did. Over her shoulder, I see Sara watching us with avid interest and not a little jealousy. It's pretty obvious she didn't believe me when I told her Tess and I are just friends. I suppose watching Tess grab my ass didn't do a whole hell of a lot to convince her. Great. That's all I need.

"Yeah?" Tess arches an eyebrow at me for throwing her attitude. "Someone had to get a handle on this mess and it sure in the hell wasn't going to be you two fuckwits."

"*Turning tricks* implies I get paid," Con calls from the back of the bar. "I provide a valuable service, free of charge."

Tess rolls her eyes so hard, for a second I'm convinced they're going to fall out of her head and bounce across the floor. "I had plans!"

Conner's disembodied laugh slams its way around the bar. "Hanging out with your cats doesn't count as plans."

"Fuck you, Gilroy—I don't have cats," Tess shouts, while she swipes chewed up cocktail straws and wadded napkins off the bar and onto the floor with a bar towel. "I have *one* cat. Singular. And for the record, Shadrach is awesome."

"One cat, plus... how many strays do you feed at the garage, again? I lost count."

Tess throws a couple of empty beer bottles into the trash. "Shut-up."

"Seventeen?"

"I hate you."

"Thirty-six?"

"You're taking me to Benny's for pancakes."

"Ask your awesome cat to take you for pancakes," Con

teased back, even though we all know he's going to do what she says. He always does.

"I'm not *asking*, Gilroy," she yells. "Pan. Cakes."

Conner laughs again, the sound of it followed by a sigh loud enough to hear from across the bar. "Yes, dear."

"That's what I like to hear." Tess did a fist pump like there was ever a question she'd be eating pancakes an hour from now. "How about you, Cap'n—pancakes?"

Their exchange eats at me. Maybe it's the ease between them. Something Cari and I will probably never get back. If Cari was around, we'd go to Benny's with them. We'd all talk and laugh over questionable food choices and too much coffee. Afterward, Cari and I would walk home and talk. Sometimes, if she was still tipsy, even after eating, I'd give her a piggyback ride. Her legs wrapped around my waist and her head on my shoulder, the highlight of my night. The thought makes me laugh but there's nothing humorous about the sound.

"Don't you mean *Predictable Patrick*?" I say quietly. One of the glasses in my hand is chipped and I throw it in the trash can, on top of the bottles Tess tossed in there. The sound of breaking glass makes me feel better, but only for a moment. When I look up, I find Tess watching me, a pained expression on her face.

"That was 100% me, Patrick," she says, shaking her head. "And we both know I'm a complete asshole which means you can't hold me responsible for what comes out of my mouth." Despite what she's saying, she looks sorry. "Please don't be mad at her because I'm thoughtless and shitty."

I dump the load of glasses I'm holding into the sink,

careful not to break anymore. "What's to be mad at, it's true isn't it?" It is the truth. That's *why* I'm mad. From the corner of my eye, I can see Tess shaking her head at me, her mouth open to argue with me.

It's 12:20AM and Cari still isn't back.

Fuck it.

"Sara, want to help me and Tess get this place cleaned up?" I say, shooting her the same grin Conner uses when he's working co-eds. "I'll pay you in pancakes?"

Sara perks up and hops off her barstool. "You've got yourself a deal."

THIRTY-FIVE

Patrick

"Hey."

I knock on the door jamb of the office before pushing it open. Declan doesn't even lift his head from the ten-key, his fingers flying over the keys while he sifts through a pile of credit card receipts, wrangling the total fuckery of tonight into some semblance of order.

"What's up?" he says, shooting me a quick look before gathering the pile of receipts and paper-clipping them together in a neat, orderly pile. It's what he does best. Declan is an expert at keeping things neat and orderly.

I open the door on the dryer and pull out the load of clothes I threw in there more than twelve hours ago. It's a hopeless, wrinkled mess that will have to be re-washed at some point but right now, I don't care. "I thought you had dinner with Jess's parents or some shit."

"I left them at the restaurant with my credit card," he says, swiping a hand over his face. He wouldn't say it but I knew the deal. He hated Jess's parents. Almost as much as the rest of us hate Jess.

"We're heading to Benny's, you want to come?" I ask, even though I know what his answer is and why. The answer is no. Because *we* includes Tess.

A frown creases the thin skin of his brow and he looks away, tucking the bundle of receipts into a zippered pouch. "Thanks, but I'm gonna head home," he says, shaking his head. "We've got a game in the morning, remember?" He sounds pissy when he says it and I jam a pair of wadded up jeans into my basket. This time *we* is him and me. We coach a little league team sponsored by our contracting company. The fact that he thinks he has to remind me, like I'm suddenly irresponsible or thoughtless, stiffens my jaw.

"No shit, Declan." I laugh, shaking my head, grabbing a bunch of clothes from the dryer to jam into my basket. "We've had a game every Sunday for the past two-and-a-half-years—you think I magically forgot?"

"I don't know what the fuck you remember or *don't* anymore, Patrick," he says, finally sitting back in his chair to glare at me. "You've been acting weird all damn day, and if I'm honest, I'm getting sick of trying to figure you out."

Declan sounds like I feel. Amped up and touchy. Angry and quick-tempered. Looking down at the clothes in my hands, I see Cari's red lace thong, peeking out between my fingers. The ones I nearly ripped off her last night, seconds before I fucked her with my tongue. She must've snuck it into my laundry at some point during the day. I almost laugh, which is crazy because nothing about this is even remotely funny. "Same here," I mutter, shoving the clothes in my hand into the basket, because I'm hoping to start some shit. Maybe if I get punched in the face enough times, I'll snap the fuck out of whatever the hell is happening to me.

"What's that supposed to mean?" he says. I don't have to look at him to know he's been spoiling for this blow-up all day, almost as much as I have, but I look anyway because I want to see his face when I say what comes out of my mouth next.

"I'm not fucking Tess," I say, dropping my laundry basket on the floor at my feet. "Not that it'd be any of your business if I was." I kick the basket across the floor and it sails through the open door and into the hallway. "You dumped her, remember? A long fucking time ago."

Declan's head snaps back like I sucker punched him in the face. All that's missing is the blood. "That's about as much your business as it is my asshole brother's," he says, the warning in his tone ringing loud and clear. "Which, in case you forgot, is none at all."

"That's where you're wrong," I say, fighting the urge to crank my hands into fists. "It is my business. Tess *is* my business." I have no idea why I'm stirring this shit up. What happened between Tess and Declan happened a long fucking time ago and it's never been any of my business before. I've always stayed out of it except to break up fights between him and Conner whenever Con gets his dick in a twist over it. Now it's my dick in a twist and I can't seem to keep my mouth shut. Conner would be so proud. "She's my friend and you *broke* her."

One second Declan is sitting behind the desk, the next he's in my face. "Shut your fucking mouth."

"Nah," I say, shaking my head, the corner of my mouth, jerking upward even though my jaw is so stiff I think it might be close to cracking. "You treated her like shit, remember? You have no right to get pissed if someone else comes along and wants to help put her back together." Even as I'm saying it, I know I'm talking to myself just as much as I'm talking to Declan. This isn't about him and Tess. Not really. This is about Cari and me. The way I've been treating her. Because let's be real—I'm just as guilty of what I'm saying as he is.

A muscle in Declan's jaw flexes. "Is that right?"

"Sure is," I answer. "And fuck you for thinking you do."

Declan doesn't answer me. The two of us stare each other down and I'm thinking this is really gonna happen, we're really going to start throwing punches. I'm about to ask him to step outside because the office is where we keep liquor shipments and there's about twenty grand worth of booze stacked on shelves behind him. I want to kick Dec's ass, not bankrupt the bar.

"Are you guys gonna kiss?" Conner pipes up from the doorway. "Because I can come back…"

I look over to see Con, his hand latched around Alisha the pinch hitter's wrist. Despite what he said, he knows what's happening, even if he doesn't know why, and he wants to tie this shit off before it gets out of control. The idea of Conner playing peacekeeper is ridiculous enough to cool my blood a bit. At least enough to keep me from throwing the first punch.

"No," I say, keeping my tone easy but I don't back down. Because that'll never fucking happen, no matter how ridiculous this situation is. "I think we're done here. What do you think, cousin?"

Declan bares his teeth before he takes a step back, putting a few inches between us. "Enjoy your pancakes," he says, moving back behind the desk. "And shut the door—you idiots are wearing me thin."

"Whatever you say, boss," I say because suddenly I'm the kind of asshole who has to have the last word, before I sail through the door, slamming it closed behind me. I pick up my laundry basket and head down the hall.

"What the fuck was that?" Conner calls after me but I don't answer. Walking through the bar without stopping, I head upstairs.

After dropping off my laundry in the apartment, I head out to my truck and grab my tool belt and head back up. Strapping it on, I go to Cari's room. The painting Chase gave her is still sitting on the floor, leaning against the bed.

My bed. The one I bought. The one she sleeps in without me.

The urge to put my foot through it is still there but I keep it in check. Instead, I survey the room, looking for the perfect place for it. She sleeps on her side, facing the alcove where she keeps her paints so I decide on the wall directly to its left. That way, she'll see it every morning when she opens her eyes.

I pull out my stud finder, running it along the drywall until it lets out a beep. Marking the spot with my pencil, I dig out a nail and sink it in with a few light taps with my hammer. Lifting the painting, I drag it down until the nail in the wall hooks around the wire strung across the back of the wooden frame. Using my level, I make sure it's as straight as an arrow.

Stepping back, I keep going until I bump into the bed and I sit down, imagining the way she'll smile when she wakes up and sees it.

Perfect.

I look at the stack of finished paintings Cari keeps covered with a canvas drop cloth. She caught me snooping once, the first day she moved in. She'd been bringing in a box from her car and I'd just hauled up the stack from her trunk. I'd started to lift the drop cloth off the top of them when she walked in.

"Please don't," she said from the doorway, dropping the box on the floor before rushing over. As soon as she said it, I stopped, holding my hands in the air.

"Sorry," I said, giving her a sheepish look. "I didn't think you'd mind."

"It's okay," she said, pushing her hair out of her face. "You don't want to look at those anyway. They're terrible."

"No peeking," I say, crossing my index finger over my chest. "Promise." And I meant it. After that, I never looked. No matter how curious I was about what she was hiding from me.

Since then, I've seen a few of Cari's finished paintings. That's how I know that whatever she's hiding under that drop cloth is anything but terrible. If they're even half as good as what I've seen her do, they're worthy of just about any museum in the world.

I'm not sure how long I've been sitting here before I realize I'm not alone anymore but when I do, my heart stutters a bit in my chest. I turn around hoping it's Cari. I want to tell her I'm sorry. That what she did doesn't matter. Not anymore. I want to tell her that I love her. That I want to be with her. I start to turn around to tell her all of it, even though I'm not sure I can but when the doorway comes into view, it doesn't matter.

Because it's not Cari standing behind me. It's Sara.

"Tess is passed out in a booth and Con and Alisha are..." She shrugs and rolls her eyes. "Anyway, I think we're finished downstairs," she says and the way she says it tells me she knows how I feel about Cari. She's known all along.

"Alright," I say, standing up to unhook my belt. "It's pancake time." I shoot her a smile, heading toward her and she moves out of the doorway to let me pass. Bypassing the kitchen, I drop my tool belt on the dining room table. "Feel free to order a side of hash browns with your pancakes," I say, joking because I don't want to talk about Cari. Not with her. "You earned it."

Sara laughs and the sound of it chases away the awkwardness between us. She doesn't want to talk about it any more than I do.

We make our way downstairs to find Alisha sitting at the bar alone, playing with her cell phone while Conner sits at a table by the door, Tess cradled in his lap. Declan is standing two feet from them, jaw clenched, keys in his hand.

"You were snoring less than thirty seconds ago," Conner

says, in an exasperated tone. "No pancakes. Not tonight—
come on, Tessie, just let me take you home. You put in a
full day at the garage and then you came here and worked
your ass off. You're wiped."

"Why are we even talking about this?" She smiles and
reaches up to cup his beard-stubbled cheek. "We both
know the only place you're taking me is Benny's," she says,
her expression turning set and stubborn. "For pancakes.
And I don't snore."

"You are a pain in my ass," he tells her, fighting a grin.
"Seriously, I can't even deal with how much of a pain you
are. And yes, you do."

Tess narrows her eyes at him, the hand on his cheek
reaching up to grab his ear to give it a jerk. "Just for that,
you're buying me pancakes *and* a side of bacon."

"Don't," he says, widening his eyes at her, tucking his ear
into his shoulder. "You almost pulled it off last time."
Finally noticing me and Sara standing over them, Con gives
up, sighing as he stands with Tess still in his arms. "I'll
throw in a hot chocolate if you take tomorrow off."

I sneak a look at Alisha, worried that Con and Tess's
antics might be making her uncomfortable but she's not
even paying attention. She's standing next to Sara like she's
ready to leave, still fucking around with her phone like
we're not even here. Like she couldn't give a shit that Con
had her bent over the bathroom sink less than fifteen
minutes ago and here he is with another chick in his lap.
Granted, that chick is Tess. But still.

From the doorway, Declan clears his throat. He's got it
propped open with his foot, his message clear. *Get the fuck*

out. He looks annoyed with the lot of us and it reminds me of when we were kids. He's only two years older than us but he's always been surly as fuck. He can usually handle the sexual innuendo that is 99% of their usual banter. What he can't handle is watching Tess and Conner take care of each other. He never could.

Tess shoots Declan a look that seems to pass right through him before focusing on her negotiations with Con. "Pancakes, bacon, hot chocolate *and* pie. And I'll come in at noon."

"Alright—noon." He grins at her. "That's probably for the best," he says, heading for the door, still carrying her. "You gotta come in and feed your cats, anyway. All forty-three of them."

"I hate you," she sighs, winding her tattooed arms around his neck. "You're the biggest bastard I've ever met in my life."

"Well now, we both know that's not true." Conner laughs, throwing his brother a look on his way out the door. "Later, bro."

Ouch.

Once we're all standing on the sidewalk, Declan shoves his key in the lock and gives it a twist. "Goodnight," he says to no one in particular before heading toward the parking lot on the side of the building.

"You sure that's a no on the pancakes?" I call after him and smile when he flips me the middle finger. Things will still be tender between us tomorrow but the worst is behind us.

A car pulls up to the curb in front of us and a guy who

looks like my eighth-grade math teacher gets out. "Someone call an Uber?"

"Yeah," Alisha pipes up, finally shoving her phone in her purse. "I'm heading to that party in Allston, you want to come?" she says. Allston is another college town a few miles from here.

Sara looks at me for a second before shaking her head. "No, I'm gonna stay here."

"Suit yourself," Alisha shrugs, opening the door to her getaway car. "Call me," she says to Con who makes a non-committal sound while giving her an awkward wave. She'll never hear from him again and they both know it.

Alisha and her Uber pull away while Con, Tess and Sara make their way down the sidewalk. They get about fifty feet ahead before Sara stops and turns back to look at me. "Are you coming?"

The last thing I need to do is buy Sara breakfast because that's just going to give her hope when there is none.

But it's 1AM and Cari still isn't home. Regardless of what I need, the last thing in the world I *want* is to lay in bed and listen for her key to hit the door. Because I don't know what the fuck I'm going to do to her when it finally does.

"Yup," I say and jog to catch up.

THIRTY-SIX

Cari

It's 3AM and I'm sneaking into my apartment like I missed curfew. I'm trying to be a considerate roommate. That's what I tell myself. That Patrick has a game in the morning and making noise when he has to wake up in a few hours would be rude. I'm sneaking around like a rebellious teenager because I'm a good person. Not because I feel guilty about staying out so late.

I shouldn't have bothered. I know he's awake and in the living room the moment I shut the door. Knowing that he's sitting on the couch, a prime seat from which to watch what he thinks is my walk of shame, waiting for me like a disapproving older brother, makes me angry. Like he has the right to criticize anything I say or do.

Sighing, I cross the living room, toward my room. The hall light is on, the soft glow of it splashed across the floor, casting the couch in shadows. I can't see him but it doesn't matter. I know he's there. "I didn't mean to keep you up," I say into the dark, tossing my clutch onto the coffee table between us. "I lost track of time."

He doesn't answer me but I think he laughs. I can hear the quiet push of it, disturbing the air between us. He's as angry and confused as I am. I need to remember that. I need to go to bed and not make things worse. I need to ignore the fact that right now, there's no such thing as *worse* when it comes to me and Patrick.

"Good night, Patrick," I say, my high heels clicking across the hardwood floor.

"You could've just asked me, you know," he says from the dark, stopping me cold. "I would've been glad to show you."

I have no idea what he's talking about but it doesn't matter. It's not his words that affect me. It's his voice. The deep hum of it shoots through me, down my spine to seat itself between my legs. I think listening to Patrick read the phone book would make me wet.

"I have no idea what you're talking about," I tell him, reaching out to steady myself on the back of a dining room chair to take off my shoes.

"The heels stay on."

It's not a request. It's an order. Hearing it, delivered from the dark, in that calm, rational voice of his makes my pulse race. I should finish taking the shoe off and throw it at his spot on the couch where I know he's sitting. I should but I don't. When I straighten myself, my heels are still on my feet.

"Turn around." Another order from the dark. I do it and come face to face with my reflection in the mirror, illuminated by the slice of light from the hallway. The mirror I hung to give Patrick a perfect view of my room from where he sits on the couch. "Take off your dress."

I don't even bother wondering why I keep doing what he says. It doesn't really matter. *Why* is a question I can't answer. All I know is that I'm going to do it.

Whatever Patrick tells me to do, I'll do it. I *want* to do it.

Reaching for my side, I tug the hidden zipper down until it stops at the top of my hip. Shrugging out of the bodice, I let it pool at my waist. I look at myself. The soft white lace of my bra plunging between my breasts, my nipples tight and swollen against it. The dark stain of my birthmark on my chest, almost black I'm so aroused. I can feel it. Damp heat tingling between my legs. Soaking through the lace of my panties. Looking past my reflection, I find the shape of him. The dark shadow of Patrick sitting on the couch behind me. "What did I do?" I say softly. "What should I've asked you?"

"Take off your bra."

Reaching between my breasts, I find the front closure of my bra and open it. My bra slides off my shoulders and drops to the floor. My breasts sway slightly, my nipples throb in time with the clench and release of my pussy. "Patrick…"

"Are you wet?"

My fingers grab onto the skirt of my dress and twist. The only thing I want more than to touch myself it for Patrick to do it for me. What the hell is he doing to me? "Yes."

My answer pulls a growl out of the dark and I can hear him shift on the couch, sliding lower in his seat to accommodate the hard-on I know he has for me. "Show me." He growls the words. The rumble of it going straight to my clit. "Lift your dress up over your ass."

Leaning forward just a bit, I pop my ass out before lifting the full skirt of my dress to settle it around my hips. Cool air hits the damp stretch of lace between my legs and I have to lift a hand to brace myself against the wall in front of me to keep myself upright. "What should I have asked you?" My voice is strained. Breathless. "What did I do?"

"Jesus…" He groans the word, the sound of it harsh and guttural. "Pull your panties down."

It's awkward with one hand but I manage it, rolling my hips and tugging until my panties are around my knees. "No more until you answer me," I tell him even though I know I don't mean it. Whatever he says, I'll do it and we both know it.

"Touch yourself, Cari," he tells me, the calm tone of his voice cracking, want and need bleeding through.

My free hand grips my skirt again, pulling it between my thighs. "No," I say, somehow resisting, stopping myself from doing what we both want. "Not until—"

"You had Tess ask my ex-girlfriend what I was like in bed." He finally answers my question, his tone solid again. Calm and sure. "Now, put your fingers in your pussy."

His matter-of-fact command, and the dirty words he uses to give it, surprises me. I'm not sure why—nothing about Patrick's behavior should surprise me anymore. But it does. Almost as much as it turns me on.

I let go of my skirt to slide a hand up the inside of my thigh. "I didn't—" The moment my fingertips make contact with the wet seam of my pussy, my brain shuts off. My fingers slip past my slick entrance to bury themselves, the heel of my hand pressed against my clit. *"Patrick..."* His name shudders its way up my throat, tumbling out of my mouth on a moan.

"How wet are you, Cari?" His calm is crumbling again, his voice broken and uneven. In the dark behind me, I hear him breathing, the sound of it ragged and heavy. "Tell me," he breathes, his tone strained.

"So wet..." I moan the words, forcing myself to keep my eyes open and focused on the mirror in front of me so I can see the shape of him behind me in the dark.

He groans again, the sound of it shaped into a curse. I can feel his eyes on me, the heat of his gaze narrowed on my throbbing center. The fingers I have buried inside of it as far as they'll go. Waiting for him to tell me what to do. *Tell me what you want.*

Like he's reading my mind, he tells me. "Fuck yourself while I watch."

I withdraw my fingers almost to their tips before burying them again, stroking myself slow and deep. The heel of my hand grinding against my clit in lazy circles.

"Let me guess what she said..." His words come out in short bursts between ragged breaths. "I'm sweet and tender, right?" Even though I can't see him, I know what he's doing. He's doing the same thing I am. He's touching himself. Getting off on watching me as much as I'm getting off on listening to him. "She said that I'm considerate. That I always let her come first. That I never made a mess. That I'm gentle and caring. That when I fucked her, it was nice. Predictable." He laughs, breath heaving and shuddering in his chest. "Is that what she told you? That I'm *predictable*?"

He knows. I'm not sure how but he knows about the unflattering nickname Tess gave him. The one I've used like a shield to defend myself against the fact that I want him. No matter how boring and predictable Patrick seemed to be, I wanted him. I still want him.

But this isn't sweet, predictable Patrick. This is the Patrick no one knows but me. The Patrick who orders me around and takes what he wants without asking for permission. There's nothing gentle or considerate about him. His question echoes off the cool brick walls, hanging in the quiet between us. I don't answer him. I'm too far gone, the only sound between us is our ragged breathing and the wet sliding of my fingers fucking my pussy. I close my eyes, opening myself to the orgasm barreling down on me.

"I think you forgot the rules." He's behind me now, the pulsating length of his cock pressed between my thighs. Feeling him there, so close to where I need him makes me whimper. "You don't come until I say so, remember?" He reaches down to pull my fingers free.

My legs begin to shake. "Patrick, please..."

Lifting my arm over my head, he covers my hand with his own, pressing it into the wall beside the mirror. "I'm a nice guy—is that what she said?" He leans over and whispers it in my ear. "I want to know."

I open my eyes and the image that greets me takes my breath away. My sweat-slicked breasts bared, nipples hard and swollen. My arms above my head, Hands trapped, pressed flat against the wall by his wide, callused palm. Patrick's chest is bare, a pair of basketball shorts yanked down around his hips. I can see the huge, swollen length of him pushed between my legs.

His hips grind slowly, sliding the shaft of his cock along the seam of my wet pussy, pushing between its folds, the head of it hitting my clit, over and over until I'm shaking uncontrollably.

"Please..."

He lifts his free hand and captures one of my breasts. "As soon as you tell me what I want to know..." He pinches my nipple hard, rolling it between his thumb and finger, tugging and caressing. "I'll let you come..." His heavy-lidded gaze locked on the hand on my breast. "I'll even help you." He rolls his hips against me and I moan, my knees buckling slightly. "Is that what she told you? That I'm a nice guy in bed."

I nod my head, swallowing hard.

Patrick slides his hand down my torso and it disappears behind the veil of my skirt a moment before I feel him. Slipping his fingers inside, he pumps them in and out of my quivering center to coat them with my arousal before finding my clit. "Words, please," he growls, rolling the swollen nub under his juice-slicked fingers.

"Yes." The words tumble out on a shuddering groan.

He pulls my hand off the wall and presses it between my legs, replacing his with mine, guiding my fingers, pressing them inside me. "You want to hear something funny?" he says, his fingers still circling my clit, the pleasure of it, his hand and mine, heavy between my legs before his fingers leave me completely. "I never fucked Sara." In the mirror, I watch him coat his cock with my arousal, his glossy fingers sliding up and down the straining length of his shaft. "Not without thinking about you."

The hand on my breast slides around my shoulder, closing around the back of my neck. "Because that's the only way I can get hard." The hand on my neck trails down my spine while his other hand pumps his cock. "Do you know how bad that fucks with someone's head? Knowing the only person he can get hard for thinks he's a fucking joke?"

The hand on my spine brushes across my lower back, fingertips dipping into the cleft of my ass, feathering and teasing against its hole and I moan. *Oh, my god…*

"I tried being with someone else and it didn't work. I tried to be the nice guy and you wouldn't let me." He presses his thumb against my puckered hole. "I don't understand what you want from me." He slips the tip of it inside, the sudden pressure of it turning me inside out while the head of his cock jerks against the juncture of my thighs with the forces of his strokes.

"*Patrick…*" The orgasm rips me apart, screaming through me, so hard and violent I feel myself sliding down, a puddle of me gushing to the floor like water. Anchoring an arm around my waist, Patrick holds me upright, the head of his cock hot between my ass cheeks.

"I'm gonna come all over your ass," he tells me, his chest heaving with the effort to keep his own orgasm at bay.

"Yes…" That's all I can say as my pussy grips and pulls at my fingers as a second orgasm pulls me under. "Come on me."

"Fuck." He lets out a roar, the fast, rhythmic pump of his

hand up and down his cock becomes frantic, seconds before I feel the hot spurts of his release against my ass cheeks. The back of my thighs. Between them.

His hand comes up to brace against the wall over my head and he leans into me, the length of his cock pressed between my slippery ass cheeks, jerking and twitching the last of his release. So much, I can feel it start to creep down the inside of my thigh.

Suddenly, his fingers close over my chin, twisting my face around, his mouth and tongue devouring mine. I want to turn around. Wrap my arms around him so he can carry me to bed but he won't let me. He keeps me where I am, breaking the kiss, turning my face again to run his tongue along my jawline.

"This is what I see every time I watch you in this mirror," he whispers in my ear before trailing his tongue up the length of my neck, gaze fused to mine. "I want you to see it too." He moves his hand between my legs, grips me by the wrist, stroking me with my fingers before pulling them free. "I want you to *feel* it, every time you look in this goddamned mirror." I watch as he lifts my fingers to his mouth and sucks them clean of my juices, the feel of his tongue against my skin almost enough to make me come again.

You broke it, you bought it.

What Conner said to me earlier replays in my brain.

"Make me feel bad," I say, feeling a perverse kind of satisfaction when his shoulders stiffen against the sharp jab of my words.

He looks away from our reflection and lets go of my

hand.

"Earlier today when I was getting ready for my date. You came up here to…" *make me come.* Remembering it, heat rushes over my body. It didn't matter that I've had more orgasms in the past 24-hours than I've had in the last six months. My body wants more. "You interrupted me while I was talking. I was going to say all you want to do is make me feel bad."

He won't look at me. All I can see is his profile in the mirror, his clean-shaven jaw flexing. His teeth grinding and clenching. For a moment, I think he's going to say something but he doesn't. He just steps back and reaches down to catch a hold of my panties, still around my knees. "Well, you know what they say about misery, Cari," he tells me, pulling them up, the crotch of them instantly soaked with my arousal and his release when they meet the juncture of my thighs. He smooths the seam of them across my hips before leaning into me to whisper in my ear again. "It loves company."

THIRTY-SEVEN

Patrick

I don't sleep. Instead, I lay in bed and wonder what the fuck is wrong with me. If the past hour did anything, it proved to me that whatever it is, it's not going to get better anytime soon.

After Benny's I ordered Sara an Uber and waited with her for it to arrive while Conner walked Tess home. I could hear them arguing one of their classics—Superman vs. Batman—their voices growing fainter and fainter the farther away they got. Sara and I made awkward small talk until her car showed up and then I walked home alone.

Despite what I said to her before she left, I'd resolved to keep my hands to myself and my dick in my pants tonight. It was somewhere between two and three o'clock in the morning. I had to be up in four hours. Regardless of my ridiculous posturing to the contrary, I had absolutely no claim on Cari. I couldn't fuck her just because I wanted to.

And holy shit, I wanted to.

But, I wasn't going to. I was going to take a hot shower

and try to steam the stench of beer and coconut rum out of my pores and then I was going to go to bed. I was not going to go to her. I wasn't going to touch her. I wasn't going to peel her panties off and taste her. Make her scream my name.

I wasn't.

When I got home, she was still gone. Still on her date and it did something to me. Twisted my guts into knots. Blurred my vision. Made it hard to breathe. Made me want to wait for her in the dark and pounce on her the second she walked through the front door.

But I stayed on track. I took a shower. I even shaved. Pulled on a pair of basketball shorts and climbed into bed.

I lasted a whole five minutes before I was up again, in the living room, waiting for her to come home.

Cari does not belong to me just because I want her to.

Cari is a grown woman who is capable of making her own decisions.

After the way I've treated her, Cari is smart to stay away from me.

These are things I told myself, over and over, while I waited for her to walk through the door. When she came home, I was going to apologize. I was going to let her apologize to *me*. We were going to move on. Try to be friends again. Put this all behind us.

Then she walked through the door and all my good intentions went out the window. What I did is the exact, polar opposite of *moving on*. I ordered her to finger fuck herself while I jerked off and came all over her ass. Not exactly something a friend would do. Not something a sane, rational person would do either.

The worst of it is, when I left her standing there, her perfect ass covered in my cum, I wasn't finished with her by half. I'd wanted more. So much more. I felt myself teetering on the brink and it took every ounce of decency I had left to force myself to walk away.

Decency.

The word flopped over in my brain and I laughed out loud, the harsh sound of it ricocheting off the walls of my room like a bullet because I'm pretty sure now I've never actually *been* decent. I've never really been the nice guy. I've just been pretending this whole time. A wolf in sheep's clothing, going through the motions to please the people around me. I'd gotten so good at it I even fooled myself.

It's different with Cari. *I'm* different with Cari. I can't pretend. Not anymore. I'm harder. Sharper. Relentless. I'm someone I don't even recognize half the time. Someone I'm not sure I like.

The only thing I'm sure of is I can't stop. I can't go back to who I was. Now that I've had her, I can't let her go.

Not now.

Not ever.

THIRTY-EIGHT

Cari

I lay in bed, listening to Patrick move around the kitchen, alternating between working up the courage to get up and talk to him and willing him to come in here and make me come again. The thought makes my pussy clench in response, reminding me that he'd walked away from me before either one of us got what we really wanted.

Huffing out a frustrated breath I force myself out of bed. Pulling a pair of pink cotton boy shorts from the top drawer of my dresser, I pull them on before gathering my hair into a messy bun. It's Sunday. I don't even have to leave my room to know what he's doing. He's standing in the kitchen, leaning against the counter, eating a quick bowl of cereal while he waits for the coffee to finish brewing so he can slam a cup before heading to his game. When I go out there, he'll say good morning and act like nothing is happening between us. Like I still can't feel his hand pressed against mine. On my breasts. Between my legs.

I'm gonna come all over your ass…

The flash of warm heat that rushes through me to settle between my legs is enough to make me have second thoughts about going out there.

I pull my door open and step into the hall, reminding myself that I live here too. I have just as much right as he does to be here. He can be as polite and proper as he wants.

In the kitchen, I find him doing exactly what I expected. He's dressed in faded jeans and a navy T-shirt with the DG Contracting logo splashed across the front. He's got a bowl of Raisin Bran in his hand and he's making quick work of it, like *here* is the last place he wants to be. Next to him, on the counter, is his ball cap. He won't put it on until he's outside. If you ask him why, he'll laugh at you and say *because I'm not an animal.*

But I know that's not true. Patrick Gilroy is a wolf, walking around in people clothes.

"Morning," I say, forcing as much cheerfulness into my tone as I can but he doesn't answer. It's like I'm not even here. Turning away from him, I open the cabinet over the coffee maker. Pulling a cup free, I reach for the coffee pot to pour a cup. Leaning over I open the refrigerator, bending to pull the carton of half and half out to add a generous dollop. Moving around the kitchen, I can feel the weighted heat of his gaze on my ass. The sensation of it stiffens my nipples instantly.

Turning around, I lean against the short length of counter across from Patrick and take a sip of coffee. "I'm not going to make the game today," I tell him, working to keep my tone light and friendly. "Chase is coming over." It's true.

Chase is coming over but not for the reason I'm letting him believe. We spent the night at the gallery, watching people fawn over his work until the showing was over. Afterward, we walked and talked until nearly three in the morning and somewhere along the way it went from a first date to two friends, just hanging out, to a quasi-job interview.

He asked me about my painting, and after nearly an hour of poking and prodding, got me to agree to show him some of my work. "Chase is coming over," I say it again because, from his reaction, you would've thought I told him we were out of toilet paper.

"I heard you the first time," he tells me, calmly. He doesn't say anything else. He knows I'm pushing him. Trying to get some sort of reaction out of him. That for all my apologies and claims to the contrary, I can't seem to stop playing games with him. He just stands there, eating his fucking Raisin Bran. Refusing to take the bait I'm dangling. It's pissing me off.

Despite the fact that he's treating me like I'm invisible, he's hard, the impressive length of it pressing against the unforgiving fabric of his jeans and he doesn't do anything to hide it. Doesn't seem embarrassed or apologize. He wants me to see it. To remember.

And it works. Seeing it reminds me of last night, the feel of his shaft against my ass, pressed between my cheeks. The frantic jerking of his hand up and down his hard length. The head of his cock bumping against my puckered hole—half promise, half threat.

Heat erupts across my chest and I catch my lower lip between my teeth to keep myself from licking my lips.

When I force my gaze upward, I find him staring right at me.

Finished with his cereal, he turns and rinses his bowl before placing it in the sink. Picking up his cap, he moves again and my breath catches in my throat when he stops right in front of me. Reaching for me, I suck in a sharp breath when his knuckles graze my nipple. He pulls my coffee cup out of my hand and takes a drink, his eyes never leaving mine. When he's finished, he doesn't give it back. Instead he leans into me. So close I can feel the hard length of him press against my belly. Close enough to bring his mouth to my ear.

"Enjoy your day," he says softly, his lips brushing the shell of my ear. Behind me, I hear the quiet click of my cup as he sets it on the counter I'm leaning against.

And then he's gone. Out the kitchen, across the living room and through the front door before I can find the strength to take a breath.

Patrick's getting really good at leaving me breathless.

THIRTY-NINE

Patrick

The situation with Cari is beyond fucked but *this* I can count on. The crack of the bat and the whip of the ball. The way the brim of my hat shades my eyes from the bright morning sun. The sting that *thwacks* into the center of my palm and radiates up my arm when I catch a fastball. Being out here, I feel like I can breathe for the first time in days.

"You look like shit," the kid I'm catching for tells me, his tone matter-of-fact. His name is Chris and he's about fifteen. A neighborhood kid—they all are, ranging in ages from thirteen to seventeen. Behind him, Declan lobs balls deep into the outfield while kids hustle to keep up.

Chris is our starting pitcher and I'm crouched about twenty yards away, hat turned backward, so he can get warmed up. "Yeah?" I say, standing to toss the ball back to him. "I'd rather look like shit than look like you."

"Ohhh," Chris shoots back with a laugh, his arm rocketing out to throw me a more than decent curveball. "Old man's got jokes."

"I'm twenty-five." I catch the ball before popping up from my crouch. "I won't be old for another five years." I throw the ball back, putting a little more zip on it than usual to make my point.

Chris keeps laughing and gives me a fastball. "Whatever you say... old man."

The kid's curve is better than decent but his fastball is a thing of wonder. Fifteen-year-old me is more than a little jealous. The ball hits my hand so hard it goes numb. "Just keep throwing the ball, asshat," I tell him. "I'll let you know if I need a Geritol break."

Chris stops for a second and cocks his head, grinning. "A what?"

I walked right into that one. "You talk too much," I say, lowering myself into a crouch, planting my feet shoulder-width apart. "Just throw the ball. We don't have all day."

The game is at ten but Dec and I try to get here at least an hour early. He picks up kids who need rides in a company van while I stop at Benny's and pick up a fuck-ton of breakfast burritos to feed the team. We tell them it's because they need the protein but the real reason is that I know a lot of these kids don't eat breakfast. To be honest, I don't think a whole lot of them eat on a regular basis at all.

My senior year in college I had a business professor who assigned my class with drafting a business plan for a non-profit—that's how Boston Batters was born. I knew from spending summers here as a kid that club ball costs a small fortune and city leagues didn't offer the kind of instruction or involvement needed to help kids develop their talent or their character. So, instead of entrance fees and expensive equipment to buy, we offer the league for free. In return, the kids are required to participate in community service projects—some we set up and some they do on their own. So far, we have ten teams in the league, each sponsored and coached by different local businesses as well as a few larger firms and corporations. We practice a few evenings a week and have games on Sunday, going on two years now. As soon as I went into business with Declan, I talked him into sponsoring our first team. Tess and I are still working on Conner. It's not the sponsoring he objects to. It's dealing with kids he isn't sold on.

"Where's my woman?" Chris called out, delivering his question with another fastball.

He's talking about Cari. The kid's had a crush on her since he joined the league, not that I can blame him. She comes to every game, somehow making jeans and a team T-shirt look downright sinful, to make sure the team stays hydrated and cheer them on.

"She's got other plans today," I say evasively.

"You guys fighting?" Chris says, concern spiking his tone. Like most of these kids, his home life isn't the greatest. *Fighting* usually involves the cops and domestic battery charges.

"No," I say shaking my head, tossing the ball back before dropping onto my haunches. "She has a date." I think I manage to say it without sounding like I want to hunt that Chase prick down and stomp his skull in.

I must've pulled it off because Chris rolls his eyes and throws me a slider. "Another douchebag?"

I catch the ball and throw it back. "He's an artist—seems

nice enough."

"*Seems nice enough,*" Chris stops and laughs. "That's what you said about that shit-face lawyer she was dating a few months back."

"I'm gonna start charging laps for language," I tell him, but only because I know I'm supposed to be a responsible adult. Truth is, I'm sure developing a gutter-mouth is the least of this kid's worries. His mom pops oxys like they're breath mints and his dad is a barely functioning alcoholic.

"Why don't you just quit dicking around and ask her out already?" Chris says, completely ignoring my threats about his language.

"Because we're just friends." I'm so used to saying it that it comes out automatically. Catching the ball, I don't toss it back. Instead, I stand and start walking, closing the distance between us.

"I don't get it," he says, pushing his hat up to scratch at his head. "According to Sean's sister, you're supposedly the *hottest guy on the planet.*" Sean is his best friend and starting shortstop. For his part, Chris looks skeptical. And a little jealous. Sean's sister is seventeen and, besides Cari, his current object of infatuation.

Even though it makes me uncomfortable, I shrug. "So?"

"So, what's the deal?" Chris widens his eyes at me and gestures broadly. "Apparently, you're not a carnival freak and Cari's a total smokeshow. It shouldn't be *that* hard to bag—"

"Don't talk about her like that." The tone of my voice, flat and heavy, is something he's never heard from me before and it shuts him down completely. Fuck. I've worked for years to get these kids to trust me and here I am practically ripping the kid's head off for stating the obvious.

Even though I want to apologize—know I should—I don't. "Declan's lining everyone for batting practice." I'm close enough to Chris to drop the ball into his gloved hand. "Why don't you go get some swings in before the other team gets here."

Chris doesn't answer, he just bobs his head once before turning to leave me behind at a moderate jog. He's halfway up third before he turns back to me and grins. "I take it back—you are a *total* carnival freak." His gaze drifts past me and the grin on his face goes from sheepish to shit-eating in less than a second. "Someone's here to see you," he says, jerking his chin in my direction before loping off to join Declan and the rest of the team.

It's not Cari. I know it's not. If it were Cari, a stampede would've broken out, Declan losing total control of the team as they all ran toward her. That's how much these kids love her. They saw her almost every Sunday without fail and they still swarm her every time they do, bombarding her with questions and telling her about their school week. She remembered every one of them—who has big tests coming up or who'd been having trouble in school—and she made sure she said something personal to each of them. So, no—it wasn't Cari.

Just like I knew who it wasn't, knew who it *was*. I put a smile on my face and turned to jog my way to the dugout where Sara waited for me behind the fence.

"Hey," I say when I'm close enough to say something without shouting. "What are you doing here?"

"Your team is playing my dad's," she said, pointing at her T-shirt. It's bright orange with the letters LH&H scrolled across the front in a fancy script font. "And as much as it hurts to break it to you, we're gonna whip your ass."

I laugh, feeling almost relieved. While we were dating, she'd asked her father, one of the founding partners of some huge law firm downtown, to sponsor a team. Even after we broke up, she insisted that her father keep up with the sponsorship but she's handed coaching over to an associate at the firm. I knew taking her out for breakfast was a mistake. That it would encourage her into believing there was a chance of us getting back together. I need to set her straight but I don't say anything about it. Not now. Instead, I give her a friendly smile. "You care to place a friendly wager on that, Ms. Howard?"

"Sure," she says, grinning ear-to-ear. "Loser buys lunch."

I return her smile and hold out my hand. "You're goin' down, Howard."

FORTY

Cari

I can't help it. Even though Chase and I hung out all night and developed what I think of as a solid foundation for a lasting friendship, I'm freaking out.

Everett Chase is in my apartment and he's looking at my paintings.

As soon as Patrick left (and I finally caught my breath), I did a quick tidy-up. The apartment itself is clean. Patrick is as close to a neat-freak as a twenty-five-year-old guy can get so the main rooms are good. It's my bedroom that's the issue. I'm kind of a slob.

Clothes on the floor. Paint splattered on the walls. Dishes—mostly coffee cups and wine glasses—crowd the table next to my easel. I scoop it all up, shoving the clothes into my hamper with a promise to do laundry later and cart the dishes to the kitchen where I give them a quick rinse before loading them into the dishwasher. I even add soap and start the wash cycle.

Shoving my overflowing hamper into my closet, I shut

the door and turn to focus on making my bed. Comforter straight and pillows fluffed, I take a last look around. Chase'll be here any minute and I want to at least look like—

The painting Chase gave me is hanging on the wall, across from my side of the bed. How I missed it earlier, I don't know, but I did. Lowering myself onto the edge of the bed, I can't help but stare at it. The dark current of water. The way the moonlight is reflected off its dappled surface. Ripples and torrents. The soft flow and steady rush. Both exhilarating and peaceful. Tranquil and terrifying. Familiar and strange.

It reminds me of Patrick.

I know he's the one who hung it for me. I can imagine him doing it. Choosing the perfect place. Setting the nail and hook at the right angle. Hanging it just so. Using his level to make sure it's straight. Not wanting to, but doing it anyway. For me.

There's a knock on the front door and when I answer it, I find Chase standing on the other side. Today, he's wearing jeans and a faded, paint-splattered T-shirt. "There's a place down the street that makes the best breakfast burritos in Boston," he says, holding up a white paper bag.

I see Benny's logo printed in red across the bag and can't help by laugh. "You should try their pancakes," I say, opening the door to let him in.

He crosses the threshold and drops the bag on the coffee table while I get a roll of paper towels from the kitchen. Benny's is good but can be a bit messy. When I get back to the living room, Chase is sitting on the couch, in Patrick's spot, halfway through his breakfast. "You live over a bar," he says between bites. "I'm jealous."

"It's Patrick's uncle's place—his grandfather lived here," I say, pulling a few paper towels from the roll.

Chase nods while he chews. "This place is pretty amazing," he says, taking in exposed brick and raised ceilings that dominate the space. "Your boyfriend's handy work?" He focuses on me, giving me a friendly grin.

"One—he's not my boyfriend." I laugh and shake my head, unwrapping my burrito. "And two—yes."

"You put up my painting," he says and I almost ask how he knew but then I realize where he's sitting. From Patrick's spot on the couch, he had a direct line of sight into my room, thanks to the mirror I hung.

"Patrick did it for me." I shove the end of my burrito in my mouth and take a bite big enough to choke a horse. I don't want to talk about my roommate.

Chase laughs, wadding up the paper that housed his recently devoured burrito. "Of course, he did," he says, tossing the paper ball into the bag.

Giving up on the burrito, I manage to swallow what's in my mouth without choking before dropping the rest on my paper towel. "You want to see my work or do you want to bust my chops?" I stand and jerk my head in the direction of the hall.

He stands. "Both—*duh*." Chase shakes his head at me while heading in the direction I'm pointing and I follow him. "Jesus." He heads directly over to the alcove where my easel and paints are set up. Standing at the bank of floor to ceiling windows overlooking the Charles, he shakes his head. "How much is Mandy paying you, Cari?"

The question makes me blush. After a few months of working for Miranda, I was financially stable enough to pay nearly ten times what Patrick originally asked for. I'd insisted he raise my rent, letting me pay half. He refused.

"Enough," I tell him, sitting on my bed. "Like I said, Patrick's uncle owns the building, so the rent is flexible."

"Where is Mr. Perfect?" He asks, taking a few steps away from the window. "Saving kids from a burning orphanage?"

I laugh because really, Chase isn't too far off from the truth. "He runs a non-profit baseball league for underprivileged kids. He started it in college—gets local businesses and corporations to sponsor teams in exchange for community service work."

"Boston Batters?"

"Yup. That's him." I'm not surprised he's heard of it, Patrick's endeavor has been covered by a few local papers. "He and his business partner/cousin coach and sponsor a team. He has a game every Sunday morning."

"Jesus." Chase laughs. "Why *isn't* he your boyfriend?"

The question digs in my chest, making it ache. I force a smile and shrug. "I'm not girlfriend material for a guy like Patrick." While I can't deny we're sexually compatible, I can't help but believe that's where it ends between us. I'm good enough to fuck but not much else.

Story of my life.

Chase cocks his head and gives me a look. "Who keeps lying to you, Cari?" Before I can respond, he sets the subject aside. "So," he says, tipping his chin at a stack of canvases leaned against the wall to his left. "Are these the pieces?"

I nod, suddenly nervous. "I still don't know why you want to look at my work," I say shaking her head. "They're hardly more than doodles."

He made another sound, moving the canvases so he could look at each of them individually. I watch him pace and hunker, lean in close and move away, looking at each of them from different angles and perspectives. "They're good," he says without bothering to look at me. "You've got a great eye. Your use of color is impeccable. Steady hand. Details are impressive. They're… good."

They're good. He's said it twice now. So why does he sound disappointed?

I look at the paintings in front of me. The first is a landscape of the river outside my window. The other two are still-lifes. The first, a cheesy fruit bowl set-up I did years ago, the second, a bouquet of tulips I bought on a whim at a farmer's market. This morning, I thought they were perfect. The best paintings I had that showcased my range and ability as an artist. Now, I see what Chase sees. They're safe. Lifeless. Technically sound but lacking in soul.

"What made you pick these pieces?" he says, turning to look at me over his shoulder.

"I don't know." I shrug. "I just thought—"

"What are these?" Turning, he zeros in on a thick stack of canvases I keep covered.

Panic squeezes my chest and pushes me to my feet. "No," I say, shaking my head. "You don't want to—"

He cuts me off again, this time by whipping the drop cloth off the stack of paintings I keep hidden. Sinking down, my ass hits the bed and I close my mouth. It's too late now.

These are the paintings I don't show anyone. The paintings I wake up in the middle of the night to work on. The ones I do in secret. The paintings I work on with the door closed. The ones no one knows about. Watching Chase flip through the stack, I feel exposed. Like he's seeing me naked.

After several long minutes, he finally pulls one free of the stack and leans it against the wall, next to the fruit bowl still-life. They look like they were painted by two entirely different artists. I stare at it. Bold colors. Broad strokes. Vague and yet the image it portrays pulls at me. It's of Patrick, the way he looked the night we met. His perfect profile caught in the glow of a red light while he drove me home.

He puts it back and pulls out another. This one shows Patrick sitting on our couch, his image captured in the reflection of the living room mirror. Another one. Patrick leaning against the kitchen counter, draining a bottle of water after one of his early morning runs. It didn't matter which canvas Chase pulled from the stack. They're all of Patrick. Painted in a dozen different ways, from a dozen different memories.

Chase doesn't ask me why I've hidden them away. He already knows. Anyone who looks at them would know. This is where my soul is. My heart. What I really want. Who I really am.

I feel unbalanced. Obsessed. Like who I really am is someone I should be apologizing for.

"I want them." His back is to me and I'm not sure I hear him correctly.

"Excuse me?"

"For the charity show I'm putting together with Mandy," he says, finally looking at me. "I want to show them."

FORTY-ONE

Patrick

Declan calls a timeout before making his way toward where I'm standing on the first baseline. "What the fuck is he doing here?" he says as soon as he's close enough to speak without being overheard. Things have been a bit stiff between us, which is understandable considering we'd been in each other's faces last night. Seeing Cari's ex-boyfriend in the bleachers at our junior league baseball game is as weird as it was aggravating. Weird and aggravating enough to make Declan forget he's pissed off at me. At least for a minute or two.

"Which one are you talking about?" I say, aiming a glare over Declan's shoulder. The fact that he isn't alone only adds to my irritation. "James or the guy sitting next to him?" James, the douchewad who cheated on her and then had the balls to put hands on her after she broke up with him over it is sitting at the top of the stack, drinking a beer and watching the game. Next to him is Travis, the *other* douchewad—the one she went out with a few nights ago. I wish I could say the fact that they seem to know each other is a surprise but it isn't. They're basically the same person for fuck's sake. Both of them are wearing brand-new jeans they probably bought for the occasion and a bright orange T-shirt with the LH&H logo on it… "Oh, shit."

"What?" Declan says, shooting a quick look over his shoulder.

"He's a lawyer," I remind him, pulling the bill of my hat down, shading my eyes. Behind the fence, James lifts his beer and tips it in my direction, toasting me. "He must work for Sara's dad's firm."

"Wow." Declan's gaze widens for a second. "And you didn't know?"

I shake my head. "Cari never mentioned which firm he was with and it's not like I cared enough to ask." I take a quick look at Sara. She's watching Declan and me from her spot in the dugout. If she knows what's going on, she deserves an Oscar for best actress because I can see the confusion on her face from here.

"You think he's looking for Cari?" Declan's tone drops, low and dangerous. There are few things that can crack my cousin's shell faster than a guy who roughs up women.

"Probably." I keep watching them. They're talking. Looking in my direction. Laughing. I get the feeling this isn't about Cari. At least not directly.

"They get back together?"

The question is valid. Declan doesn't know about me and Cari. The only reason Conner and Tess know is because those meddling assholes orchestrated the whole thing. Even though it's an honest question, the thought of that douche nozzle anywhere near her makes me dizzy. "No." I shake my head that one word heavy enough to shut down my cousin's assumption. "She's not with him."

"Alright." Dec rolls his neck and I hear it pop. Even though he and I were ready to beat the shit out of each other less than twelve hours ago, he'll back me, whatever it takes. I don't even have to ask. "What do you want to do?"

"Fuck it," I say, jerking my hat off my head to slap it against my thigh. "Let's get this game over with so we can have a little chat." I pull my hat over my head again and walk away.

The game ends thirty minutes later in a tie. As soon as it does, James and Travis bounce, high-tailing it to the parking lot and into James' douchemobile before I can wade through the sea of kids and parents I'm surrounded by. Before he pulls out of the parking lot, he gives his horn a brisk honk and sticks his hand out his open window to wave at me.

"What was all that about?" Sara says, standing next to me while our teams walk past each other and slap hands in a show of good sportsmanship.

"I don't know, Sara—you tell me," I say to her, shooting her a heavy dose of side-eye. "Why didn't you tell me James Templeton works for your father?"

She turns toward me and shakes her head. "Who?"

"Cari's ex-boyfriend," I tell her. "The guy who almost ripped her arm off the night you and I met."

Recognition dawns on her face and she turns, looking toward the empty space where James' car had been parked just a few seconds ago. "That was him?" she says, looking back at me with wide eyes. "He works for my dad?"

The kids are done and Declan is rounding our team up on the other side of the field around an ice chest full of water. "I don't know why else he'd be here, wearing an LH&H shirt, do you? I mean," I laugh and shake my head. "It's not like he has any fucking kids."

"My parents are divorced. I grew up in Chicago. Before I came here for college, I saw my father twice a year." Sara narrows her eyes at me. "I have no idea who works at his firm and who doesn't," she says, jerking her chin at a park worker laying chalk lines on one of the neighboring ball fields. "For all I know, that guy over there just made junior partner."

It isn't her anger that deflates me. It's the hurt I see on her face when she realizes what I'm accusing her of. That she somehow set this whole thing up. "I'm sorry, Sara," I say, reaching out to give her hand a quick squeeze. "He caused a lot of trouble for Cari, for a long time. Seeing him here was a surprise." *And not the good kind, either.*

Sara nods. "Maybe he was just here to watch the game," she says, offering an explanation. It makes sense. James was a climber and the firm-sponsored team was coached by a founding partner's daughter. It could be that he was here to kiss ass. Use the game as a way to get in good and score points with Sara's dad. It made total sense. Exactly the kind of thing a guy like James would do.

I'm not buying it for a second.

"You're probably right," I say, smiling in an attempt to put the last few minutes behind us. "Burgers and beers at

Gilroy's?"

"It was a tie," Sara says, giving me a relieved smile. She's as eager to put it behind it as I am.

"That's why we're going Dutch," I tell her, starting to walk away, toward where Declan is collecting equipment and passing out water. "Meet you there in thirty minutes?"

She laughs. "Last one there buys the beer?"

I grin at her over my shoulder. "You're on."

FORTY-TWO

Cari

I can hear them as soon as I open the front door to our apartment. Laughter. Music. The loud clack of pool balls. The smell of burgers cooking on the flat grill. Gilroy's is closed on Sunday but what good is having access to the family bar if you don't abuse your privileges every once in a while?

"Sounds like a party," Chase says on the stairs behind me. "Are we invited?"

Even though I'm not entirely sure we are, I nod my head and laugh. "Being a member has its privileges."

The first thing I see when I hit the ground floor is Conner and Tess playing pool. As usual, they're bickering over something. When she sees me, Tess straightens up from a bend and gives me a look before aiming one at the bar. I follow her gaze and my stomach does a slow roll before slamming itself into my throat. Sara is sitting there, talking to Patrick while he makes drinks. He's laughing at something she's saying and he slides a college girl special across the bar. As soon as he sees me, he stops laughing, letting his gaze settle on Chase. "Hey, man," he says, recovering quickly. "Want a beer?" He smiles while he says it but I saw it in his eyes. He's jealous. Knowing that shouldn't make me feel good, but it does.

Behind me, Chase laughs and leans over my shoulder. "Tell me again about how you're not his type," he says in my ear before straightening himself to walk around me to approach the bar. "Sure," he says, taking the stool next to Sara while Patrick draws him a beer.

"Cari?" Patrick says, looking at me, a glass in his hand. He's asking me if I want a drink.

"No, thanks," I say, shaking my head. "I'll take a burger though." I say it loud, so Declan can hear me in the kitchen, my request answered by a far-off laugh. I know it's Declan in the kitchen. If given a choice, it's where he prefers to spend his time when he's working a shift at Gilroy's. I think it's because it keeps him sequestered and away from Tess when she's here but that's just my guess.

Leaving Patrick and Chase at the bar with Sara, I make my way to the pool table where Tess is waiting for me.

"Well, that was quick," she says as soon as I'm within earshot and I give Conner a quick look to see if he's listening. He looks focused on lining up a shot but I know him. He's listening to every word we say.

"What?" I say, even though I'm certain I don't want to know what she's talking about.

"Second date with Mr. Arty-fartsy in less than 24-hours," she says, she leans against the pool table and arches an eyebrow in my direction. "You worked Cap'n out of your system in record time." Behind her, Conner takes his shot and sinks a solid.

"His name is Chase. And we're just friends," I say quickly when I see the smirk on Tess's face.

Conner proves he's eavesdropping by laughing out loud. "I swear, I've heard that somewhere before," he says, cocking back his cue before letting it fly, breaking up a tight cluster of balls at the other end of the table.

His words, and the meaning behind them, stain my cheeks a bright red. "He wants to show my work at the charity benefit he's putting together with my boss."

"Oh, yeah," Conner says, shooting a glance at Chase who's looks like he's in deep conversation with Sara. Behind them, Patrick rounds the bar with a pitcher and a stack of pints, headed our way. "And what does he want from you?"

The question yanks the rug out from under me. "Why," I say, feeling like he just punched me in the gut. "Because I'm not good enough? Because no one would want to show my paintings unless I fucked them for it?"

Conner's shoulders go stiff and he suddenly looks uncomfortable. "That's not what—"

"Yes, it is," I say, shutting down his excuses. "It's exactly what you meant."

"What's going on?" Patrick says behind me and I turn to watch him set the pitcher and glasses down before he divides an expectant look between me and Conner.

"I was just telling Tess and Conner that Chase wants to show some of my paintings at the benefit show he's putting together with Mandy." Saying it makes me feel proud. Something I haven't felt nearly enough.

"Seriously?" Patrick lifts the pitcher and pours a pint before handing it to Tess. "That's fantastic." He smiles at me and I smile back because this moment feels so normal, so right, that I can't help *but* smile. This is the Patrick I know. This is the Patrick I know how to handle.

"Thanks," I say, cheeks flushed. "It's not a big deal—just a charity thing he's working on with Miranda."

As soon as Tess and Conner resume their game, Patrick leans into me. "So, how's your date going?"

I don't know what happened. I really don't. Maybe it was Conner's snide comment about having to seduce Chase to get him interested in my work or maybe it's the fact that this is the second time in as many days that Patrick and Sara have been hanging out. Hell, maybe it's the fact that despite all the orgasms he's been giving me, Patrick hasn't fucked me in days and it's making me irritable. I don't know what it is, but it's something. And it's enough to make me snap.

"You know what, Patrick," I say, narrowing my eyes on his face. "Fuck you."

His pint stalls halfway to his mouth, the smirk withering on his lips. "Excuse me?"

I resist the urge to smack the glass out of his hand. "You heard me." I take a step back so I can look him full in the face. He doesn't look amused. That's okay because neither am I. "You've made your opinion of me clear." Just thinking about it, the things he's done to me over the past few days—the things I've begged him to do—sends a rush of heat across my chest. Whatever he thinks of me, whatever he's done—it's my fault. I pushed him. I asked for it. I know that but right now, I don't care. "Now, let *me* be clear—I don't give a shit. You want to fuck me, fine. You want to make me feel like shit, great. But it's not going to be both. Got it?"

My voice rings in my ears, echoing around the bar and the people in it. They're all quiet. Too quiet. I keep my glare trained on Patrick's face, ignoring the flush that erupts across my chest and neck. They're all staring at us. Waiting to see what happens next.

Patrick lowers his glass, setting it on the table, never taking his eyes off me. "Loud and clear, Ms. Faraday," he says, his tone so calm I'm able to pretend the last thirty seconds happened in my head and not in front of God and everybody. The thought is comforting but it only lasts a second before someone clears their throat—my bet's on Conner—and breaks the spell.

I don't wait for him to say anything else. I don't wait for Tess to rescue me with a smartass comment or for Chase to make his excuses and leave.

I just turn on my heel and bolt.

FORTY-THREE

Patrick

Before I can move a muscle or say a word, Cari is gone. I don't watch her but I can hear the fast, heavy stomp of her feet on the stair as she heads back up to our apartment.

What the fuck.

"That was Conner's fault," Tess says in a rush and I look up to see her shifting from one boot to the other, uncomfortable with the scene she just witnessed and possibly her part in creating it. "He inferred that she had to sleep with the art guy to get him to show her work."

"*Inferred*?" I look at Conner.

If possible, he looks even more uncomfortable than Tess. "She misunderstood," he mutters, giving me a shrug, which means, *she understood perfectly.*

I sigh, scrubbing a hand over my face. "I need the two of you to do me a favor." I drop my hand, dividing a look between them both. "Stay the fuck out of our business. Whatever's going on between us, it's between *us*," I say, thumping my clenched fist against the table. "It's our business. Not yours."

Tess nods her head quickly, ready to surrender, but Conner gives me the kind of mutinous glare that spells trouble. Before he can start mouthing off, I point a finger at him. "And the next time you open your mouth at her, you better think long and hard about what's about to come out of it because the next time you *infer* anything negative about her character, I'm going to fucking kill you." I don't wait to see if he takes me seriously and I don't wait for him to say something else that will undoubtedly piss me off. I don't say goodbye to Sara and I don't even look at Chase. The cat's out of the bag now. They all know what's going on with me and Cari and I don't care.

I just head upstairs.

She left the front door hanging open like she was in such a hurry to get away from me that she couldn't spend the precious seconds it would take to shut it. Pushing my way through it, I hear the music resume downstairs. It'd take a hell of a lot more than a minor blow-up to derail Conner's good time. I'd bet money he's already trying to figure out a way to get into Sara's pants now that I've made it obvious to her that I'm otherwise occupied.

She's in her room with the door closed. Painting. I know that's what she'd doing because it's the only time she shuts her door—but only sometimes. Sometimes she welcomes me in when she paints and others, she shuts me out. I have no idea why. Never understood the difference in why or when but I've always respected it. Until now.

Pushing her door open, I stand in the doorway, watching her and for a moment, she's a person I've never seen. She's got her long hair piled on top of her head and earbuds plugged into her ears. She's changed out of her shorts and tank and into a paint-splattered T-shirt. This one is hers, short enough that the hem of it barely skims the top of the pair of pink boy shorts she's got on. Tight enough to give me a clear view of her dusky-pink nipples, pushing against the paper-thin fabric. Watching her, my cock is instantly hard.

If I didn't know better, I'd say this was another game of hers. Painting in her panties. But I know it's not. She doesn't even know I'm standing here watching her.

The wide, flat brush in her hand, isn't one I've ever seen her use. I watch her, slashing and cutting bright colors across the canvas, her movements fast. Almost violent. She looks hurt. Angry. That's the way she's painting, her arms and hands telegraphing her emotions into the canvas. When she lets me watch her paint, there's nothing violent about it. Her movements are precise. Careful. Her brushes small and fine. The colors that tip them muted and refined.

Whatever she's doing, wherever she is, it's not something I'm supposed to see. It's not a place I'm allowed to follow.

Then she drops her brush to swipe a wide stripe of bright color across her bare thigh. Seeing her do that, something familiar, makes me feel better. I'm able to recognize her for a moment and that gives me permission to cross the threshold to her room.

I sit on the edge of her bed and let my gaze wander around the space. She cleaned up—her table clear of cups and glasses. The carton of Chinese takeout that's been there for a month finally gone. She cleaned up for Chase. She invited him into her room.

Something ugly fares in my chest.

Of course, she brought him into her room, you fuckwit. She had to in order to show him her paintings.

Logical. True. Doesn't matter. Isn't working. That something ugly in my chest starts to strangle me. Chokes me so hard I can feel the pressure of it ringing in my ears.

Cari does not belong to me just because I want her to.

Cari is a grown woman who is capable of making her own decisions.

After the way I've treated her, Cari is smart to stay away from me.

I repeat my mantra over and over, letting my gaze rove the room to distract myself from the irrational jealousy pounding through my veins. I see a trio of her paintings leaned against the wall behind her. A landscape and two still-lifes. I've seen them before. She showed them to me and I told her they were beautiful. I meant it. I have no doubt that these are the painting that Chase wants to show. Despite what my asshole cousin says, I know Cari didn't have to do anything to get Chase interested in her work. All she had to do was show it to him.

Something catches my eye from the corner of the space— wide slashes of bold color across canvas—and I look. It's a painting, completely different than the ones she's showed me. It's propped against the stack of finished canvases she usually keeps covered with a drop cloth. I suddenly understand why she keeps them hidden. Why she won't let me look at them.

It's because they're of me.

I can't say that for sure—that they're all of me—but the one I'm looking at is. In the painting, I'm leaning against the kitchen counter, bare-chested, drinking a bottle of water after one of my runs. The angle shows my profile through the open door to Cari's room.

While I've been watching her, she's been watching me. Painting me.

"What are you doing in here?"

Her voice, sharp and angry, cuts across the room, jerking my gaze in her direction. She's glaring at me, pissed off, but there's a flush on her chest, creeping up her neck. She looks guilty. Like I caught her doing something dirty. She knows I saw the painting. She knows I recognize myself. I feel like I've violated her. Like looking at the painting has stripped us both bare and words bobble in my mouth, too thick and stupid to find their way out.

She jerks the earbuds out of her ears with one hand while she drops the other to swipe the brush against her thigh. I see it for what it is now. A nervous habit. I make her nervous. Unsure of herself. But that doesn't stop her from being angry.

"What?" She demands again, her glare falling to my hard-on, outlined perfectly against my thigh even though my jeans are a little baggy.

She thinks I came up to fuck her again.

Jesus. What kind of animal does she think I am?

She doesn't think *anything. She knows exactly what kind of animal you are. The kind who orders her to masturbate while he jerks off on her ass.*

"I—" I can feel my gaze start to stray back to the painting but I force myself to focus on her instead. "Conner's a dick. I know you'd never fuck someone to get them interested in your art." I blurt it out and watch her eyes narrow on me, suspicion replacing anger. "Besides, you wouldn't have to. Chase—anyone—would have to be blind not to see how talented you are."

The tables have turned between us. She's angry. She's the aggressor and it's knocking me off balance. I stand up before I can make a total ass of myself. "Just wanted you to know," I tell her, making my way through her open door.

Crossing the living room, I keep waiting for her to come after me. Call after me. Stop me from leaving. In the reflection of the mirror, I can see her. Earbuds plugged back in. Her arm guiding the brush across the canvas in front of her, movements still big and fast. Angry and violent.

It's like I never said a word.

FORTY-FOUR

Cari

I put my earbuds in but don't turn the music back on untilI hear the front door slam shut. I stare at the canvas in front of me. My arms move. My hands transfer paint from brush to canvas, the bright slashes of color that cover it taking shape. I don't even think about it. I just paint. Let everything I've been feeling and thinking and wanting for the past three days flow through me. My hand and brush an extension of my heart.

I paint until my arms are tired. Until I feel empty and the roar inside my head is silenced to a whisper. I drop my brush and take a step back to look at the image in front of me. Patrick again but this time, not just him. This time it's him and me. Us together. Me, naked to the waist, the bodice of my dress pooled around my hips. Panties around my knees. Skirt hiked up over my ass. One hand braced above the mirror. The other between my legs. Anyone looking at this painting, that's all they'd see. Me. Alone. But Patrick is there. In the deep slice of black reflected back to me in the mirror I'm posed in front of. Watching me.

Even though it's still wet, I lift the canvas from my easel and carry it into the living room. Pulling the full-length mirror from the wall, I set it aside and hang the painting on its hook.

I want you to feel it, every time you look in this goddamned mirror...

Looking at the painting, remembering what he said to me last night, I couldn't agree with Patrick more.

I smell it first. Grilled meat and greasy French fries and my stomach rumbles. Besides the single bite of breakfast burrito a few hours ago, I haven't eaten anything today. I turn away from the painting in front of me, toward the smell, expecting to find Tess in the doorway, eating a cheeseburger. Or maybe Chase—the guy likes his food. But it's not either of them.

Jerking my earbuds out of my ears I feel my gaze narrow to a glare. "I'm not in the mood for your grease monkey/love guru routine."

Unflappable as usual, Conner gives me a grin. "Come on, Legs," he says, coming through the doorway. He's carrying a burger basket from downstairs. "I brought you an olive branch." Walking in like he owns the place he breezes past me, like I'm not standing here in my underwear, and sets the plastic, paper-lined basket full of food on the dining room table. "The least you can do is let me apologize."

My stomach rumbles again and I turn to pull a chair away from the table. "This isn't an olive branch," I tell him, sliding into my seat. "It's a cheeseburger." I lift the top bun and peer at the ketchup smeared cheese underneath.

"Lisa's not down there is she?"

Conner laughs and looks at me like I'm crazy before pulling out and sitting in the chair across from me. "It's Sunday," he tells me like it's the answer to my question. He left the door to the apartment standing open and I can hear music again—The Rolling Stones—and the quiet murmur of voices. I imagine Patrick down there, deep in conversation with Sara. Perfect Sara, with her *save-the-world* ideals and rich family. Perfect Patrick and Perfect Sara. They belong together. A match made in perfect people heaven.

It's enough to make me want to vomit.

Giving him a sloppy shrug, I take a chance on the burger. "What time is it, anyway?" I ask around a mouthful of food, too hungry and pissed to care if I gross Conner out by talking with my mouth full.

"After four…" Conner leans back in his chair, his gaze floating over my shoulder. I know what he's looking at. The painting hanging behind me. I watch, amazed as a flush creeps up his neck. He's embarrassed. The guy couldn't care less that I'm sitting two feet away from him, braless and in my underwear but seeing my bare ass on a canvas is freaking him out. To be honest, it'd probably freak me out too if I wasn't so pissed.

"Is there something wrong?" I say, shoving more food in my mouth.

"No," he clears his throat and looks away. "Your guy said to tell you he had to go but that he'd be in touch about which paintings he wants for the benefit show."

Hearing him talk about my work reminds me of why I'm

mad at him. "He's not my guy," I tell him, dragging a pair of fries through the pool of ketchup he was thoughtful enough to squirt into the basket. I shove the fries into my mouth, as unladylike as I can possibly get.

"If you're trying to gross me out, you're gonna have to try a lot harder than that," Conner tells me, eyebrow arched at my questionable manners. "You forget who my best friend is."

Tess. She has the table manners of a toddler. "Whatever." I give him another shrug. "Chase is just a friend."

"I get that," Conner says, looking me in the eye. "I also get why he'd want to show your work..." His gaze strays over my shoulder again before refocusing on my face. "You're way more talented than you make yourself out to be."

I narrow my eyes on his face. "What would you know about?" I say. I'm irritable and angry and looking at him makes it impossible not to think of Patrick, which doesn't help my mood.

"About art?" he says, giving me a one-shoulder shrug. "Enough to know you'd never have to sell your ass to land a show."

Sell my ass... I stare at him for a second before I start to laugh. "Is that it?" I swallow the food in my mouth, mainly so I don't choke to death when I scoff at him. "Is that your lame attempt at an apology?"

Conner laughs, reaching out to swipe a fry from my basket. "You've gotta cut me slack here, Legs," he says, chomping the fry in half. "I don't have much practice at it."

I nod my head in agreement. "It's because you're a self-centered egomaniac, isn't it?"

He presses a hand to his chest like I offended him. "I was going to say it's because I'm never wrong..." he cocks his head at me and shrugs. "But, yeah—that too."

We're both quiet for a moment. While I polish off my burger, Conner studies the painting behind me. The embarrassed flush is still there but beneath the embarrassment is something else. Something that looks a lot like envy.

"He loves you, you know." He says it quietly like he's telling me a secret. Something he doesn't really want to say out loud. I probably shouldn't laugh but I do. Hard enough to bring tears to my eyes.

"He loves *fucking* me," I tell him, wiping at my eyes. "There's a difference, Conner." I sit back, pushing the basket of cold fries in his direction. "You, of all people, should know that."

"Are you serious?" He hisses at me before rubbing a rough hand over his jaw. "You asked for this, Cari." He stands up, knuckles thumping on the table between us. "You made it happen—*on a bet.*" He lets out a rough laugh at the look on my face. "Yeah, I know about that."

I'm going to kill Tess.

"So, what?" I say, giving him quite possibly the lamest excuse in the history of excuses.

He gives me a look that says I can't possibly be as stupid as I sound. "*Sooo,* can you honestly say you're surprised or angry over the way this shit is shaking out?"

"Yes." I blurt it out, surprised that it's true.

He waves his hand around the room. "You strut around

here for six fucking months, throwing your tits and ass in his face at every available opportunity and then when he finally breaks and takes what you're offering, you get your feelings hurt." He's glaring at me the way he glares at Declan over Tess. Like I'm something Patrick needs to be protected from, not the other way around. "What did you expect?" He laughs again. "And why do you even care?" he barks at me, picking up the basket, purposely looking at the painting over my shoulder. "It's just about the sex, right? Seeing how far you could push him until he broke. You could never get serious about a guy like Patrick. He's not rich and slick enough for you."

That's what I told Tess. That's what I told myself. It's not supposed to matter. I don't know what I expected but it wasn't this. I didn't expect it to matter. The stack of paintings in my room call me a liar. The one behind me argues the opposite. I clench my teeth against the stabbing in my chest. "I'm more than a pair of tits and ass."

"I know that. He knows that—" He stabs his finger at the canvas behind me. "Matter of fact, I think you're the only person around here who *doesn't* know it."

It's like he slapped me. Inside, I'm reeling. I can't catch my breath. But that's what it's usually like when someone hits you with the truth, right? "Are you finished?" I say through gritted teeth, refusing to cry in front of him.

"Yeah." He runs a frustrated hand over his head before dropping it to his side. "I'm finished." Conner walks past me out the door and down the stairs. As soon as he's gone, I put my earbuds in and go back to my room

FORTY-FIVE

Patrick

I wake up to rain. The steady beat of it pounding against my bedroom window, insistent. Demanding. So loud I can feel it vibrating against my eardrums. I lay here, listening to it for a while, waiting for what I know is coming.

Fifteen minutes later, Declan texts me.

Declan: Job site is Washed out. I'll let The crew know we're taking the day.

I stare at my phone for a few seconds before responding. Things are back to normal between him and me. After the show, Cari and I put on for everyone yesterday afternoon, I think he actually feels sorry for me. Which makes me feel like a giant pussy. Irritated, I punch my finger against the screen, sending him my abbreviated answer.

Me: Thx

I drop my phone and stare at the crack in my ceiling. My new favorite thing to do. A week ago, I would've been thrilled to have a Monday called on account of rain. A whole day to myself. A whole day to work on my own building designs. Designs I'll probably never get to see built but I draw them anyway, just so I can dream. A week ago, a rainy day would've been perfect. Today—right now—it feels like the walls are closing in on me.

There isn't a room in this place where I haven't touched Cari—or touched myself while thinking about touching her. Like clockwork, my dick twitches just thinking about it. If I have to stay in this apartment all goddamned day, I'll either wind up jerking off until my brains leak out my ears or hanging myself in the fucking shower.

Getting out of bed, I pull on the first shirt I find. It's the shirt I wore Saturday night and it smells horrible but I don't give a shit. Next, I pull on a pair of socks that, God help me, smell even worse than the shirt, before leaving my room.

The rain is louder in the living room, it lashes against the skylights in the ceiling, drowning out the sound of everything else. I sit down to pull on my shoes but the minute my ass hits the couch, my gaze lifts to the spot on the wall where the mirror is. Or was. She took it down sometime yesterday and replaced it with a painting that isn't like any of her paintings that I've ever seen.

She painted us. That way *she* sees us. The way she thinks I see her and I can't look at it for more than a few seconds before I have to look away.

Seeing it from her perspective makes me feel like shit.

Shoes on, I grab my keys and head out the door.

I run as far and as fast as I can. I'm soaked through within seconds of stepping out onto the sidewalk but I don't care. The streets are flooded, businesses and shops shuddered against the rain. The few commuters brave or maybe dumb enough to try to make it to work drive impossibly slow, water sloshing above their wheel wells, windshield wipers slapping uselessly at the rain. As they drive by at a crawl, they all stare at me like I'm nuts. Like trying to operate a vehicle in this shit is any smarter than running around in it.

I don't care. I just keep running. Until my legs are numb and too heavy to lift. Until my fingers won't work right and my elbows scream when I try to unbend them. Until rivers of water stream down my back and pool in my shoes.

I don't care. I just keep running.

But running myself into the ground doesn't stop me from thinking. Every time I blink, every time I close my eyes, I see that painting. Not the one she hung in the living room. The one I saw propped against the stack of hidden canvases in her room, The one of me in the kitchen.

Watching her while, all the while, she was watching me.

I can't stop thinking about it because it changes everything. Everything I ever thought or felt about what's been going on for the past six months. The past four days. The past three years. About how Cari feels and what she thinks about me. Wants from me. What made her do the things she did. What made me react the way I did when I figured out she was doing them on purpose. Right now, I think none of it really matters.

I love her. And I think she loves me.

I stop running and go home.

FORTY-SIX

Cari

It's raining inside my room, cold drops of water hit my arm and face and I screw my eyes shut even tighter for a moment. The clouds rolled in sometime around 3AM. I watched them swell and bulge from my place behind my easel, scrape and tumble their way across the skyline until they burst. Then I crawled between the sheets of my bed and let the deafening sound of it pull me under.

Another drop of water hits my cheek, rolls to slide across the bridge of my nose and I groan softly. I turn my head and look up, expecting to see a fast leak from the skylight above my bed. Instead of a leaky skylight, I see Patrick.

Patrick is in my bedroom.

And he isn't just in my bedroom, he's standing over me, soaking wet, inches from where I'm lying, his T-shirt and shorts sodden. His shoes sopping, water puddling on the floor and on my mattress.

"What time is it?" I lift my head and turn but I can't quite make out the display on my alarm clock.

He shrugs. "I don't know," he says, still looking at me. "Early."

"Did you go for a run?" I say. It's a stupid question. Unless he took a shower, fully clothed, that's exactly what he did.

He grins at me before squeegeeing rain off his face with his hand. "Yup."

"Are you crazy?" Another stupid question. I'm pretty sure we're both crazy.

Instead of answering me, he just grins some more while he toes off his runners.

"What do you think you're doing?" My gaze strays behind him to the painting of him still propped against the stack and I feel heat erupt across my chest. Even though I know he's already seen it, I feel naked. Exposed. Much more exposed and naked than the painting I hung in the living room. When I look back at him, he's got his socks off and he drops them onto the floor next to his shoes.

"You're going to be late for work," I tell him even though he said it was *early*, I have no idea what time it is. "Declan's going to have a—"

"I'm not going to work today." Patrick catches the hem of his shirt, still grinning. "Neither are you," he says, peeling his shirt off, up over his head before letting it hit the floor with a wet *thwack*. "Not unless you have a boat somewhere."

I shake my head and sit up. "It's Monday," I say, feeling around in the bed for my phone. I haven't seen it since yesterday afternoon and I have no idea where I left it. "We're expecting a shipment today. Miranda—"

"It's in the kitchen," he tells me, laughing a little because he knows exactly what I'm looking for. "Dead as a doornail." He hooks his thumbs into the waistband of his shorts and boxer briefs and takes them off together, discarding them as unceremoniously as he did his shirt. "I texted her for you. She said the shipment is delayed because of the rain and she'll see you tomorrow." He's completely naked, so perfect and beautiful that I can't look away even though the sight of him makes it hard to breathe.

"I can't stay here," I say, shaking my head again. I don't have the mental or emotional strength to handle Patrick right now. An entire day trapped in this apartment with him will probably kill me.

He cocks his head at me. "Why not?"

"Because—" I stare up at him, my eyes widened slightly. *Because you're angry at me. Because being around you makes* me *angry. And horny. And stupid.* "Because."

He laughs at me. "Because?" he says, totally okay with the fact that he's stark naked in my bedroom. "That's not a reason, Cari. That's a conjunction."

My eyes narrow on his face. "Whatever." I throw my covers back and turn, moving away from him, toward the other side of the bed. I'll take a shower and get dressed. Boston might be on a rainy-day schedule but I know Tess is at the garage, business as usual. It's only two blocks away. I can make it. I'll go hang out with her. Where it's safe. I'll have to put up with Conner's bullshit but—

Patrick's hand closes over my ankle, dragging me back across the bed. I flip myself over so I can glare up at him.

Jesus. Does he have to be so naked? And perfect?

"What?" I say the word through gritted teeth, jerking against his hand still clamped around my leg.

"Tell me why." He's not smiling anymore. Even though he keeps asking the question, he looks like he's afraid of the answer. "Why can't you stay here with me?"

I squeeze my eyes shut against the sight of him so I can think straight. So I don't have to look at him when I say it because I'm just as afraid of the answer as he is. "Because I'm tired, Patrick," I say. "I'm tired and I don't want to do this today." I look up at him, shaking my head. "Not today, okay?"

He loosens his grip on my ankle but doesn't let go. "Do what?"

"This. Us—whatever *this* is." I look away, swallowing against the lump in my throat. "Not today, okay?"

The hand on my ankle loosens even more, its fingers gentle as they slide up the length of my calf to stroke the back of my knee. My nipples stiffen instantly, my panties dampening almost as fast. "Patrick," I whisper. "Please…" I'm not sure if I'm asking him to stop touching me so I can run away or to keep his hands on me so I won't. "Please."

"Delay the game on account of rain?" he says, a slight smirk lifting the corner of his mouth, but there's something else. Something solemn about the way he's looking at me. Something that squeezes around the edges of my heart. He's asking for a truce. A time-out. He doesn't want to fight anymore. Play games anymore. At least for today.

It's ridiculous, the idea that we can stop fighting and fucking with each other, just because it's raining and I open my mouth to tell him so. Instead, I nod my head. "Okay," I say softly, my heart in my throat.

"Okay," he echoes, a slow smile spreads across his face and he lets me go so I can scoot over on the bed to make room for him.

He slips under the covers and reaches for me. I expect his hands to close over my breasts. Reach between my legs. Tear off the paint splattered T-shirt and boy shorts I fell into bed wearing. To get me naked so he can live out whatever unfulfilled fantasy he's still harboring about us.

Instead, he pulls me close, turning me in his arms so my back is pressed against his wet chest, instantly soaking the back of the shirt I'm wearing, the mattress and sheets under us. "You're wet," I say because I'm nervous and I can't seem to stop saying stupid, lame things.

"I know," he says, pressing a soft kiss against the back of my neck. "Sorry about your bed." His lips brush against my nape when he says it and I melt a little. Tucking an arm under the pillow we're sharing, his other arm circles my waist, his hand cupped around my ribcage. I lay there for a moment, my breathing shallow. His cock presses against my backside, reminding me of Saturday night. How he waited for me in the dark. The things he did to me. The things I did to myself because he told me to. No, that's not fair. I didn't do anything I didn't want to do. Patrick doesn't have to *make* me do anything. All he has to do it say the words and I'm more than willing to comply.

"It's your bed," I whisper, pressing my thighs together to try to back off some of the heat building between them. "I'm just borrowing it."

"You're the reason I bought this bed." The hand on my ribcage shifts, his thumb brushing across my breast, my nipple stiffening under his touch. "I couldn't stop thinking about getting you into it," he says softly, his breath warm against my skin. "The things I'd do to you once I did."

The pad of his thumb skates across my nipple again. The feather-light pressure of it tingles against my clit and I'm instantly soaked. "Show me," I say, breathless, waiting for him to touch me. Wanting him to.

"I am," he says, his arm tightening around my waist, pulling me closer, holding me against him. His chest moves against my back, his breathing slow and even. His mouth a fraction of an inch from the back of my neck. His thumb curved around the swell of my breast. Rain batters the roof and windows, the beating of it furious and wild— completely at odds with the slow and steady drum of his heart, keeping time with mine.

FORTY-SEVEN

Patrick

For the second time this morning, I wake up to rain. The torrent of water sloshing against the skylight above the bed, a fast, steady drum. The rhythm of it holds me in a trance. Half-asleep, I can feel Cari pressed against me. The rise and fall of her chest beneath my arm, her hand settled on top of mine. The swell of her hips, her ass pressed against me. For a second, I think it's a dream. The kind I've had almost every night since she moved in. The kind that has me waking up hard, frustrated and alone.

I'm throbbing, so stiff and swollen it's almost painful and I flex my hips, instinctively trying to relieve the pressure. The ache gives way to pleasure and I realize this isn't a dream. I'm in Cari's bed. She's pressed against me, shifting in her sleep at the feel of my cock against her ass. I do it again, half-aware that if I don't stop, I'm going to come all over her sheets like a teenager. Right now, I don't care. I do it again. And again.

Cari stirs, a soft, breathless moan escaping her mouth as

she rocks her hips against me. The hand resting on top of mine reaches back, her fingers digging into my ass, holding me against her, meeting my thrusts.

With a groan, I back off, putting space between her hips and mine even as the hand on her ribs searches for the hem of her T-shirt. She moans again, the sound of it tinged with disappointment.

"*Shhh...*" Finding the hem of her shirt, I slip my hand under it, my fingers skimming along her belly until it closes over her breast. "No games," I whisper into the curve of her neck. "Not today." Her nipple is already stiff, so sensitive her breath catches in her throat when the rough skin of my palm brushes against her tender flesh. I caress her, my mouth on the back of her neck. Teeth scraping along the slope of her shoulder, Tongue tracing along the shell of her ear. "I'm going to fuck you," I say softly against her flushed skin, pressing my lips to the tender spot behind her earlobe. "Come inside you."

"Yes..." Her fingers, still gripping my ass, dig in deeper, trying to pull me close again. "Patrick, please..."

I almost give in. I almost jerk her panties down and move her thighs apart so I can slip my bare cock between them. So I can pound myself into her wet, swollen pussy from behind. Fill her up with my cum. Instead, I move over her, turning her onto her back, spreading her thighs so I can kneel between them.

I look at her, my throat going dry at the picture she makes beneath me. Her blue eyes are dark, heavy-lidded with desire. Lush mouth slightly open, lower lip caught between her teeth. Hair, a honey-colored tangle around flushed cheeks. Her T-shirt rides high on her ribcage, exposing the underside of her tits. "Jesus, Cari..." I use both of my hands to push it up even farther until it's bunched under her arms, banded softly across her chest, her nipples stiffening and swelling beneath my gaze. I cup them, squeezing their hard peaks until she cries out. Leaning over her, I tongue her nipples, sucking them into my mouth, my hips flexing against hers, rubbing my cock along the crotch of her boy shorts. "I want to fuck you so bad..."

She moans again, arching into my mouth as my hand trails down the soft skin of her belly, to skim along the waistband of her panties. She lifts her hips from the bed so I can peel them off, the seam of her bare pussy grazing against the head of my cock. I groan and sit up, pressing her back against the bed, the gesture pulling a frustrated moan from her throat. "You said no more games." She sounds desperate, her tone edgy and breathless. "You said..."

Her thighs are covered in paint. Layered stripes where she swiped her brush against them. For some reason, it's hot as fuck and I grip her thighs, spreading her wide, holding her to the bed while I trace the pad of my thumb up the glossy length of her slit. "No games," I tell her, the feel of how wet she is for me going straight to my dick. "I'm putting my cock in you..." I rub her arousal across the top of her thigh, so wet it smears the stripes of dried paint together. I do it again, liking the way the colors bleed together on her skin.

"Then do it," she says, the demanding, needy tone of her

voice putting a grin on my face. "Quit teasing me and put your—" her words break away on a shuddering moan when I press my paint-smeared thumb against her clit.

"I'm not playing games... I'm putting my cock inside you, Cari." My thumb skims along the seam of her pussy again, trailing color in their wake. "But not yet." I lean over to press an almost chaste kiss against her belly. "Because if I do, I'm going to fuck you and I won't be able to stop..." I dip my head, trailing my tongue along the sensitive place where the inside of her thigh meets her pelvis. "And I plan on taking my time with you." My head dips even farther, my hands tightening their grip on her thighs as I press my tongue against the bottom of her, pushing it inside before dragging it up the length of her slit.

"Oh, my god."

The taste of her pussy, the slightly astringent paint mixed with the achingly sweet juices of her arousal, snaps my self-control. A growl, long and low, erupts from my chest, the taste of her turning me into something savage. Something wild. Shifting my hold on her, I slide my arms under her, wrapping them around the backs of her thighs until my hands are gripping her from behind. Spreading her even wider, my shoulders pressing into the cradle of her hips so hard, I'm afraid I'm going to break her. I can't stop. I fuck her with my tongue, My mouth. Sucking her clit. Nipping it with my teeth, my thumbs hooked into her folds, opening her so I can taste every part of her. Claim every last inch.

She's close to coming, her thighs quivering in my grip, her breath coming in short, violent bursts. I look up, aiming my gaze up the length of her body, watching her undulate under the unrelenting pressure of my mouth. She closes a hand over her breast, her fingers squeezing and rolling her swollen nipple when her other hand cups the back of my head, holding me against her like she's afraid I'm going to pull away.

"Can I come, Patrick?"

She's asking for permission to come and the question shoots straight down my spine, gripping my cock like a fist. I press my hips flat against the bed, my own orgasm suddenly so fucking close I have to dig my elbows into the bed to keep myself from lunging up to bury my cock inside her.

"Patrick, please..." She's begging me now, her plea coming between soft little pants. "Please, can I—"

I can't answer her, not without taking my mouth off her and if I do that, there's no way I'm not fucking her with my cock. Instead, I latch my mouth around her clit and suck.

"*Come.*"

She screams the word, her legs breaking free of my grip to slam closed around my head as she arches herself off the bed, her fingers tightening their grip on my hair, her hand alternating between pressing me close and pulling my mouth away from her. She's sobbing, coming apart underneath me while I lap and suck every last drop of sweetness from her throbbing pussy.

She screams again and I ease the pressure of my mouth, feathering her swollen center with gentle kisses and soft strokes of my tongue until she's quiet and content.

We lay here for a while, listening to the rain outside, while I lick and stroke her until she's writhing and panting under my mouth again and my balls are so tight and swollen I can barely breathe.

"Patrick..." She reaches for me, her fingers wrapped around my shoulder, trying to pull me to her.

I grin up at her from between her legs. "I'll be right back," I say, pressing a kiss to the inside of her thigh before levering my shoulders off the bed.

Her fingers tighten around my arm holding me in place. "Where are you going," she says, eyes narrowed on my face, so suspicious I have to laugh.

"I have to get a condom," I tell her pulling out of her grip but instead of moving off the bed, I stretch out beside her and she turns onto her side so she can look at me. Running a hand over her hip, I trace my fingertips along the inside of her thigh, my throbbing cock pressed against her hip. "Unless you've got one handy..."

She sighs, the breath of it shuddering across my skin. "I don't." She shifts beneath my hand, the movement pressing it higher, into the juncture of her thighs. "It's okay," she says, shaping her hand around mine to cup it against her, pushing my fingers past her entrance and I groan at the feel of her, soft and wet, against my hand.

"*Christ...*" I bury my face in her neck, stroking two of my fingers deep inside her and she cries out. I'm about ready to lose it, my dick straining and twitching against her hip like it's trying to find its way inside her on its own. "Cari—"

Her fingers close over the length of me, her thumb sweeping over the head of my cock, smearing the pre-cum that's leaking from it at a steady drip. Her fist glides from tip to base and I almost swallow my tongue, while I stroke my fingers inside her again and again, my hips flexing against her grip, pumping my cock inside her hand. I've touched her so many times over the past four days, had my mouth and my hands and my cock on every inch of her but this is the first time she's touched me. It's the first time I've *let* her touch me.

The realization almost has me coming in her hand.

I grab her by the wrist to stop her hand from pushing me over the edge. It doesn't help. "If I don't get a condom right now, I'm not going to make it." It's an embarrassing thing to say, that I'm so worked up that I can't touch her without coming but it's true. That's how crazy she makes me. How far she's worked herself under my skin. I squeezed my eyes shut, fighting off the orgasm that's spiraling up my cock. "Cari, we can't—"

"Yes, we can." She says it against my mouth, rocking her hips against the hand between her thighs, my fingers sliding in and out of her pussy. "I want to."

I'm trying to force myself to concentrate on what she's saying. What it means. But all I can think about is her hand on my dick and the feel of her fucking herself with my fingers. "What?" Jesus Christ, she's going to fucking kill me.

"I want you bare inside me." She whispers it against my mouth and my cock jerks in her grip. "I want to feel you…"

"No games, Cari." I groan, tightening my grip on her wrist, trying to pull away. She's playing with me. "We said no games. Not today."

"No games…" she presses her mouth against mine, the

hand on my cock, easing up enough for me to comprehend what she's saying. "I haven't been with anyone else since I moved in. Just you, Patrick." She kisses me, her lips soft and slightly parted. Breaking out of my grasp, her hand slides down the length of my erection to cup my balls. "Have you..."

There's been no one. Not in months. Not since I broke up with Sara, a few months after Cari moved in. There's been no one and she knows it. "You know I haven't."

"Then it's okay to fuck me bare," she whispers it in my ear like we're sharing a dirty little secret, no one else needs to know. "I want you to."

I know she's on the pill. She keeps them in our medicine cabinet. I've seen her take them. "I've never done it before," I tell her, not because I'm reluctant but because I want her to know that it means something to me.

"Neither have I."

Neither have I.

I move over her, into the cradle of her thighs, the head of my cock throbbing against her. "No one else." It's not a question but she breathes her answer out on a sigh.

No one else.

I slide my bare cock inside her on a long, slow stroke that turns her words into a soft, shuddering moan. Her knees come up, her ankles locked around my hips, hers raised off the bed so I can fuck her deep, plunging in and out her pussy with slow, languid thrusts that pulls soft, mewling cries from her open mouth. Braced above her on one elbow, my hips flexing and pumping against hers, I reach down to press my fingers against her throbbing clit, stroking her most sensitive spot, keeping a steady rhythm that slowly drives us both to the brink.

"Patrick..." my name tears out of her throat on a sob. "Please..." her hips rock against my cock and my hand. "Can I—"

I shift my elbow, clamping my hand over her mouth before she can say it. "Don't," I drop my head into the crook of her neck, pumping and plunging my cock into her faster and faster. "If you say it, I'll come and I'm not ready. Not yet."

She moans against my palm, her short, blunt fingernails digging into my shoulders but she nods her head. I move, my hand sliding it off her mouth as I pull myself up until I'm kneeling between her legs again. Turning her over, I pull her hips off the bed and palm her ass cheeks, spreading her pussy wide for my cock. "Touch yourself," I say gruffly, watching while she slides her hand between her legs, her fingers going straight for her clit. I give her short, shallow thrusts, my balls feeling like they're on fire. If I fuck her like this, I'm not going to last long but I can't seem to stop. "Tell me how good it feels."

"So good," she moans softly. I can feel her fingers brushing against the base of my cock every time she rolls them over the swollen bundle of nerves at the center of her. "Your bare cock feels so good inside me."

Fuck. I reach up to clamp a hand over her shoulder, pushing her into the bed so I can take her deeper, so I can bottom out on every stroke. I pound into her, my hips smacking against her ass, my engorged balls slapping against her wet slit. She's moaning, face turned to the side, eyes half-closed, her thighs and ass shaking uncontrollably while she fights off the orgasm that's barreling down on her.

"Come for me, Cari," I tell her and she immediately stiffens under me, moaning while her pussy clamps down on my cock like a vice, shuddering and flexing around it while I fuck her through her orgasm.

Suddenly, I can't hold out anymore. "Shit. I'm gonna come in your pussy." The words come out low and guttural. "I'm going to fill this tight little pussy up with my cum." I have no idea where it comes from. Before Cari, I never would've said something like that out loud. Even now, not angry, not trying to punish her, I can't seem to stop myself from saying filthy things to her.

"Yes," she pants softly between thrusts. "Come in me."

I groan, my orgasm blowing through me, rocketing and spiraling up the length of my cock. I keep fucking her, my hips pistoning against her ass while I fill her up with my cum. My deep, hard thrusts trigger another release for her and she gasps, pushing back against me, milking me of mine.

We're both quiet now, the only sound between us is our ragged breathing as it slowly returns to normal. I don't know what to do. This is usually the part where I say something shitty to her and walk away. She seems to be as confused as I am, lying beneath me, her ass fused to my hips while my dick twitches and jerks the last of my release.

She stiffens beneath me like she's waiting for me to play my part. Be the same asshole I've been for the past four days. Outside, the rain is still pouring down. Rivers of water flood down the skylight, the sky beyond it a bruised and battered gray.

"It's still raining," I say, taking my hand off her shoulder to smooth its wide palm down the length of her spine and she smiles, relaxing under my touch.

It's still raining. No games. Not today.

Still buried inside her, still kneeling between her thighs, I brace my hands against her lower back and turn her over. I could stay inside her forever. Just the thought gets me hard again and she moans, her hips flexing under my hands. I look down at where we're joined and smile. "I made a mess," I tell her, brushing my thumb across her cum-covered thigh, smearing and mixing it with the remnants of the paint that's still dried there.

She laughs, the sound of it squeezing around my heart. It's been too long since I've made her laugh. "I don't mind," she tells me, laughing again when I swat the side her ass.

No games. Not today.

I stretch out along the length of her, propping myself up on my elbows, so I don't crush her. "Are you hungry?" I say, brushing the tangle of her hair away from her face.

She looks up at me and nods, a slow smile spreading across her face.

"Great," I kiss the tip of her nose. "You shower while I cook."

She rolls her eyes. "You can't cook, Patrick."

Still inside her, I give her a single, slow thrust before I force myself to pull away from her. "I can do a lot of things you don't know about Ms. Faraday. You'd be surprised," I tell her as I move off the bed and through the door.

FORTY-EIGHT

Cari

When I get out of the shower, Patrick's nowhere to be found. For a second, I think he left. Then I notice the front door to the apartment is wide open, the smell of bacon wafting up the stairs along with the sound of the jukebox cranked up—21 Pilots. My favorite. Beneath the thumping beat of the music, I can hear the rain.

In my room, I dry quickly and take my hair down from the sloppy bun I threw it in to shower. Inspecting myself in the mirror, I notice a few flecks of paint that I missed and I rub at them, trying to scrub them off. Finally, I give up and get dressed, pulling on a pair of clean underwear, the skimpiest I can find, and a soft yellow T-shirt dress, worn thin from years of wear.

Plaiting my hair into a quick braid, I secure it with a hair tie before taking another cursory glance in the mirror. No make-up. My hair barely combed. Bare feet and a dress that I should've tossed out years ago. I grimace at my reflection and consider changing. A nicer dress. Some mascara.

Maybe take a few minutes to do my hair. It's what I'd do if I were going on a date with a guy like Trevor or James. I'd spend a solid hour powdering and perfuming myself to perfection.

I sigh, reaching down to catch the hem of my dress, intent on changing.

Just as I've got the dress halfway off, the music downstairs goes quiet. "You're beautiful—now get your ass down here before your food gets cold," Patrick yells up the stairs, his voice thick with laughter. He can't even see me and he knows what I'm doing.

Embarrassed, I drop the hem of my dress.

When I walk into the bar, Patrick's by the front door, wearing a pair of track pants and nothing else, hunched in front of a neat, double-stacked row of sandbags lined against its bottom. "Where did you get sandbags?" I ask, looking around for signs of water damage. Everything looks fine.

As soon as he hears my voice, Patrick stands and turns toward me. "My uncle learned his lesson with Hurricane Sandy," he says. "He keeps them in the office." His gaze, traveling the length of me, reminding me I didn't put on a bra. "I put them down before I left on my run this morning. They're holding up." Inches from me, a slow smile spreads across his face. I think he's going to kiss me but he doesn't. True to form, Patrick keeps surprising me. "Told ya so," he says softly, his hand reaching up to lift the loose braid of my hair off my shoulder.

"Told me what?" I say, swaying into him a little, trying to get him to kiss me. Touch me. Anything that will tell me that everything is still okay.

Rubbing his fingers along the length of my braid, he gives it a gentle tug, pulling my mouth to within a breath of his. "You're beautiful." He grins at me, his lips brushing against mine briefly, too brief to be called a kiss, before he takes a step back. "And your food is cold."

He leaves me there, unkissed. Untouched. Completely off balance. I watch him walk away, skirting around the bar to disappear into the small kitchen behind it. "Sit down, Cari," he calls from the kitchen like he knows I'm still standing here. Like he knows I'm confused and likes it that way.

Because I feel like an idiot, just standing there, I take a seat at the bar. Looking around, I realize that while it looks and sounds like Armageddon outside, things in here look relatively normal. "How do we have power?"

"Paddy, again," he says, the words squeezed around a laugh. "After Sandy, he invested in a generator big enough to power the whole block." Patrick appears behind the bar, a plate in his hand. "Lucky for us." He sets the plate in front of me with a small flourish. On the plate is an omelet stuffed with veggies, a pile of perfectly crispy bacon and wedges of buttered toast. "All we have in the fridge upstairs is blueberry yogurt and bottled water. And ketchup." He gives me a lopsided grin, the one that shows me his dimple and loosens the hinges in my knees, holding a fork out to me in his outstretched hand. "Neither one of us has been very focused on food lately."

He isn't wrong. Still, the observation makes me glad my chest is covered because it suddenly goes hot. I clear my throat and take the fork. "This looks really good," I say, using the tine of my fork to lift the edge of the omelet. "Is there—"

"Mushrooms?" he says, leaning in close to swipe a piece of bacon from my plate. "No. You're allergic." He says it like he's reminding me, chewing thoughtfully. "And the toast is sourdough. Extra butter."

Veggie omelet with bacon and sourdough toast. Extra butter. It's what I order when we go to Benny's for breakfast—besides pancakes, of course.

"Are you sure Declan's not back there?" I joke because he remembered that I'm allergic to mushrooms and that I like sourdough toast with extra butter and for a second, I can't handle it.

I can't handle him. How perfect he is. How beautiful. How this is all going to end as soon as he remembers he can do a hell of a lot better than someone like me.

He seems to know it too because he backs off with a smile. "Declan's not the only Gilroy who knows his way around a kitchen." He shoves the rest of his bacon in his mouth and wipes his hands on the bar towel slung over his shoulder. "Finish your breakfast, I'll be back."

I dig in while he heads back upstairs, disappearing long enough to make me wonder—and a bit nervous—about what he's doing. I'm halfway through my breakfast and about ready to go look for him when he comes back, hauling both of our laundry baskets down the stairs, mine balanced on top of his.

"What are you doing?" I ask, dropping my fork to slide out of my seat. "You don't have to do my laundry."

He drops the baskets and laughs. Really laughs. "Cari, I've been doing your laundry for the past six months—" he says it the same way he told me I'm allergic to mushrooms. Like he's reminding me. "one thong at a time."

Picking up the baskets again, he heads for the office where his uncle keeps a stackable washer and dryer. As he passes by me, he pauses long enough to press a quick kiss to the corner of my mouth. "It's still raining outside," he says softly, reminding me again, looking straight into my eyes for a moment before he continues on his way. "Finish your breakfast," he calls over his shoulder before he disappears into the office. I boost myself into my stool and pick up my fork.

Doing what Patrick says seems to be habit-forming.

FORTY-NINE

Cari

After the load of laundry is started and I'm finished with my breakfast, I help Patrick clean the kitchen. Standing next to each other at the sink, he washes while I dry. It's nice, the two of us like this.

It won't last. It can't.

The thought has me bobbling the plate in my hand and he reaches out to take it from me before I drop it. Break it.

Drying the plate, he puts it with the rest of the clean dishes. "You okay?" he says, bending his knees a bit so he can look me in the eye.

"What?" I take the bar rag from his hand and turn away, pretending it's because I want to wipe down the counters when what I really want to do is get away from the way he's looking at me. Like he can see right through me. Knows exactly what I'm thinking. Feeling. "Yeah, just—are you sure your uncle is okay with us using the kitchen like this?" I lean over the prep area, wiping its spotless surface clean.

He doesn't answer me right away and I stop what I'm doing to look at him. "Are we going to get in trouble?" I ask, looking around the kitchen, suddenly worried that we didn't put things back the way we found them.

He grins at me and shakes his head. "Trouble?" He takes the bar towel from me and tosses it in the sink. "No. We're not going to get in trouble for using the kitchen." He takes my hand and pulls me through the door, toward the pool table. Letting go of my hand, he stoops to stick a key into the side of the table, releasing the balls in a loud, clanking rush. "Loser folds," he says, straightening himself to choose a pool cue.

I'm better than the average pool player but Patrick is a shark. We both know I'm going to end up folding laundry but I take the cue he's offering me. "You're on."

An hour and three games later, Patrick dumps a basket of warm, clean laundry onto the pool table. "Get busy," he tells me, fishing a random sock out of the pile with a shit-eating grin.

"*Get busy,*" I mimic him, picking up one of his T-shirts, matching its corners carefully before folding in half. He laughs at me before digging in to help me.

"No one likes a sore loser, Cari," he tells me, folding a pair of my yoga pants.

"No one likes an asshole either," I shoot back, arching an eyebrow at him and he laughs, tossing a sock at my face.

"You do," he says, pointing at himself, laughing. "Exhibit A."

We fall into another stretch of silence, sorting and folding our laundry, this one heavier than the last. He folds one of my sundresses. A pair of my underwear. I watch him, standing there bare-chested, track pants slung low on his hips—so perfect I want to cry—purposely picking my clothes from the pile so he can fold them for me. Mushrooms and toast. My favorite songs on the jukebox. Doing my laundry. It's so normal I can't breathe. I'm suffocating—not because he's coming on too strong or because he's smothering me. Because I know that sooner or later, he's going to figure it out. That girls like me don't belong with guys like him. That he can do better. That he *is* better and I don't want to wait until I'm comfortable and secure for the other shoe to drop. I want out. I want it over. Over and done with.

"I sneak my panties into your laundry on purpose." From the corner of my eye, I can see that my admission stalls his hands for a second.

"Sadly, touching your underwear is the highlight of my week," he says, shooting me a lopsided grin.

Because making things worse is sorta my things, I keep talking. "I don't forget my lunch," I tell him, gaze focused on the Oxford I'm folding. "I leave it on purpose so you'll bring it to me."

The grin on his face dims a bit. "I like taking it to you."

I snatch another one of his shirts from the pile. "I know my robe is see-through. That's why I wear it."

His hands go still around the pair of shorts he's folding. "I figured."

"I went out with Chase to make you jealous."

I'm almost relieved when I see him drop the smile

completely. "Anything else you want to get off your chest?"

Anything else? There's plenty. I could go on for days and days about how calculating and manipulative I've been. A million reasons why he should run from me, as far and fast as he can. "I walked in on you in the shower on purpose because I knew what you were doing." I reach out, pluck something random from the pile in front of me. "I heard you say my name."

He sighs, nodding his head. "Why are you doing this?" he finally says, tossing a matched pair of socks onto his pile of clothes. He looks wary like I'm an animal who might try to bite him. "Did I say something—do something wrong?"

"I like assholes, right?" I say, forcing myself to look him in the eye. "I must be pretty fucked up if I can only get hot for guys who treat me like shit, right?" I point at him. "Exhibit A."

"That's not—" It's like I spit on him, his head jerking back on his neck, mouth slightly open like he can't decide what to do or say next. Finally, he makes a choice. "I don't want to do this." He reaches out to cup my face. "I don't want to fight anymore."

I raise myself on my toes to press my mouth to his, reveling in the way he stiffens for a moment like he's not sure kissing me back is the right thing to do. It spurs me on. Makes me bold. Slipping my tongue between his lips, I lick and tease his mouth, my hands sliding down his back, my fingers playing at the waistband of his pants, slipping inside to grip his bare ass, pulling Patrick as close as I can get him. Pushing my breasts against his bare chest, the thin cotton of my dress abrades my swollen nipples until he gives in. Groans into my mouth.

It sounds like my name.

Without breaking contact, I turn us, so he's leaning against the pool table. The movement seems to rouse him and he drags his mouth away from mine. "Wait," he says, eyes squeezed shut, breath heavy in his chest, hands gripped around my arms to set me away. "Let's just take a—"

I slip out of his grip and sink to my knees, snagging the elastic waistband of his track pants, taking them with me, exposing his rock-hard shaft. Before he can stop me, I reach out to wrap my hand around the base of his cock. "Cari," he groans, a low, animal sound, half encouragement, half warning.

I ignore the warning, raising myself on my knees so I can run my tongue along the rigid line of tendon between his stomach and his pelvis and his abdominal muscles contract, flexing hard before he shudders out a curse. "This isn't what I meant," he growls at me. "We don't have to—"

I run my tongue up the length of him. "You said you didn't want to fight," I say before taking him into my mouth, opening wide, pulling him in as deep as I can, I relax, taking deep breaths through my nose, forcing my throat to relax to accommodate his size. When I've taken him as deep as I can, I flatten my tongue, giving him a long, hard suck while bobbing my head, licking every inch of him I can reach while my hand does the rest, stroking and pumping against the base of his cock.

"Oh, fuck..." He shifts backward, hands braced against

the side of the pool table, arms locked straight, hips flexing instinctively against the suction of my mouth. "Cari…" He leans forward a bit so he can look down at me. The second we make eye contact, his cock jerks in my mouth. "Stop," he gasps even as one of his hands reaches down, threading through my hair to lightly cup the back of my head, encouraging me to do the exact opposite.

I don't stop, my hand gripping and stroking his shaft while my tongue skims along the head, gathering the salty drops of pre-cum that weep from its tip. "Fuck, Cari…" he curses again, fingers tightening in my hair to pull me back, tipping my face up so I can look at him. "You're pushing me."

A thrill shudders through me, remembering what happened the last time I antagonized him. I want it again. To snap his self-control. To catch a glimpse of what's lurking behind Patrick's calm, good guy exterior. To feel it pounding into my bones. Taste it in my mouth. Hear the growl of it vibrating in his chest. Feel its echo in my own.

Gaze locked on his, I pull against the grip he has on my hair, locking my mouth around the head of his cock, pulling him slowly into my mouth

"*Goddamn it*," he groans, the fingers wrapped in my hair jerk painfully tight for a second before flattening against the base of my skull, his other hand falling off the pool table, to wrap around the base of his cock.

"Suck." The demand sounds like a curse, punctuated with a thrust of his hips that bumps the head of his cock against the back of my throat. I do what he says, licking and sucking while he fucks my mouth with short, fast thrusts.

"I'm gonna come in your mouth," he warns me low and guttural, loosening his grip on my head so I can pull away. Instead, I wrap my free hand around the back of his thigh, pulling him closer. His harsh, ragged breathing and the wet suction of my mouth, the only sound between us.

"Cari—*shit…*" The hand around his cock tightens into a fist as the first thick, salty stream hits the back of my throat. I keep swallowing, each pull of my throat triggering another release until he's gripping my head with both hands now, eyes squeezed shut, hips jerking and shuddering against me. When he's finished, I rock back on my knees and wipe my mouth clean. I know he's watching me, his hooded green gaze sweeping over me before settling on my lips.

Despite having just come in my mouth, he's still hard. Like he's nowhere near satisfied. He stares at me for a moment, his jaw tense and ticking against the clench he has on his teeth. Finally, he seems to make up his mind about something. About me and I have to lock down the part of me that wants to apologize. Take it back.

"Stand up," he says, leaning back against the pool table to watch while I comply. As soon as I'm on my feet, he issues another order. "Take it off."

I hesitate a fraction of a second, long enough to see another warning flash in his eyes. God help me, it makes me wet. I pull my dress over my head and drop it on the floor. The cool air hits my nipples and they stiffen instantly, my breasts growing heavy, tender beneath his hooded green glare.

Pants still around his thighs, Patrick's reached down to wrap a hand around his cock, still wet from my mouth. He slides his hand down slowly, from head to base while I watch, transfixed. "Is this what you want?" The words are soft, his chest rising and falling slowly. Calm. Controlled.

Angry.

"Yes." And it is, but not like this. I want what we had before—the two of us, moving together. His breath on my neck. His hands in my hair. The rain outside my window, lulling me into a sense of security that won't last. Can't last.

This way is better. I understand it. Can control it.

Survive it once it's gone.

Without warning, Patrick reaches for me, his fingers wrapping around my wrist to jerk me toward him, clamping a hand around my neck to bend me over the pool table while the other reaches between my legs, pushing the wet crotch of my panties to the side to press two of his fingers against their juncture. My hips jerk against the pressure of them, trying to take them in and he growls again, low in this throat. "You don't have to make me angry, you know," he tells me, giving me what I want, stroking his fingers so deep inside me I cry out. "If you want it rough, all you have to do is say so—I'm a nice guy, remember?" He keeps fucking me with his hand, long, fluid strokes that turn my knees to water. "I'm more than happy to accommodate."

Without warning, he pulls his hand from between my legs and wraps it around the crotch of my flimsy, lace panties. Giving his arm a quick, violent jerk, he rips them in two. "No more *fucking* underwear," he growls in my ear while the hand on my neck slides down the length of my back to grip my hips, pulling them away from the pool table. I feel his fingers dig into my ass cheeks, spreading me open while he leans over me. "Say *yes, Patrick*," he tells me, the head of his cock pressing against me like it has a life of its own. Like it can't wait to get inside me.

"Yes…" I rock back, trying to take him in. Pushing him to fuck me, rough and dirty.

"Good enough." He slams his cock into me, filling my pussy so quickly I feel it clench and I try to straighten myself off the table.

His hand clamps around the back of my neck again, holding me down, pushing me against the pool table, the soft felt of its surface brushing and abrading my swollen nipples while he pounds his hips against my ass, fucking me so fast and hard I can't catch my breath.

"Clit," he says through clenched teeth and I reach down to press my trembling fingers against my clit. Waves of pleasure crash over me, his cock plunging and pumping into me, the head of him grazing my g-spot with every thrust.

Within seconds I'm teetering on the edge of an orgasm. Squeezing my eyes shut, I gasp the word. "Can—"

"No." The hand on my hip streaks up my back to wrap around my braid, using it like a leash to jerk my head up. "Watch."

I do what he says. I watch. Me, bent over the pool table, tits bouncing with every thrust. Patrick behind me, fucking me so hard I can feel the edge of the table grinding against my hip bone. I squeeze my eyes shut, my orgasm shuddering through me, threatening to break free. "Patrick..."

"*Come.*" He roars the word, his fingers around the back of my neck tightening, hard enough to bruise. His cock slams into me once, twice before I'm coming, the orgasm so intense, my vision goes dark around the edges, my pussy gripping and milking him so hard it almost hurts and my lungs are seizing in my chest.

He lets go of my hair. As soon as he does, I fall forward, my cheek pressed against soft, warm felt. I close my eyes and pretend the feeling of him inside me will last forever. That I didn't just fuck everything up, all over again.

As soon as he's finished, he pulls out and jerks his pants up. Opening my eyes, I angle my head so I can see his reflection in the window. He doesn't look angry or disappointed anymore.

He looks resigned. Like he finally understands me.

"I'm going upstairs. I've got some work to do," he tells me, his tone terse. Like he's talking to someone he barely knows. I watch in the window as he walks away. Climbs the stairs and disappears.

Outside, it keeps raining.

FIFTY

Patrick

It rained into the night and all day Tuesday.

During the day, Cari painted with the door closed and I worked at my drafting table, catching up on work or working on plans for buildings that will never be built. When we got hungry, we'd wander down to the bar and ate. When we got bored or needed a break, we'd watch movies.

And we fucked.

A lot.

But that's all it was. Fucking. After we both got off, we'd part ways like nothing happened. We didn't talk about it. We didn't talk at all.

But at night, after I turned off the generator downstairs and the entire building was dark and quiet, I'd strip off my clothes and climb into her bed. I'd stare at the sky and listen to the rain—waiting for it to lull me to sleep and wishing she'd let me hold her.

I hate myself for what happened. What I did. The way I

treated her. It doesn't matter that she wanted it. Pushed me into it. I'll never be able to touch her again without remembering.

It's Wednesday and I wake up to feel the sun streaming through the skylight above me, warm against my back. I know right away she's not in bed next to me. Opening my eyes, I see her. She's wearing one of my old shirts. It hits her mid-thigh, her hair gathered up in a hasty ponytail high on her head, paint soaked into her cuticles. Drying on her hands and legs. A smudge of bright yellow across her cheek. She's the most beautiful thing I've ever seen.

She flicks her gaze between me and the canvas, dabbing her brush against her palette now and then. When she realizes I'm awake, that I'm watching her, a flush creeps up from beneath the neckline of her shirt, turning her neck bright pink. She looks away from me, dropping the paintbrush in her hand to draw it against her thigh. After a couple strokes, she lifts the brush again and keeps painting.

I lay here and watch her, until she steps away from her easel, dropping her brush into the coffee cup full of murky water she keeps next to it. I've teased her a thousand times about how often she's picked it up and almost taken a drink in one of her post-paint dazes. Instead of teasing her, I turn over to look at the cloudless sky above my head—a bright, brilliant blue that makes it hard to breathe—and wonder how we got here. How we ended up in a place where it's expected for us to use and hurt each other.

I guess *how* doesn't really matter. What matters is I don't want to do it anymore. I don't want to hurt her. I don't want to punish her. I don't want to blame her. And I don't want to be the type of guy who would do those things to her. Not anymore.

But I know there's no going back. Not for either of us.

Maybe Conner was right. Maybe Cari and I were never friends to begin with. Maybe this is always where we were headed. Maybe this is where we end.

Unable to stand another second of it, I leave her bed. I leave her room. I leave the apartment. Because if this is where we end, it's the last place I want to be.

When I get to the jobsite, I find low-level pandemonium. Panicked about storm damage, our multimillionaire client and his poodle-toting trophy wife showed up as soon as the roads cleared. When I pull up, Declan has them corralled under the canopy we keep set up for shade, telling them they were absolutely not going to assess the damage for themselves. They're going to go home and wait for a call from the insurance company. It's what Declan is good at. Controlling a situation and the people in it.

Let him deal with it. These days, I can't even control myself.

Half of my usual crew is milling around, dodging debris—ruined building materials and trash litter almost the entire site. As soon as they see me pull up, they start moving with a purpose. "No one's leaving until this shit is cleaned up. Jeff—" I bellow without breaking my stride and he appears at the top of the stairs. "How bad is it?"

Jeff shakes his head like he's trying to figure out a way to tell me I've got less than six months to live. "Lot of broken glass. Drywall's soaked. Roof's completely peeled back on the south end."

Fuck me. Life is awesome.

"Alright." I nod, keeping calm because none of this is his fault. I look at my watch. It's 10AM. "You call everyone not here and tell them that unless they've got a legit and provable emergency, that their ass better be here by noon if they expect to keep their job. At noon, you call every temp we've got on call and replace the assholes who don't show."

Jeff gives me a bug-eyed look. "Yes, boss."

"And keep those fuckwits out there in line," I add, careful to keep my voice down. "The clients are here and they're freaked. The last thing we need is them seeing the crew standing around, jerking each other off."

Fifteen minutes later, I hear the slamming of car doors and tires crunching over gravel. Sufficiently talked off a ledge, our clients are heading home. Declan finds me standing in what's supposed to be the gourmet kitchen. "Didn't you get my text?" he says, clipboard in hand. If there's anything Declan loves more than telling people what to do, it's checklists. "We're delayed until I can get an inspector out here to assess the damage."

"No." I haven't checked my phone in three days. I don't even know where it is. Dropped out of my pocket. Kicked in a corner somewhere. "And even if I had, I'd still be here."

He cracks what passes as a smile for Declan. "Cabin fever?"

"Yeah—something like that." I shrug, changing the subject because I don't want to think about what I've been doing for the past three days, much less talk about it. "We're gonna have to strip it down to the studs and start over." The roof can be repaired and windows can be replaced. My main concern is water damage. Mold can be toxic. "That'll put us behind schedule and over budget."

Declan set his jaw, following the trajectory of my gaze. "Yeah..." he says, slapping the clipboard against his thigh. "We should know what we're up against by the time the crew is finished with clean-up." The money really isn't a concern—that's what insurance is for—but a rebuild is going to throw our entire build schedule off by months. I'm suddenly regretting telling Jeff to fire people who don't show to help with clean up. Declan tips his hardhat back a bit to scratch his head before resetting it "How'd the bar hold up under the weather?"

"Good," I say, giving him the first genuine smile I've managed in days. "I cranked up the genny and set the sandbags like your dad showed me. There might be some exterior damage but everything inside held up."

"That's good," he says, looking relieved. "I talked to Dad this morning and he was headed that way to make sure—"

"Hello?" The female voice called out from the front of the house, timid and unsure. "Is there a Patrick Gilroy here? I have a package for him."

A package? No one would send me a package here. I shoot Declan a puzzled look. He looks as skeptical as I feel. I cross the kitchen and cut through the butler's pantry and into the dining room.

"Can I help you?" I say to the woman standing in the foyer. She's on the phone with her head down. Through the open doorway, I can see a dark-colored sedan and my crew watching like they're in the middle of a live-action TeleNovela. I can see the FastPass hanging from the review and the bright yellow fleet sticker on the windshield. It's a company car.

As soon as she hears me, she whispers, "He's here," into the phone before hanging it up. Looking at me, she smiles. She's young and pretty. "Are you Patrick Gilroy?"

Behind me, Declan clears his throat. "What's this about?"

Ignoring him, the woman repeats her question, looking right at me. "Are you Patrick Gilroy?" It's obvious she knows who I am but she needs me to confirm my identity. For a second, I consider saying no, just to see what she'll do.

But what will that accomplish? Not a goddamn thing.

"Yes," I say, nodding my head. "I'm Patrick Gilroy."

She produces a thick packet of papers, tri-folded and stapled together at the top. Still smiling, she pushes it into my hand. "You've been served."

FIFTY-ONE

Cari

When I woke up this morning, I rolled over to find Patrick asleep beside me. Stretched out on his stomach, sheets pooled at his waist, face soft and so achingly perfect I felt the overwhelming urge to reach out and touch it. Him. Any part of Patrick I could reach. I wanted to feel him under my hands, just to prove to myself that he was still here. To convince myself that I hadn't messed everything up as bad as I thought I did.

Instead, I got up and painted him.

Because of course I had. I'd gotten on my knees and reduced everything that happened between us down to nothing more than sex. Proved to him that he was no better than any other guy I've been with. That he's going to use me and leave me, just like the rest of them.

I've been painting Patrick for three years—dozens of times between the first time we kissed in the front seat of his car to the last—and I've hidden them all away. Never admitted to anyone how I really feel or what I want because, deep down, I know they're things I don't deserve. I painted him this morning because it's the only way I can make him stay. Keep him with me.

I'm not sure when he wakes up but suddenly he's watching me and for a few seconds I can't breathe. He doesn't say anything. Tell me to stop. Laugh at me for being pathetic. Yell at me for ruining everything. He just watches me paint him, his eyes dark and unreadable.

As soon as I put my brush down, he gets up and walks out. Fifteen minutes later, he's gone. No goodbye, he just leaves, the sound of the door closing behind him sounds final. It sounds like an ending and as soon as I hear it, I crawled into my bed—*our bed*—and lay in the spot where he slept in the sun. And I cried myself to sleep.

I find my phone where Patrick said it was—on the kitchen counter. He plugged it into the charge cord he keeps next to the coffee pot, a sticky note stuck to its screen.

It won't work if you kill it.
P.

I peel the note off my phone and press it to the front of the fridge. Turning it on, I watch texts and voicemails roll across my screen. My parents. Tess. Miranda. Chase.

I call my parents back first and spend the next thirty-minutes convincing my parents that I'm okay. Next, I call Miranda.

"This is Miranda McIntyre." Her clipped, professional voice breaks through the third ring.

"Hi, Miranda—it's Cari," I say, suddenly afraid that my MIA routine is going to cost me my job. Patrick sent her a text on Monday but it's mid-morning on Wednesday. A lot of time between then and now. "I'm really sorr—"

"I know who it is and you have nothing to be sorry for," she tells me, giving me a slight, exasperated sigh. "Unless of course, you're calling me to apologize for holding out on me."

"Holding out?" For one insane second, I think she's talking about my thing with Patrick. I know she's into him—I'd call it a crush if Miranda did crushes, which she doesn't. What she does is chew through men like a wood chipper, tearing into them and leaving their mangled, bloody pieces behind her while she keeps on chewing.

"Chase called me," she says. When I don't say anything coherent, she sighs again. "About your paintings."

Oh. God. "He shouldn't have done that." I manage to get it out without vomiting. "They're terrible," I say because old habits die hard. "I mean they're not—"

"I'll be by tomorrow to look them over," she says like I haven't said a word. "Around noon? We'll go to lunch afterward."

"Okay." It sounds like a question, so I clear my throat and try again. "Sounds good."

"Good. Take the day, I'll see you tomorrow."

And then she hangs up on me.

Not sure what to do with myself after that, I check my texts. Several from Chase, all variations of *I told Miranda that I came by your place to check out your work. Please don't kill me.*

I text back.

Me: I know. It's okay.

I hit send and scroll through the rest of my texts. Wedged between texts from Tess and even more from Chase, is a text from a blocked number. Attached to it is a video file.

Something prickles along my scalp, an uneasy feeling, telling me not to open it. That whatever it is, I don't want to see it. I ignore the feeling and retrieve the message.

I recognize myself immediately. On all fours in the middle of an unfamiliar bed in a swanky hotel room. Horrified and confused, my heart hammers in my chest, trying to remember… then I recognize James' bare, white ass fucking me from behind. His face isn't in the camera's frame but I know it's him.

Oh, my God.

I watch it the way I'd watch a sex tape of someone else. With pity and disgust and a healthy dose of scathing judgment.

What kind of stupid girl would let someone make a sex tape of them?

But I *didn't* let him. I wouldn't even send him pictures of myself when he asked for nudes. If I wouldn't take a topless selfie, I sure as hell wouldn't consent to a sex tape.

The part of my brain that's still working catches hold of something. Something that has bile rising in my throat and me lunging for the sink, so I don't throw up all over the kitchen floor.

The video is time stamped for Saturday night. The night I didn't get home until 3AM. The night I went out with

Chase to make Patrick jealous.

Phone clenched in my hand, head in the sink, I breathe my way through the nausea. James made a sex tape of us without my consent. Somehow manipulating the time stamp. I wish I could say I'm surprised. That the James I dated for almost a year would never do something like that but that would be a lie. This is exactly the sort of thing he'd do.

The only thing I don't understand is why he waited so long to use it against me. I don't have to wait for my answer. My phone buzzes in my hand. Another text from the same blocked number.

> **Unknown:** I wonder what your boy scout
> would have to say about seeing his slut
> girlfriend getting fucked like a dog.
> Shall we find out?

FIFTY-TWO

Cari

Tess stares at my phone, her lip curled in the same kind of judgmental disgust I felt when I watched it. She's always known I'm no vestal virgin but knowing is different than having proof shoved in your face—and that's exactly what I did.

Barely taking time to put on a pair of pants, I tore out of the apartment and down the stairs. I didn't even stop when Patrick's uncle called after me as I bolted out the bar's fire exit.

I ran for the garage, heart hammering in my chest. By the time I careened through the open bay where Tess was working on a vintage Chevy, I felt like I was going to have a stroke.

"What the shit?" she said, head poking out from under the hood, wrench mid-twist when I slammed into the side of the truck. One look at my face and she drops the wrench. "Fuck, what's wrong?" she practically shouts. "Con—"

"*No*," I screech at her, shaking my head. She's calling for Conner. He already thinks I'm a heartless whore who's just killing time by fucking his cousin. "Please."

Conner walks through the door leading to the alley, a box of dry cat food in one hand a purring calico in the other. "You call me?" he says, glancing at me before focusing on Tess. "Something wrong?"

Quick on her feet, Tess reaches into her pocket and pulls out her cell. "Say *I love cats*," she chirps before snapping a picture. Turning her phone to face her, she smiles at the screen. "That's going on Facebook."

Conner narrows his eyes at her for a second before shrugging. "Go for it. Pussies love me." He flashes her a lop-sided grin before heading into his office, cat perched on his shoulder.

"You're disgusting," Tess calls after him. As soon as he's gone, Tess pockets her phone. "What is happening?" she says quietly, grabbing me by both shoulders. "Cari, tell me what's wrong?"

I can't say it. I just hand her my phone.

It takes her a few minutes to say anything. "Dirty motherfucker," she hisses under her breath, glaring at the video. Using her thumb to navigate my phone, she looks up at me. "He sent this Sunday night?"

"I guess." I shrug because I don't know why it

matters. "I just got it this morning. I..." I don't even know what to say. That I all but ignored my phone because Patrick and I spent the last two days fucking each other's brains out. That aside from Monday, we haven't said more than two words to each other. That like everything else, I fucked it all up.

Tess waves her hand like she doesn't care. "Whatever—listen," she says, and I brace myself for the tirade I know is coming. Every horrible thing I've ever said about myself is going to come out of her mouth and it's going to kill me. "It's going to be okay, do you hear me? We're not going to let that piece of shit get away with this." She puts her arms around me, and even though the top of her head barely hits my ear, I feel myself crumple against her like a piece of wet paper.

"He did something to the time stamp," I tell her. "It says the video was made the night I went out with Chase. You can't see James' face in the video. He's going to show it to Patrick and he's going to think—"

Tess pulls away just enough to bring us nose to nose. "Give Cap'n some credit, will ya?" she smiles and shakes her head. "He knows who you are."

I take a step back, rubbing the tips of my fingers under my eyes. They come away wet. "That's what I'm afraid of."

She frowns at me, her heart-shaped pixie face scrunched up. "I hate it when you do that shit," she says, handing my phone back. "And don't say *do what*. You know *what*—" she says before I can ask. "I hate it when you talk about yourself like—"

Conner comes out of his office like it's on fire, calico wrapped around his legs. "Hey—" he's peeling off his grease-stained coveralls to reveal a pair of worn jeans and T-shirt. "I'm heading over to the bar," he says, giving his coveralls a jerk to get them over his boots. "Dec and Patrick are meeting me for a beer." He tosses the coveralls in the direction of the washing machine in the corner and leaves before either of us can ask any questions. The cat strolls back into his office.

"Enjoy your beer," Tess shouts after him. "I'll just be here, posting your cat pictures."

Conner flips her off before he disappears around the side of the building. As soon as he's gone, she slams the hood on the truck and pulls a faded blue bandana from her back pocket. "Have you talked to Chase about it?"

I shake my head. "Not yet." I lean against the Ford's rear wheel-well and sigh. "But I'm going to have to." A sex tape could damage Chase's career. It wouldn't matter that it's not him. He took me to his latest opening. The same night the tape is time stamped. We were seen together—people will draw their own conclusions. "Miranda," I mumble, rubbing circles against my temples with my fingertips. Chase tells her he wants to show my paintings a few days before a video that supposedly shows the two of us having sex surfaces? She'll never take me seriously as an artist. No one will. "I'll have to tell her too… I just don't understand," I say, dropping my hands. "he waited until Patrick and I—but how did he even know?"

"Sara."

I look up to see Tess, hands buried in her bandana. "Sara?"

"Yeah—*fucking* Sara," Tess scoffs, shoving her bandana back in her pocket. "Sara *Howard*—her dad is one of the *H*s in LH&H—the law firm Douchey McSextape works for."

Douchey McSextape. If I wasn't fighting the urge to pass out, I'd be laughing my ass off. "How do you know that?"

Tess shrugs. "I heard Declan telling Con about how James and that other dickbag you were dating—the one who followed you into the bathroom—"

James says hi.

"Trevor." I feel numb.

"Yeah, that one." Tess waves an impatient hand between us. "Anyway, they showed up at their game, Sunday morning. Sara was there too—she coaches a team in Patrick's league—so, it has to be her, right?"

She was there Sunday afternoon. She saw me with Chase. She overheard the blow-up between Patrick and me—the one where I pretty much told the world we were hooking up. Despite the fact that she was Patrick's girlfriend, I always liked her and I thought she liked me.

"He was there," I tell her, building an alternate theory in my head. "At the opening Chase took me to... he tried to talk to me and Chase had him shut out of the event."

"James?" Tess looks at me like I'm nuts. "You ran into your asshole ex and failed to mention it?"

"I…" I shake my head. "I've had a lot on my mind lately." Before I can say anything else, my phone vibrates in my hand. Another text from the same blocked number James used to send me the video.

Unknown: My office in one hour or the tape goes viral. No one else. Just you.

I show the text to Tess.

"You can't actually be thinking of going there by yourself," Tess says, looking at me like I've suffered some sort of brain injury. "Seriously?"

"What else can I do," I say, shoving my phone into the back pocket of my jeans.

"Tell Patrick what's going on. Let me go with you. Call the police." Tess is practically yelling, ticking her fingers off, one by one. "I can think of about a million other things you should do besides go see your sleazy ex-boyfriend by yourself—shall I continue?"

"I'll be okay," I tell her, even though I'm almost certain it's not true. "I'll text you before I go in. If I don't call you fifteen minutes after that, you can tell anyone you want, okay?"

"No." Tess shakes her head at me. "Not okay."

Too bad it's not her choice. "I'll text you," I say, before walking out the door.

Thank you so much for reading PUSHING PATRICK! Keep reading for a sneak peek at book #2 in the The Gilroy Clan…

CLAIMING CARI

Patrick

The way my cousins are looking at me, I feel like I've been punched in the gut. Declan and I left Jeff in charge of the site and hightailed it back to the bar. As soon as we got here, he called Con. Now the three of us are stuffed into Conner's booth at the back, nursing a pitcher while Paddy gives us the stink-eye.

He knows something's going on—the three of us don't just show up together to day-drink on a random Wednesday—but he won't ask what it is. He'll wait for one of us to break and spill about whatever trouble we got ourselves into. It's worked for the past twenty-five years, and Paddy isn't one to mess with perfection.

"Well?" Declan hisses across the table at his brother. Conner holds up a finger while another slides down the page he's speed-reading. He flips the page and does it again, and then one more time before he refolds the packet of paper and slides it towards me.

"It's a sexual harassment suit," he says leaning back in the booth. "I'd also like to take this opportunity to point out that I'm not the one she filed it against."

"Not funny, asshole," I growl, snatching the packet of papers off the table. I open them and scan the first page.

Lisa is suing me.

James, Cari's asshole ex is representing her.

That's as far as I got before I totally lost my shit. "Especially since you're the reason I hooked up with her in the first place."

"That's weird." Conner cocks his head at me, looking confused. "I don't remember putting your dick in her mouth."

"What's her claim." Declan cuts in before Conner, and I can really tear into each other.

"That the Cap'n here took her upstairs and forced her to perform sex acts on him in order to keep her job," Conner says, shaking his head.

"So, rape?" I feel like Conner just punched me in the face. "She's saying I raped her?"

"Is he going to be arrested?" Declan says it before Conner can answer me.

"No," Conner shoots me a look, and for a second I think he's almost sorry about this whole mess. "It's a civil suit at this point—but if she wins and she could because basically, it's your word against hers—it'll render criminal charges a foregone conclusion."

Criminal charges. "You're saying I could actually go to prison over this shit?" It's not prison I'm worried about. Not really. I founded a charity-based baseball league for kids. If I go to prison on trumped-up rape charges, the fact that I'm innocent won't matter. I'll go from a young, successful businessman who cares about his community to a sexual predator who started a charity so he could hang out with kids all day. "You were here," I say, desperate to make this go away. "You know that's not how it happened."

"Yeah..." Conner nods his head. "but I'm also your cousin. And your friend. And a bit of a whore. My word won't help. Might even hurt."

Shit. I close my eyes. Everything about that night is a blur. "Cari—"

"Is your girlfriend." Con shrugs. "Same thing."

She's not my girlfriend. She's not my anything anymore. It's on the tip of my tongue to say it, but I don't. "Lisa was in full octopus-mode Saturday night," I say instead. "I don't know how many times I told her to back off."

"Anyone see it besides family and a couple hundred drunk college kids?" Conner asks, forcing me to shake my head no. "Then it didn't happen."

I scrub a hand over my face and bite the bullet. "What does she want?" Maybe if I just pay her, I can make it all go away.

"James did his homework," Con says. "He knows exactly what you're worth."

"How much?" I say, suddenly impatient.

"Enough to wipe out your liquid assets."

Fuck. It's only money, right? Even as I think it, I know it's not. It's not just money. It's my legacy. Our legacy. Not to mention that paying her off is all but an admission of guilt. "I'm sorry—both of you. I should've—"

Conner leans forward and gets in his brother's face. "You're awful quiet for someone who's usually a judgy asshole." I look at Declan, but he's not looking at me. He's not looking at Conner either. He's staring at the lawsuit I'm being slapped with. "You got something to share with the rest of us?"

Like he's made up his mind about something, Declan sighs. "What if it wasn't just he said/she said? What if we can prove Lisa went upstairs willingly? That she made repeated advances toward him Saturday night and that he turned her down? That *she* harassed *him*?" He's talking to his brother like I'm not even there. Before I even get mad about it, Conner gets in on the act.

"Then I'd say we have a shot at getting this whole shitshow shut down before it even gets started," Con says, still eyeing his brother. "How do you propose we do that?"

"I had security cameras installed… a while ago."

Both Conner and I look at each other. Neither one of us knew anything about it.

"You what?" we say at the same time, loud enough to earn a look from my uncle. "Say that again," Conner says quietly. "It sounded like you said you had hidden cameras installed in this bar without informing its owner."

Declan glances at me but looks away quickly. I look at the pool table and think about what happened on it a few days ago. I know from the way Declan won't look at me that he saw it all. I shift in my seat, unaware that I'm making a lunge for him until Conner's hand lands heavily on my chest, stopping me in my tracks. "How long ago?"

Declan squirms in his seat. "Long enough that I've got it all on tape. The altercation between Cari's ex and Patrick the night she broke up with him. Lisa following him up the stairs willingly. The way she wouldn't leave him alone, even after being shut down a hundred times."

It suddenly makes sense. "Conner didn't tell you about Lisa and me, did he?"

"I—" Declan runs a hand through his hair.

"Why?" I say. "Because you don't trust me?"

"I got a better question." Conner's voice lowered with each word until it was barely more than a whisper. "How long is *long enough*?"

Now Declan sets his jaw and looks away.

Conner pounds his fist into the table to get his brother's attention. "How. Fucking. Long."

Declan finally shrugs and opens his mouth. "Eight months."

Conner sat back in his seat again, a strange mixture of pity and disdain on his face. "Don't worry, Patrick," he says, still eyeing his brother. "This doesn't have anything to do with you." The corner of his mouth turns up in something that looks more like a sneer than a smile. "It's about Tess—right, Dec?"

"Does it matter?" Declan says defensive like he'd been caught doing something wrong but doesn't want to admit it. "It's a good thing I did it or this whole thing would—"

"Eight months ago, he found a pair of Tess's panties in a desk drawer in the office," Conner says to me, laughing. "My guess is he had the cameras installed to see if he could catch us fucking, after hours." Now he looks at Declan again, all traces of humor gone. "What the hell were you going to do if you *did* catch us on tape? Jerk off while watching your little brother fuck your ex—"

Before I can stop him, Declan launches himself across the table and grabs Conner by the shirt and they both crash through the booth partition before hitting the floor, yelling and cursing. Declan lands on top and punches Conner square in the mouth. Conner grabs Declan by the shirt and jerks him in close. "The sad part of it all is I know you took them," Conner says, grinding the words between bloody teeth. "You *took* them. Do you even know how fucking pathetic you are?" Before Declan can respond, Conner jerks up and head-butts him in the nose before rolling him over and straddling his chest.

It all happens in the space of about thirty seconds. Long enough for my uncle to fill a large plastic pitcher with ice water and walk it to where his sons are trying to kill each other. He tosses the entire contents of the pitcher on his sons, and when the water hits, they fly apart like a pair of spitting cats.

Paddy lets his gaze roll over the damage his sons did to the bar. "Have I told ya how happy I am that this shite isn't my responsibility anymore?" he says to me before tossing me the pitcher. "Since the three of you don't look to have actual jobs today, I'm going home." He looks at his sons, soaking wet and seething on the floor at his feet. "Your Mam wants you both to Sunday dinner—hope you're healed by then." My aunt Mary rules with an iron-fist. If either of them rolls into dinner with bruises, she's going to give them a few lumps to go with them. "You too, Altarboy." He points at me before heading for the door leaving Declan and Conner, bleeding in a pool of water and melting ice and me holding the bag.

Before any of us can say anything, the side door flies open and Tess streaks into the bar, a tiny blur in overalls and boots. "Patrick, I need to—" She stops short and stares at the aftermath. "What the—no. You know what?" She holds up her hand silencing them before they even open their mouths. "I don't give a shit." She looks at me. "Cari's in trouble."

Claiming Cari is available now by Ardor Press!

Made in the USA
Coppell, TX
14 April 2023

15613405R00203